Praise for *Guilt*

Carter Taylor Seaton immerses the reader in history – not just the facts, not just the dates, but the humanity. You will live and breathe these characters. You will rage and rejoice with them, and remember this novel for a long, long time.

S.G. Redling, author of *Flowertown*

The author has earned the rights of giftedness in the portrayal of this moving story that creates a deeply emotional visualization of the awful truths and scars of racism on the lives of innocent people.

Guilt is exquisitely written with extraordinary detail, not allowing the reader to escape the real torment and persistence of racial agony. This book is highly recommended!

Maurice R. Cooley,
Marshall University
Distinguished Visiting Scholar
Vice President and Dean,
Intercultural and Student Affairs, retired

❦

Carter Seaton's latest book is a propulsive story that doubles as a murder mystery and a savvy examination of race and class. Seaton entrances readers with strong characters, impeccable prose, and brisk pacing. She is a consummate storyteller.

Eliot Parker, author of *A Final Call*

I am a judge and I can tell you I that this book is spot on. The story lets us see the situation from several different people's point of view. All of this puts the judge in a very difficult situation. But in the end, the right things happen and you will be satisfied with another wonderful Carter Seaton book.

Judge Dan O'Hanlon

❦

The dilemma of Judge Alexander "Xander" Betts is one of history, guilt, and two restless souls: Leon's and his. In the end their souls are finally at rest.

Marie E. Redd,
Former West Virginia State Senator

This novel of suspense, racism, and the complexities of right and wrong follows the life of a boy who chooses not to tell what he knows about a crime. The story touches on American history from the Civil Rights movement through the Vietnam war to the Covid pandemic; it moves forward with great momentum and a potent mix of personal dilemma and cultural context.

Meredith Sue Willis,
author of *Their Houses*, *Out of the Mountains*, and others

Praise for other books
by the same author

Father's Troubles

Carter Taylor Seaton's *Father's Troubles* is an engrossing, splendidly written story of family secrets played
our against a background of time and change...

Terry Kay, author of *To Dance with the White Dog*

The author is a born story teller, and her ability to
establish place, create character, and maintains suspense made *Father's Troubles* one of the best books I've
read.

Virginia Spencer Carr,
biographer of Carson McCullers

Hippie Homesteaders

This book was waiting to be written... and only
Carter Taylor Seaton could have written it.

Lee Maynard, author of the Crum trilogy

The Rebel in the Red Jeep

A superb biography of a West Virginia icon. Carter Seaton has done a wonderful job capturing the essence of Ken Hechler.

> Jean Edward Smith, author of *Bush*, *Eisenhower* and *FDR*

The Other Morgans

Drawing on her family history and a deep knowledge of the life and culture of the region that comes from years as a social activist and researcher, Carter Taylor Seaton delights readers as she takes them with AJ on a richly-textured journey that explores insights about culture, class, race, and history from the founding of America up through the present time in the West Virginia hills and the Virginia high country.

> Bonnie Proudfoot, author of *Goshen Road*

An engrossing and unforgettable story that is certain to ring true with Appalachian readers and beyond.

> Rada Hassib, author of *In the language of Miracles* and *A Pure Heart*

❦

The Other Morgans is artful and brilliant, filled with colorful narratives and a tone akin to Joyce Carol Oates.

Eliot Parker, Author of *Shapshots*

❦

This fast-paced novel will sweep you up in its lush detail, its close observation of characters, and its enduring love of the land and its people.

Lee Martin, author of *Yours, Jean*

❦

Feisty AJ Porter may be more at home on her West Virginia farm than in a fancy city country club, but woe to anyone who underestimates her business acumen and strength of character. AJ's flawless sense of what matters most in life makes *The Other Morgans* a superb story, both timely and timeless.

Donna Meredith,
Associate editor of *Southern Literary Review*
and author of *Buried Seeds*

Guilt

CARTER TAYLOR SEATON

A Blackwater Press book

First published in the United States of America
by Blackwater Press, LLC

Printed and bound in Canada by Imprimerie Gauvin

Library of Congress Control Number: 2023936483
ISBN: 979-8-9877181-3-1

Cover design by Eilidh Muldoon

Blackwater Press
120 Capitol Street
Charleston, WV 25301
United States

blackwaterpress.com

The arc of the moral universe is long, but it bends toward justice.

The Reverend Dr. Martin Luther King, Jr.

October 22, 2020

Judge Alexander L. Betts sits in his bookshelf-lined chambers staring at the testimony transcripts and evidence reports on his long walnut desk. What's missing is a small envelope, one he'd turned over to the police as soon as he'd read it. As usual, classical music floats from the Alexa Echo his son gave him last Christmas. He knows what the documents say, he's just trying to decide what to do. And he remembers what was inside that small envelope.

Glancing at the Seth Thomas clock on his desk, he begins to get nervous when he sees he's got only thirty minutes before court begins and he has to pronounce his decision on Sylvester "Sly" Thompson's fate, but the case haunts him. *It's too damn much like Leon's. But, this time I've got to do the right thing.* But, his mind returns once more to the threat in that small envelope: CONVICT THOMPSON OR ELSE. When he'd read the inch-tall words on the one-sheet message the week before, it had given him chills and had brought his mother's words into the present.

Now, the chills return and her voice echoes in his ears again. *Don't cause no trouble. You know what'll happen.*

Remembering her tales of life in the 1950s deep south, he *does* know what can happen. He imagines someone burning a cross at his home or worse. *Hell, I remember those. It wasn't that long ago. And, since Charlottesville, nothing would surprise me.* He sighs, and, hopeful the police will find the sender soon, he forces himself to focus on the official documents.

Before COVID-19 closed the courts, Thompson had stood before him accused of raping and strangling an elderly white woman named Maybelle Anderson. Betts had asked for a few days before rendering his decision and then the courts closed. Now, the shut-down has been lifted and Thompson finally has been scheduled to hear the judge's decision. For six years this was a cold case; but in 2018, following the murder of another white woman, Beulah Curtis, the police reopened the Anderson case and arrested Thompson for both crimes. In the newer case, the woman's pocketbook had been taken and later found in Thompson's south Atlanta apartment. He told the police, however, that he had found it on the street. In the Anderson case, nothing had been stolen, therefore Thompson's attorney claimed that nothing linked him to Mrs. Anderson's death even though the circumstances were similar: both had been raped and strangled with their own scarves. His lawyer further argued that the police were determined to close the books on the cold case and thus chose Thompson as the scapegoat.

For whatever reason, Thompson had chosen a bench trial rather than a jury trial. In all Betts' years on the bench, this was the first time such a request had been made of him. Maybe, as a Black man, Thompson had felt he would draw a white jury, which he assumed would be prejudiced. Betts could understand that. It had happened to Leon and countless other Black men and boys. And, in drawing a Black judge, Thompson's attorney surely must have assumed there would be a favorable bias toward his client.

Betts knows all this; but he also knows the notoriety of the case means the public is eager to see a Black man the press has termed an "old-lady serial killer" taken off the streets. He knows his re-election is fast approaching and that he was elected by a slim margin the last time. Although he knows full well that in the South, in Georgia, a Black judge is always vulnerable to the whims of the white voters who would be eager to see one defeated, with that threatening letter, this is the least of his worries. Betts knows he's on dangerous ground. And that scares the hell out of him.

Betts thumbs through the reports, the transcripts of the trial, and the police files one more time. Fingerprints taken at the Anderson home had been tested against Thompson's months after the murder when he'd been arrested for breaking and entering, but they did not match. Then, six years later, police said they *did* match. When Thompson was arrested for the second murder, the state claimed he confessed to both crimes. However, the confession was not recorded, and notes were not taken by the police. Betts had seen the handwritten confession in the police reports, but it was unsigned and undated. At his first hearing, Thompson denied having made it at all.

Although antigens in Thompson's semen made it a possible match to that of the semen found on the body of Mrs. Anderson, Betts is extremely hesitant to rely on those results in making his decision. He knows there have been several firings of crime lab personnel for failure to follow proper DNA testing procedures. The state, of course, had argued that tiny difference was irrelevant and that the tests had proved it was Thompson's semen.

The case is so similar to Leon's that Betts can't ignore it.

Just like Leon, I don't think he's guilty. Once more, the evidence is circumstantial. And look at that alleged confession. I call bullshit on that. I think the police rushed to judgment just like back then. But if I let Thompson go and I'm wrong, other women are likely to be in danger. Furthermore, if I let him go, whoever wrote that letter might act – doing God knows what. What if they do something to Charlene? Could never forgive myself. And a cross burning would sure raise a ruckus in Roswell. God! At the very least, I'll probably face a backlash at the polls this November.

It's a murder case so I don't have much sentencing leeway. Assuming I find him guilty, my choices are life with parole, life without parole, or the death penalty. I'll never sentence him to death; I've had enough of that. And I don't want to be like old Judge Bishop back then... allowing no room for leniency. I want to be fair, do what's right. Of course, I'll follow the law, but I want to err on the side of mercy, not just apply justice.

Still, one wrong move in the public's eye, and who knows what might happen. God, I feel like I'm sixteen and back in Blanchard's Bottom again. I know what Mama would say but... I've got to do the right thing this time. If I can't, I'm no better than I was back then. A coward. A chicken-shit kid.

1960
XANDER BETTS

If I'da knowed what was gonna happen, I nevah woulda listened to Mama. But I most always minded my mama. If she told me to take out the trash, I did. If she told me to get a job, I did. So, when Mama told me to keep my big mouth shut, I did. Like she said, nobody gonna believe me no how. Turns out I shoulda ignored her.

Everbody calls me Xander, have since I was a baby. When I was a little kid, my daddy die of a heart attack and we hadda move to the projects. Ladonna jes a baby then, and I was in first grade. Had us a nice house before that, but after he die, Mama said we can't afford it no more. Mama sure had her hands full with us kids and havin to work, so I took care of Ladonna when I wasn't at school.

Back then, all us folks at Booker T. Washington apartments was Negroes. One of the first guys I met there was Louie Peppa. He lived across the courtyard, so I saw him whenevah he come out on his stoop. We got to be good friends right off. His daddy dead too, but he gots a older brother name Leon. Leon don't live with Louie. Think he stay with his sister but I nevah met her. He come around lots, though. I like him. He joke with me and Louie all time. Call me "kid."

Money tight, so I delivers stuff for Bill Feeney at his grocery store down the street to help Mama out. He a white man, so gettin a job there a big deal. I give mosta my pay to Mama, but she let me save some for college. She don't want me workin labor jobs when I grow up like she do. When I was in grade school she clean and iron for them white ladies over by Withlacoochie Park. Later on, she wait tables up to the country club. Now, she cook at Tiny's Kitchen. Folks, colored and white, come from all over Blanchard's Bottom, Georgia, for Livvie Betts' pies.

Mista Feeney let me work after school and on Saturdays takin stuff on my bicycle to folks all over town. And boy, could I tell you a story or two 'bout what some peoples order. Miz Butterworth over to Blanchard Street get her hair dye from us. When I brings it, she meet me on her porch holdin this orange cat name Petey big as a baby lion. She all time wearin long robes and fuzzy bedroom slippers with bunny ears. I swear she dye her hair so she match that cat. She look like Little Orphan Annie in the funny papers. Love to talk, too. Always wantin to know 'bout my life. She say, "You doin good in school?" or "You gots a girlfriend yet?" I always answer, "yes'm" or "no'm." She all time tellin me what her neighbors do, too. Who been messin round with who. Who can't make they kids behave; all sorts of stuff. That's why I nevah tell her nothin.

Up in Jordantown, they's a old guy still wears his Army uniform. Says I oughta call him Major. Maybe he *was* a major, but he got such thick glasses I can't see how he evah got in the Army in the first place. Like the bottom of a Coke bottle. I take him some kinda tonic for his rheumatics. Some days it so bad he come to the door with two canes. I bet sometimes he wish he still a young man over to Fort Bennin. I woulda.

Some folks not home when I come, so I leaves they order on the porch. Then I leave out lickety-split 'cause I don't want no trouble. They might be police around or the Klan. Mama all time warnin me 'bout the Klan. But they's good people here, too. One lady over to Woodvale always home. Evah time I come she ax me in for lemonade and cookies. She knowed it a hard ride up the hill to her house. I thank her but say I have it on the porch. I know better'n to go in a white lady's house.

When I'm not out deliverin, I'm sort of a watchman for Mista Feeney. He gots this colored girlfriend, Annie Sowards. She come see him sometimes, lots of times, really. He say to me, "Alexander, I be workin in my office a while, you hear?" He all time call me Alexander. "If anybody come axin for me, you ring this buzzer and I come runnin." His office in the back of the store near that door open on the alley for the delivery guys. That where Miz Annie come in, too. Shoot, he don't fool me none. I know what goin on in that office. One time, I was back there gettin a school book outta my bike basket and I hear em talkin real quiet-like. She start into gigglin like a little girl, then she moan like somethin feel real good. When Mista Feeney come back to the front counter he got a red face and a big ole shit-eatin grin. Another time, I seen lipstick on his collar. He don't fool me one bit but I don't say nothin to nobody. I needs this job.

The day this whole mess start back in early February, Mista Feeney in the blackest mood I evah seen. Usually, he cut the fool, jokin and carryin on. But, that day, he hardly say nothin to me 'cept, "I'll do the deliveries today, Alexander." He wearin a cap, too. One of them caps with its top all smashed down on the bill. Nevah wore no cap before. But it don't hide them scratches on his face, if that what he tryin do. All over his cheeks, they was. Red, and terrible sore-lookin. Look like he done lost a fight with a cat big as Petey. Glad he doin the deliverin, though; it was drizzly and colder'n a witch's tit. No kind of weather to be ridin my bike. So, I work all day cleanin the storeroom and don't see him 'til the next day. By then, I knowed Leon been arrested.

FEBRUARY 13, 1960
XANDER

When I got home for supper that day, they's a gang of old guys talkin on the playground near our apartment. Can't hear what they sayin but they look all riled up 'bout somethin. I think maybe the Klan back like Mama all time worryin. They marched all over town last year. Some folk laugh at em, but not me. Scared me outta my skin. I remember they rally and them big ole burnin crosses out to Malcom Road, too. They burnt one in Miz Lester's yard, too, 'cause she been preachin civil rights. I thought she was real brave but I worry they comin back and startin up again.

I hurried in the house and they's Mama sittin on the sofa with a long face. She usually over to the stove fixin supper, but not that day. "Sit down, Alexander. Got some bad news," she said. My stomach did a flip-flop. When she use my full name always means somethin bad. Either I done somethin wrong or she got real bad news. *She sick? One of the kids hurt? Klan back?*

"Leon Peppa got hisself arrested today. Say he killed a woman over to the jook joint on Sixth Avenue. Say he beat and stabbed her. Raped her too."

"Noooo." My voice all choked up and my mind don't wanna believe what she sayin. I been knowin Leon since I was little. I plop down on the sofa and say, "Mama, Leon the nicest guy I know next to Louie. He wouldn't hurt nobody. I nevah seen him fight, get mad, nothin. Who they say he killed?"

"That Annie Sowards works there. I sees her sometimes when I'm shoppin, but I nevah really knowed her."

My stomach do another flip-flop and my face got all hot. Thought I might puke right there on the floor. "Mama, *I* knows her. She come see Mista Feeney over to the store all the time. When she there, he tell me let him know if anybody lookin for him."

"That don't mean nothin, son. Maybe she jes a good customer."

"Shoot. I seen lipstick on Mista Feeney collar one time after she left outta there. I think they got somethin goin on. Know what I mean?"

"Don't you be makin up stories, you hear now? Could be from his wife, you know." Mama nevah want to believe bad stuff 'bout nobody.

"I'm not; I swear. Today, when I come to work, he look like he been in a fight with a wildcat. Scratches all over his face. In a terrible mood, too. Maybe they got inna fight and he killed her," I said.

"Alexander Lee Betts, I don't care what you think. You keep your mouth shut with them crazy notions on what Mista Feeney mighta done. You just guessin and makin stuff up. Ain't nobody gonna listen to you no way." All her words had hard edges. "Colored kid talkin gossip? Shoot! Good way to get your butt fired. We sure don't be needin that."

"Okay Mama, but…"

"Don't you 'but' me, young man." She look like she gonna slap the fire outta me. "Besides, they say Leon say he done it. All we can do is pray for Annie Sowards' soul. Pray for Leon, his whole family, and Mista Feeney too. I want you get on your knees and pray with me, right now, you hear?" Mama's a church-goin, Bible-totin Christian. Belong to the First AME Church. Been prayin ovah her family and other folks long as I can remember. So far it hasn't took on me, though. I know right from wrong but I'm not so sure prayin help nothin. When I was little, she pray my daddy wouldn't have another heart attack or die but the good Lord didn't see fit to keep that from happenin. Sorta lost faith in him then.

Anyway, I done what Mama said, but all time I was thinkin 'bout Leon and Louie, not Annie Sowards, Mista Feeney, nor the Lord. I jes want to get out to the stoop see if Louie out there. Need to hear his side of the story. Mama kept on prayin but I wasn't payin her no mind. Finally, she said, "And Lord, please give Alexander Betts the sense to keep his big mouth shut. Amen." That part I heard.

February 13, 1960

That morning, Leon Pepper was sound asleep when his sister Mae Ellen came running up the steps hollering, "Lord, Leon, get your ass up. Police at the door. They want to talk to you."

It took Leon a minute to figure out what she was saying, but after he did, he just sat there trying to figure out what they could possibly want. Shaking his head, he shuffled downstairs. Outside the storm door stood three cops, all white. "Shit. This ain't gonna be good," he muttered.

He opened the door, saying, "I'm Leon Peppa, what ya'll want with me?"

The policeman with red frizzy hair sticking out of his hat said, "Step out here so we can talk to you. We need to ask you a few questions."

"Bout what?" Leon said, as he stepped outside into the chilly air.

"Where were you last night?" the red headed policeman, Sergeant Thad Kelly, asked.

"Out drinkin with my buddy, Linc Cousey. After,

I come on home and went to bed. We *was* pretty drunk but we ain't caused no trouble. Don't recollect much else. Why?"

"You go near Stanley's Jook Joint?" This time the shortest of the three asked the question. To Leon, that cop, Lieutenant Matthew Blevins, looked mean because one of his eyes didn't open all the way. The third man, Detective Ralph Settle, was quiet, but was taking notes in a small, leather-bound notebook.

"I reckon we walk by there. My buddy, Linc, he wave at Miz Annie, that gal work there. Why?"

Sergeant. Kelly said, "She's dead. We think you might know something about her murder. So, you'll need to come with us."

Holy shit! Leon tried to think what he'd done after he and Linc had split up.

Kelly grabbed Leon's arm, turned him around, and snapped a pair of handcuffs on his wrists. Leon could hear Mae Ellen crying behind the glass door, "Lord, Leon, what you done now?"

The group walked to the patrol car; Kelly shoved Leon in. Kelly and the detective squeezed in on either side of Leon. Before Blevins started the car, Kelly said, "You got blood on your jacket. Where'd that come from?"

Leon looked, thought a minute, and said, "Couple days ago I was cleanin at the meat market. Musta got it on me then."

"You still wearing clothes from several days ago?"

"We ain't got no washin machine. Can't afford no laundromat, know what I mean?"

"Uh, huh," Kelly said, but he sounded like he didn't believe him. Kelly turned and started inspecting the rest of Leon's clothing. "Looks like blood on your shoes and pants, too. You been wearing them all this time, too?"

"Like I say, no money for no laundry business."

Blevins started the car. "Where we goin?" Leon asked.

"Gonna take you down to Stanley's. Something we want to show you," Kelly said, sticking his jaw in Leon's face so close he could smell the officer's cigarette breath.

"Why, what you want me to see?"

"Like I said, Miz Annie was killed last night, and we think you ought to see her since you were there."

"Lord, no! I weren't there. Ain't gonna look at no dead person."

Kelly slapped Leon across the side of his head. Leon's ears rang but he could still hear him say, "You are, 'cause if you don't tell us what you done before we get down there we're gonna show you."

"Ain't done nothin. We was goin over town when we seen her. Goin back home, I was fixin to go in say hey to her, but I passed out. Woke up out front, still drunk, and come on home."

Kelly hit Leon again. "You killed Miz Annie, didn't you? Raped her, too."

"I nevah," Leon yelled. "I done told you, I passed out, don't remember nothin after that."

In response, Kelly punched Leon in the stomach.

"I don't... I ain't... I swear..." Leon said, grimacing.

He punched Leon again. "If you don't tell us, you're going in there to see to what you did."

The patrol car pulled up in front of Stanley's where a group of Negroes were standing on the sidewalk.

"Don't make me go look at no dead body. I tell you what happened down to the station, but don't make me go in there. Bad luck to look on dead folks. Look there, they's my friends... don't want them seein me, neither."

"No, you're gonna tell us now. You killed her, didn't you." Kelly hit Leon again, this time in the ribs. Leon groaned, tried to take a breath, but could not.

"Stop, stop." Leon yelled, once he recovered. "I tell you. But don't make me go in there. I ain't for sure. I mighta done it... don't recollect. I was too drunk."

Kelly tapped Blevins on the back. Blevins put the car in gear and they headed downtown to the police station.

FEBRUARY 14, 1960
XANDER

Once supper was over, I went lookin for Louie but his stoop empty. I wanted to know what made em go lookin for Leon in the first place. Rain had stopped, but the wind was blowin leaves and shit all over them patchy yards. Decided not to ring they bell. They don't need me botherin em. Instead, I went to the paper box and bought me a afternoon *Observer*. Smack dab on the front page, sure enough, they's a picture of Leon, police right behind him. Big old headline: WOMAN RAPED, SLAIN. SUSPECT HELD.

Story said her boss found her when he came to work. She beat up so bad he couldn't hardly tell if it was her. Said her clothes was all disarranged and she stabbed, too. Sure glad they didn't show no pictures. Said she killed last night. Don't say how come they decide to go get Leon, but it said he confessed. I ain't believin that shit... bet the police beat him so he say that. Wouldn't be the first time, that for sure. Cops

19

around here come in the jook joints all time, beatin crap outta anybody give em shit. Anytime they sees one of us, it's "Hey boy, what you doin over here?" We don't have a good answer, they slap us around.

Next day everbody at school talkin 'bout it. Louie didn't come that day, and not the next neither. Didn't see him til Saturday. He out on the stoop that mornin so I went over. "Hey, Louie, where you been?"

"Home. Don't want to hear no peoples talkin 'bout Leon, ya know?"

"Yeah, but you skip much more school your sorry ass be in big trouble." I want to hear Louie say Leon didn't do it but I don't want to ask. Promised Mama I wouldn't say nothin 'bout Mista Feeney. Turns out, I don't have to ask. Louie jes blurt it out.

"Xander, I swear he nevah killed that woman. He ain't no criminal. Done some joy ridin in a stolen car when he's a kid and spent time at Milledgeville for it. But he nevah killed no one. He said he mighta done it 'cause the police say he gotta go see her all bloody and dead. He's bad scared a dead people, ya know? I know that's a ole superstition but he still believe it. He told Mama police said he's got to tell or they's gonna take him in there. All his buddies out front hangin around, too. Remember that Irish cop come in Porter's all time? He the one arrested Leon. So, he sorta confessed. Leon ain't nevah said, but I bet that cop whomped up on him, you know? But, when they got down to the police station, he tell them he *ain't* done it. Said he were bad drunk and don't know what he done. Xander, you know he wouldn't nevah hurt nobody. My mama can't quit cryin. Scared half to death. Ain't got no money for no lawyer. Reckon they get him one?"

"Don't know, Louie, maybe… don't know nothin 'bout such stuff. I hope they do, though. Colored boy on trial for murder without a good lawyer be bad, real bad. Only thin be worse be if she white. Where's Leon now, county jail?"

"Yeah. Mama talk to him this mornin but she don't want to go see him down there. They ain't gonna let me come. Too young, they say. Hope they don't beat him up in there, too."

"Yeah, me too. What made them go lookin for Leon?"

"Ain't sure. Somebody musta seen him around there and call the police or told the guy owns it."

We talked a while longer, but the more we did, the sadder Louie looked. Made me sad, too. I finally said I gotta go to work and headed back home across BTW. Felt like shit 'cause I couldn't tell Louie 'bout Mista Feeney. Mighta made him feel better, but I'da been in deep shit with Mama. Besides, I didn't have no proof, no how.

At work, the customers talkin all 'bout Leon, too, but I jes caught part of what they's sayin. When Mista Feeney got the orders ready to deliver, I'm glad. I wanted to get away from hearin 'bout him everywhere. That night I couldn't sleep. The gal next door was playin her radio up real loud. Sounded like that late-night station over in Tennessee I listen to sometimes. They's playin "Annie Had a Baby." Gotta great beat. But if I sing it around our place, Mama'd tan my skinny, colored ass. She think it's nasty. Made me think of Miz Annie Sowards. Maybe *she* havin a baby. Maybe it Mista Feeney's baby. Maybe that why he killed her.

May 16, 1960

❝Baxta, here." Gerald Baxter, II, answered the telephone like he always did, then sent a stream of tobacco juice into the spittoon beside his desk. As usual, he was absorbed with whatever was in front of him on his incredibly messy desk, and another phone call always meant more work, so he skipped the pleasantries. Frankly, he thought, it was a goddam miracle he could find anything on there now.

"Baxta, it's Judge Bishop. I'm, uh, appointin you to handle a criminal case for me. Can you do that?"

Goddamit, how the hell am I gonna tackle a criminal case? I'm a real estate attorney, now, not a criminal one. He considered objecting but instead said, "Yes, sir," with more enthusiasm than he actually felt. He knew it didn't pay to piss off Judge Michael Bishop. "Tell me about it," he said with a sigh.

"No need," Bishop replied curtly. "I'm sendin the file over this afternoon." With that, the phone went dead. Judge Bishop didn't mince or waste words.

When Baxter returned from lunch, there sat the

new file, right on top of the teetering pile that had been there for days. Inside was a copy of the February 16 arraignment of one Leon Pepper – a Negro, on the charge of murder, a police booking sheet listing his name, age, address, and prior arrest, a statement saying he'd waived his preliminary hearing, a copy of the grand jury indictment charging him with the murder of Annie Sowards – a Negress, and a form on which he'd scrawled his name, stating he was indigent and therefore needed a court-appointed attorney. Baxter studied the papers a little while longer, called the jail to set up a time to go see this Leon Pepper, and went back to work on the case he'd hoped to settle by next week. He'd done criminal work in the early days of his practice, until it had earned him an ulcer, so he knew he'd have to brush up on a few things before this one came to court.

The weather the next day was typical for June in south Georgia, that is to say, tropical. As he walked the five blocks to the Hitchins County jail, huge, wet rings began to bloom under Baxter's arms. *Shit. Martha's gonna complain about another dry-cleanin bill.* Approaching the old brick fortress, he mopped his face and neck. Once he was seated in the small visiting room to wait for Leon Pepper, he wondered how many Negro kids had passed through here.

Before he'd stopped doing criminal work, he'd defended a few, some successfully, some not. There'd been car thefts, assaults, breaking and entering cases, and forgeries, but this would be his first murder case. The room smelled stale. Like too many men who'd showered infrequently had recently vacated it. Its tan walls looked like the inside of a school coat closet with scuffs and black marks marring its surface. The door opened and in shuffled a tall, thin Negro dressed in orange, hands cuffed in front of him, shackles on his ankles. The guard shut the door, ushered Pepper to the chair across the table from Baxter, and returned to stand with his back to the door.

"Mista Peppa, I'm Gerald Baxta, the second, and I've, uh, been appointed as your defense attorney."

Pepper frowned. "Who done that?" he said. "Why can't I get me a colored lawyer? I want a colored man, not some white Georgia cracker." His belligerent tone seemed to chill Baxter who chewed the inside of one cheek before answering.

"Because, as far as I know, there isn't one in Blanchard's Bottom. Now, uh, if you want help, I'm here to defend you. If you don't, it's all the same to me. I'll leave." He turned to go.

"No, wait. Don't go," Pepper said. "Sorry. I jes nevah expect no white man wanna help a nigger."

"Well, apparently, I'm not like most of the white men you've known. I want to help anyone who needs a good lawyer, regardless of their color. We okay with that?"

"Yeah," Pepper muttered. "Sorry. I jes nevah knew no white man want to help me before."

"Very well. Now, I'd like to ask you a few questions. Is that all right?" Baxter opened his briefcase and took out a legal pad and pen.

"Sure," Pepper replied. "Call me Leon if you

wants. Ain't used to bein called no Mista." Despite suggesting Baxter call him by his first name, he chuckled as if the title had pleased him.

"I believe I'll stick with Mista Peppa, if that's okay with you. When we get to court, that's what I'll call you and I, uh, don't want to get used to usin your first name. You hear?" Baxter looked around for a spittoon and had to settle for the nearby wastebasket.

Pepper nodded but his brow furrowed when Baxter said the word "court."

Baxter pulled an official-looking paper from under the legal pad and put his finger on a section of it. "Now, Mista Peppa, you've been accused of killin Miz Annie Sowards on, let's see, February twelfth. Can you tell me what happened that night?" Baxter smiled at this boy who looked a sight younger than his twenty-one years, hoping to put him at ease.

"Mista Baxta, I ain't nevah killed no one. Not Miz Annie, not no one. I done told them cops that but they don't nevah believe me. This one cop, Kelly, he got me in the car and evah time I say that, he smack me. They's gonna make me go see her, too. I beg em not to, but they say they is. Finally, I think I said I mighta done it but don't know for sure. They got me all confused. I was drunk and don't recollect nothin after I passed out. Could be, but I got no reason be killin that gal. I ain't even hardly knowin her. When we got down to the station, I told them I was sure I ain't done it. I only say that before so Kelly'd stop whalin on me."

"You were still drunk when they arrested you?

Must have been one hell of a binge."

"Nah, but I was bad hungover. I ain't much of a drinker. But that night I tied one on pretty good. Drinkin don't really agree with me. I gets drunk easy, you know what I mean?

Baxter chuckled, "Yeah, I know. It takes only one glass of beer to get my wife tipsy."

Pepper smiled. "Yes, sir. Me too."

"You say the cops beat you? Is that why you confessed, or sort of confessed?" He scribbled something on his legal pad.

Pepper nodded. "Yeah, but they nevah gonna admit it no how. You knows that. I seen too many guys whaled on by cops then them cops lie and swear the guy done fell or somethin. My little brother and his buddy seen a bunch of cops watch some white boys threaten to beat the tar outta them but they didn't do nothin... jes watch."

"I know. I've heard it happens regularly. I'm sure Blanchard's Bottom isn't the only place, either. Okay, let's back up. Start at the beginnin and tell me about that evenin. Where you were, everythin."

"Well, if I'd knowed how that night would go, I nevah woulda went with Linc Cousey."

"Who is Linc Cousey?"

"Me and Linc been friends since grade school. Even after I drop out in tenth grade to help support my family. With Daddy dead and Mama a maid, we was always broke. But, me and Linc cats around when I ain't workin. Til I got sent up to Milledgeville for joy ridin in a car ain't mine, that is. I mean, we's still

friends, but I don't nevah see him til I got out 'bout
five years ago. Then we start up again jes like I ain't
nevah left. After Milledgeville, I nevah could get no
steady work, though… oh, a odd job here and there,
but nothin steady, ya know? Sometimes, if I wins a
little at poker, then I buys; but most the time, Linc do.
He work city sanitation, so he got money.

"He came over 'bout eleven and wants me go get
a bottle. I say, 'Man, I drunk a pint of rum already.
I'ma watch me some TV.' But he say, 'Aw, come on
man. I'm buyin.' Well, that done it."

"I see," said Baxter, looking up from the notes
he'd been writing. "What time did you leave the
house? Do you remember?"

"Not sure but it was late and Buster's place down
by Booker T. done closed. Linc say, 'Les us walk on
downtown 'cause that store over by Polk's Corner
stay open late. On the way, we passed by Stanley's
Jook Joint. Miz Annie Sowards behind the bar workin
like always, so, Linc wave at her. She wave back all
smilin and stuff. Most of the time, Stanley's busy, but
I reckon he don't make much that night, 'cause they's
only one guy sittin at the end of the counter. Can't
hardly see him too good, but I knowed he's white."

"You have no idea who it was?" Baxter asked,
making another note.

"No, couldn't see him good enough," Pepper
repeated.

"Go on. What happened then?"

"Well, Linc say, 'Man, she a fine-lookin thin,
ain't she? Like to get me a taste of that brown sugar.'"

Pepper laughed. "Linc a big flirt. But, I smack him on the shoulder. 'What you talkin 'bout, nigga?' I say. 'She ain't gonna have nothin to do with your sorry ass. Man, she twice your age. Besides, ain't she married?'"

"I told him peoples say she all friendly when folks in there but don't give you no call be talkin like that."

"Get to the point, Mista Peppa. Where'd you go next?"

"Sorry, sir. We got our bottle downtown and share it on the way back over to Booker T. I ain't in the mood for no TV now, so after Linc went on home, I walked over by Chicken Little's Restaurant. Musta been after midnight when I seen Miz Annie and that white fella again. This time, she sweepin up even if it still ain't closin time, so I thinks I'ma go in and say hey. I don't know her too good, but she look awful tired. Thought she might could use a rest. She musta work all day long and into the night servin.

"So, I open the screen door to go in and say hey to Miz Annie, but she don't pay me no mind. I nevah got the inside door open, though. Musta passed out first 'cause I don't recollect nothin else."

"Okay, Mista Peppa, I believe I've got it. Let me, uh, get the police records, read their report, and then I'll get back to you. Okay?"

"Thank you, sir. Appreciate you takin my case."

"Don't thank me, son; thank the judge."

Baxter motioned to the guard. He came forward and pulled Pepper to his feet.

"Next time," Baxter said, gathering his papers as the guard and his prisoner walked out the door. Pepper didn't respond.

SPRING-SUMMER 1960
XANDER

Next few weeks I only seen Louie at school. I likes school, but he don't. Maybe it's harder for him than me. Lots of times he skip and get in trouble. Not me. I studies hard. One of my junior high teachers said I was smart enough for college, so I had me some classes he didn't. Maybe, if I'm lucky, I get a scholarship 'cause Mama sure can't afford it. Little bit of money I makes sure won't pay for it, neither. Last year, my English teacher said the same thing and gave me extra work to do. Said it was college level stuff. Man, I studied even harder and didn't see Louie much, like when we was little.

But Louie and me's best friends, so it make me sad we don't run around together like we used to. I reckon it my fault. I sorta stays away, afraid I tell him what I knows 'bout Mista Feeney. But, I'm also scared Louie think I don't wanna be his friend no more, 'cause I'm not comin round. Not true, though. Me and him used to have some swell times, so I miss doin stuff with him.

But Louie look so much like Leon, I can't help thinkin 'bout Leon when we's together. That make me feel bad. When I do see Louie, he tell me what's happenin with Leon but he don't act like he did before. Now, he act mad, like he thinks the whole world gangin up on him and his family. Maybe he think I'm part of that, too.

After school let out for summer, I miss Louie more than evah. One night, after the Fourth of July, I was sittin on my stoop tryin to cool off when I saw Louie's door open. Hoped it'd be him but it wasn't; it was his little sister, Sarah Beth. When their screen door bang shut behind her, reminded me of how it did that when we was little, how it slap against the wood frame when me and Louie ran outside after supper to play hide and seek in Satterwhite Cemetery. When we was older, we rode our bikes to the picture show. We loved those westerns. For a quarter you gots a ticket, popcorn, and a candy bar. After, we ride all over town, especially in spring before it gots too hot. Crepe myrtles in the medians be droopin low. We see who could hit them hardest when we rode by. Them bright pink petals fly off them branches like a big pink explosion. When they land, they made the street look like a pink puddle, so we'd pretend it's water and ride through it. Last year, we open up one of them fire hydrants, too, so the little kids could cool off. Ran like hell when the police came. Woulda whaled the tar outta us. Nevah caught us, though, 'cause we knowed all the places in the projects to hide.

Goin to work that summer worse than evah, too.

Some days Mista Feeney joke around and I think he back to normal, then he be all grumpy and snappy. Maybe he thinkin 'bout Annie, 'bout what he done, if he really killed her. Not knowin how he gonna act day to day was hard, so I stayed outta his way much as I could. Don't want to get my ass fire just 'cause he feelin all guilty or whatevah.

Around the first of August, I was sittin on my stoop when Louie came outta his place and walk over. "Hey, Xander," he hollered. "Ain't seen you all summer. What you been doin?"

I look up, smile, and wave; then I remembered: *Don't bring up anythin 'bout Leon.* "Hey Louie, just workin," I say, as he sits down beside me. "How you been? Sorry I ain't been over. Mista Feeney been workin my butt off. What you been up to?"

Louie sighs, "Not much. Jes tryin stay outta trouble. Mama don't need nobody else gettin in trouble, you know? I been home, mostly."

I nod. I wanna ax 'bout Leon, but thinks better of it. I start in talkin 'bout things we done in the past. "'Member that time we was in junior high and we was walkin home down them railroad tracks with some guys from the projects? Remember them two gangs of white boys from Jordantown cut us off?"

Louie frown. "Oh yeah, one gang blockin our way... turn 'round, and they's another gang right behind us. Oh, man! They's six or eight of us, twenty-five or thirty of them. Sure looked like they's fixin to fight."

"Oh, yeah. They was for sure. I remember lookin

through that bunch in front and seein that policeman jes park there by the tracks. He jes watchin it all… nevah moved, jes sat and watch." Louie's frown got deeper. "Fuckin cops."

I laugh. "Yeah, but remember, we broke through that one gang and ran – we was probably only three blocks from home. When he got outta his car and come after *us*, he's yellin, 'Come're, you boy. I saw you down there startin that fight.' But, by then we was runnin like hell and didn't stop."

Now, Louie laughin, too. "We knowed all them shortcuts home. And when we got to Booker T., they couldn't find us no way. He'd a loved watchin that fight if we stayed and let em beat the shit outta us."

"Oh, yeah. He'd a loved it, for sure," I say.

Suddenly, Louie frown again. "Sure hopes they ain't whuppin up on Leon down to the jail."

I think they might could be but I want to make Louie feel better so I change the subject. "Hey, remember that other thin we use do for fun to make cops mad?"

Louie shake his head. "Nuh uh."

"Remember when we promise those people that park by Booker T. for the football games we gonna protect they cars if they pay us?"

He chuckles. "Suckers. Cops knew we was doin it, too. Remember when they come and we run like hell? No matter how many times we pull that shit, they nevah caught us." Louie wrap his arms around his knees and rock back and forth laughin. "We out foxed them evah time, ain't we?'

"Sure did. Let's us do it again. Reckon we can get the other kids to help?"

Louie frowned. "Maybe. Depend on what happen to Leon. Gotta stick close to home if… if you know."

I nod. I do know. Mama said the trial gonna start in September. She hears stuff down to the café, so I trust what she says. I know Leon be sent to the electric chair if he get convicted. I don't want to think on it, and I'm sure Louie don't either, so I ax if he know that girl next to me, the one with the record player. He say no, but then he went off talkin 'bout some other girls he want to date. He name a bunch til he decide to go on home. When he walk off, I was glad we don't talk 'bout Leon no more.

August 2, 1960

After his first interview with Leon Pepper in May, Baxter had asked the prosecutor for Leon's statement and any other evidence, including the witness list. Although they weren't required to provide it, the state had finally agreed to share, but Baxter thought they'd also taken their own sweet time. Finally, by early July, he had the autopsy report, pictures from the crime scene, Pepper's statement in which he denied killing the woman, and the detective's notes. And, he'd gotten something he hadn't expected. The police had located the hammer that allegedly killed Mrs. Sowards, so there were photos of it, too. The afternoon after they'd arrested Pepper, the police had found it in an empty lot at the end of block in which Stanley's was located. It was covered in blood. Baxter made a note to ask Pepper if he'd had anything to do with it being there.

He called the jail, told them he was coming in, and asked them to get Pepper to a private room. When Baxter arrived, Pepper was sitting with his head in his shackled hands. He had a pretty good growth of beard and needed a haircut. Baxter noticed that he didn't smell all that good either. *Apparently, the niceties of groomin are low on his priority list.*

"Peppa, we need to talk," Baxter said without preamble. He was irritated. Pepper hadn't mentioned this hammer or told him he knew anything about it.

"Afternoon, Mista Baxta. What we got to talk 'bout?" He smiled innocently.

"You know anythin about a hammer? The one that they say killed Miz Sowards?"

At that, his head drooped until his chin nearly hit his chest. He sighed as if a great weight had been lifted.

"Yeah, I know 'bout a hammer; don't know if it's the same one, though. I been thinkin on that since I been up in here. I recollect when I woke up in front of Stanley's, it was in my hand. Don't know how it got there, but I knowed it ain't mine. I just knowed I had to get rid of it. When I was walkin around, I throwed it in some empty lot."

Baxter exploded. "In the name of God, man! You mean to tell me that knowin she'd been killed with a hammer and that you had one in your hand when you woke up, you never thought to mention it to me?"

"I nevah knowed that's how she's killed. That's a fact, Mista Baxta. It don't mean nothin so I nevah seen no reason to tell you 'bout it. Jes a hammer ain't mine. First, I think I might could use it, you know, but then I remember my mama tellin me nevah take

38

nothin ain't mine. Besides, I done learnt my lesson 'bout that after Milledgeville. So, I throwed it away. Nevah thought no more 'bout it."

His eyes were pleading with Baxter to believe his story, but Baxter still wasn't sure he was being truthful.

"Mista Peppa, I can't defend you if you don't tell me everythin. If you're lyin to me, you're as good as fried. You hearin me?" Baxter yelled. "Nothin I hate more than havin a client lie to me."

Pepper flared then. "I swear, I nevah remembered it when we was talkin before. I ain't lyin, Mista Baxta. When I tossed it, I didn't know nothin 'bout no murder. Now, I see I shoulda let you know when I first recollect 'bout it, but I nevah knowed them police had it."

Realizing that yelling was only frightening Pepper, Baxter calmed down. He knew having a frightened client wasn't going to help his case. "Well, they do. And I must say it doesn't look good for you to have thrown it away. Didn't you see the blood on it when you woke up?"

"I didn't see nothin. It was dark. I was drunk, but I knowed it weren't mine, so I just tossed it."

"Which hand was it in? Do you recall?"

"Left. It was in my left hand. Why?"

"You're right handed, aren't you?" Incredulous that Pepper couldn't see why that mattered, he stared at him.

"I am. That's a fact," he said still not understanding Baxter's point.

"Then it's unlikely you used it with your left.

Understand?"

"Oh, yeah. Nevah gave that much thought." He still looked puzzled. He glanced down at his hands as if he had to think deeply in order to see the significance of that detail.

"Okay, Mista Peppa. Now, think; is there anything else, anything at all, you also might have recollected since you've been here? Think carefully. Leave out nothin."

"No, sir. I swear. Nothin else. Sorry I ain't told you before."

Baxter stood and put out his hand. "I'll be in touch, Mista Peppa."

Pepper tried to reach toward the offered hand but with his shackles it was impossible for him to return the handshake. As the guard came forward, Baxter left.

When Baxter walked in his front door that night, his wife, Martha, knew immediately he'd had a horrendous day and was in a black mood. After all, they'd been married almost thirty years. She'd seen that scowl many times when he was worried or upset. When her husband headed straight for the bar without giving her a kiss, she said, "Uh oh, what's wrong?"

"Lemme get a drink and I'll tell you." With a stiff Scotch and water in hand, he settled into his easy chair and motioned for her to take the sofa. Loosening his tie, he said, "You know that kid I was appointed to defend, Leon Peppa? I think he's lied to me. Either that or he's not right bright, bless his heart. But the evidence he didn't tell me about will probably damn him. I swear, I ought to tell Judge Bishop I can't do this."

"Honey, you know you can't do that. Judge Bishop would have a conniption fit."

"I know. You're right; but I don't know if I can get this kid off. I feel sorry for him, and I really don't think he did it, but you know Blanchard's Bottom."

"What about it?" She looked puzzled.

On his stubby fingers, he ticked off the things bothering him. "One, the police found the hammer they believe killed Annie Sowards. Two, Mista Peppa has suddenly remembered that he woke up with said hammer in his hand. And three, he admits he threw the damn thin in the vacant lot right where the police recovered it. Now, how do you think a jury's gonna feel about all that?"

"Oh, Gerald, that certainly doesn't sound good. I'm so sorry. What *are* you gonna do?"

"I don't know yet. But since I can't quit, much as I'd like to, I've got to find some way to defend him. Blanchard's Bottom has been pretty quiet when it comes to Negras and whites gettin along. While other cities have had outright riots, we've been lucky, you know? But this will be an all-white jury, and that'll certainly stir up shit if he's convicted."

"Language, Gerald." Martha had always been the more conservative of the couple; perhaps because she did church volunteer work and Gerald was nearly always with men whose language could get salty. They'd never had children, to her regret. Gerald thought her volunteerism served as a good antidote, however. Their marriage had worked well for nearly thirty years.

"Sorry. Seriously, there haven't been many problems here at all, except for when that Negra doctor, Conaty, got murdered. And that was a while back. Even with the bus boycott and Martin Luther King stirrin things up, the whites here still tolerate the Negras as long as they, uh, stay in their own part of town. But that jury won't have a shred of sympathy for an unemployed colored kid. It would be even worse if she'd been white, but as it is, I'm still afraid he doesn't stand a chance."

AUGUST 5, 1960

Louie Pepper approached the Hitchins County Jail, but he stopped short of the steps. *If I'da knowed how scary that jail house would be, I nevah woulda lied 'bout my age to go see Leon.* Once he got inside, he worried some official would ask for identification, would want to verify his age, but no one approached him at all. It was as if they didn't even see him.

At the front desk he stopped. "Where I go see a prisoner, sir?" The man barely lifted his head as he pointed toward the end of the hall. "Room 123."

At the entrance to that room sat another man at a desk. This one smiled at Louie as if he could tell the kid was too young to be there but didn't care.

"I'm here to see Leon Peppa. I'm his brother," Louie said.

The man picked up a phone receiver and after a moment said, "Pepper. Leon Pepper," then hung up. A minute later the door opened, and he pointed at Louie and cocked his head toward the door as if to say, "go on in."

Once inside, he took a seat and looked around. The stink of the room assaulted Louie's nostrils. *Smell like bleach water, like they jes mop. Noisy, too. Lots of people waitin. If Mama knowed I was here, she whale the tar outta me. Ain't nevah tellin her, neither.*

Leon came in with a puzzled but dejected look on his face and took a seat across from his little brother. Louie was disappointed. He thought Leon would be glad to see him but instead, his brother growled, "What the fuck you doin here? I told you and Mama not to come."

"Nice to see you too, Leon. Shit! Thought you be glad see somebody from home. Mama don't wanna see you in here, but I do. I leave out if you want, but long as I'm here, might as well talk." Louie stared at him waitin to see if he was gonna calm down. *He looks skinnier and his hair all nappy. He used to keep it all grease down with pomade, but not now. Look all wild and outta shape. One eye look like it got a shiner, too.*

Leon sighed. "Okay, you right. Let's talk. How Mama doin?"

"Okay, I reckon. Don't tell me if she ain't. She don't nevah tell me what you say on the phone, neither. That how come I came… see for myself. How ya doin?"

Leon sighed again like he didn't want to tell his brother how things really were. "I'm managin. Me and my cellmate plays cards, walk the yard. He a big music guy, all time ax if I know this song or that. He hum a tune and I try to guess it. Passes time, you know? Little Richard, Clyde McPhatter, Laverne

Baker, James Brown. I'm pretty good at guessin."
Leon's smile made Louie think it was the best thing
that happened to him all day, every day.

"What that lawyer say? Got a trial date yet?"

"Ain't heard nothin, yet. Last time he came here,
he got all pissed off. Said the police done found a
hammer they say killed Miz Annie. I told him when
I come to that night, I got one in my hand. Nevah
knowed how it got there, though. Weren't mine, so I
throwed it in the lot down the street. He pissed I ain't
told him before. Ax did I think I should have told him.
I said, reckon I shoulda, but I nevah thought nothin
'bout it. I nevah killed that girl... nevah knowed a
hammer killed her, neither."

Louie didn't respond but nodded his head. *He act
like he don't get how bad that sound. He ain't nevah did have
walkin around sense, no how. His story sound fishy to me. Want
to believe him, ya know, but even if it ain't true, ain't no jury
gonna believe him no how...'specially a white one.*

"Nevah told Mama 'bout that, so you keeps your
damn mouth shut, hear me? She worried enough."
Leon leaned so close to Louie that he could smell his
body odor.

Louie pulled away. "I promise, Leon. I promise."

Leon sat back. "See you do."

After a minute's silence, Louie asks, "How you
get that shiner? Ain't beatin you in here is they?"

"Nah, some guy and me got into it in the yard.
We's wrasslin and he clip me with his elbow. Don't tell
Mama 'bout that, neither, you hear!"

"Okay." Louie didn't believe that story either, but

he nodded anyway. "They feedin you good?"

"Nah, taste like shit. Wish I could get me one of Stanley's fried boloney sandwiches."

"You ain't heard? Stanley's done closed. Right after Miz Annie killed, Mista Stanley close up tight. Said customers ain't comin where no murder happen. He right, ya know?"

"Yeah, I reckon. Too bad. He had him some fine boloney sandwiches."

After that Leon stopped talking. He sat there staring off into space as if he'd run out of words. Louie was lost for something else to talk about, as well, so the two sat in silence until Leon began to look around like he was ready to leave, to go back to his cell.

The guard noticed him and came toward the pair. Leon stood up. "Reckon I gotta go, Louie. Tell Mama I loves her."

"Can't. Mama don't know I come." Louie grinned.

"You little shit," Leon said, but he grinned too. "See you, Louie."

"See you, Leon," *I wanna be glad I came, but seein him walk away almost make me cry. I ain't nevah comin back here.*

SEPTEMBER 7, 1960
XANDER

The day Leon's trial started, I went to the court-house for the first time. It was right after Labor Day. First time skippin school, too. Knew I was gonna be in trouble, but I jes had to go.

When I was inside, I stared up at that big ole dome and swallowed hard. I'm scared to death somebody stop me, ax what my colored ass was doin there, and how come I wasn't in school. Kept lookin around at them cops standin up against the walls. One hocked a tobacco stream at a nearby spittoon and missed. Acted like it don't matter; jes kept right on talkin to his buddy. Nevah did like cops. Give me the heebie-jeebies. After I read the signs sayin the courtrooms was on the second floor, I climbed those marble stairs. Wandered around tryin to find the right one. I'm scared to ax anybody but I sure didn't want to go in the wrong room. It was as quiet as Satterwhite Cemetery at night. I could hear my shoes squeakin on the marble floors. *Hope folks in the other courtrooms can't hear em.* Finally, I saw Louie and his mama down the hall, so I walked toward them.

"Hey, Xander, what you doin here? Ain't seen you in a while. How you know Leon's trial started today?" Louie says.

"Mama heard it down to the café. Sorry I haven't been around much lately. Been mowin grass and deliverin for Mista Feeney. Tryin to save up for college, ya know?"

"Glad you're here," Louie said. His mama stared straight ahead. Nevah even nodded hello. She look more scared than me.

We find seats up near the front of the courtroom where we can hear real good. They's two tables in front of a tall desk way high up on this platform. I slides into a pew sorta like in Mama's church. Louie beside me. His mama on the end starin off into space like she tryin not to cry. Her face look all puffy like she already done cried a bunch. Other guys I seen around Booker T. come in and sit near us. Some got on their church clothes. We don't nod to each other, though. Like we don't wanna admit we's all from Booker T. I see the man owns the jook joint where Miz Annie Sowards killed, but I don't recognize any of the other peoples. Louie looks around too, but he don't act like he know anybody either. One guy holdin a notebook so I reckon he from the *Observer*.

Pretty soon, Leon come in from a side door near the front of the room. He gots a policeman on each side and he handcuffed. Look all skinny and wore out, like they don't let him sleep much. He don't even look at his mama or Louie. Some other guys, white guys in suits, walk to the tables and sit down. Leon the only Negro up there. Then a man in a uniform yell, "All rise," and a old gray-haired man, wearin some kind of choir robe, walk up a few steps to that platform and sit down behind the high desk.

Remind me of that revival preacher come set up a tent near the projects when I was a kid. Mama made us go. He worn a ratty-lookin dark-red robe and yell to the top of his lungs. Mama tried get me to go down front and get saved, but I grabbed hold of the chair like I was hangin on to a sinkin boat. She finally gave up. I don't really believe in it, but I'm prayin hard this robe-wearin guy won't yell like that preacher. Can't hurt none, I figure.

"The Superior Court of the State of Georgia is now in session. The Honorable Judge Michael Bishop presidin. You may be seated," says the guy in the uniform.

I watch Leon standin there in what look like orange pajamas. Seems defeated already and his trial hardly even started. yet. Makes me sad, 'cause *I* think Leon defeated already, too. Mama's all time tellin me God made everbody equal, but it's not so; hasn't been since Bible days. I remember readin one story how one of Noah's boys was Black. Right off the bat, brothers not equal. When I read that, I wonder why God done it.

And I knowed enough history to know why Leon's gonna pay for somethin he didn't do. Granny Sue told me 'bout slave ships brought our peoples here from

Africa. She said 'bout the time of the Civil War, her mama, Icey, got sent down the river to Georgia from Virginia for runnin away from her no-account master been rapin her. I'm not sure, but I think that why my hair's reddish and I'm a lot lighter skinned than Mama. Not sure 'bout Leon's peoples but I figure they sure didn't come here by themselves, neither.

I'd read 'bout all the lynchin and murderin in the South, too. Granny Sue told me when Negroes got elected to Congress durin Reconstruction, white folks got scared and ran them out. I seen pictures of great-grandpappy Hiram all suited up headin for the statehouse, proud as punch. Ain't any pictures of it, of course, but a few years after the Republicans got run outta office by the Democrats, Hiram end up swingin from a tree outside Atlanta. Mama said Granny Sue nevah said why they done that to her pap, but that's when she took all her kids and run off to Blanchard's Bottom.

Mama always say thins was better here when she a kid. Colored doctors, dentists, and lawyers all practice with no trouble. But lookin at the scowlin faces of them white men in the crowd, I wonder if they ain't sons of the men that acquitted that white Mista Klingman when he killed our Dr. Conaty. Everbody knowed he done it; they's witnesses, so colored folks marched. Then the KKK showed up, burnin crosses and harassin folks. Seem like evah time we try fightin back, thins gets worse. Klan shows up, cops start in beatin on folks or ignorin laws say we's equal.

Been readin *Ebony* and *Jet* down to Feeney's, too

so I know what's happenin now. Folks startin to resist, tryin to eat where they ain't been allowed before, and tryin integrate schools. I been hearin 'bout Dr. King, too. Wish I could be like him, but I'm not that brave. They bombed his house, for God's sake.

Now, I sit here watchin Leon on trial for murderin Miz Annie Sowards. Make me furious! All them white folk up there in charge. Wish I could tell *somebody* what I knows. If I do, Bill Feeney be up there, not Leon. As it is, can't do nothin 'bout it. First off, I promise Mama. Second, I'm too scared. So, I just know Leon gonna pay.

SEPTEMBER 7, 1960

The morning of Leon Pepper's trial, Gerald Baxter still wasn't sure how to defend his client. He thought the evidence was purely circumstantial, but that hammer weighed heavily on his mind. Baxter knew that on that score, Pepper was between a rock and a hard place. *If he'd had it when they arrested him, it would have been bad; but throwin it away is almost as bad.* Either way, it was damning evidence, despite that it was in his left hand. Sadly, Baxter wasn't sure how to overcome it. He knew that Riley Connick, the prosecutor, could even question *that*, since no one actually had seen Pepper passed out. It was only his word that it was in his left hand. Some of the other issues Baxter felt he could blame on sloppy police work, the mere coincidence that Leon had been at Stanley's when he passed out, and the lack of witnesses to put him inside the joint; but that hammer. *Geez.*

As Pepper entered the courtroom, Baxter's first thought was that he wished he'd bought him a suit, told him to clean up a bit. Even *he* thought Pepper looked like a criminal with that scruffy beard, that raggedy hair. He made a mental note to change that if the trial went on past today. As an added precaution, he leaned over and asked Harry Spano to remind him to do it. He was a good lawyer and a compassionate man who Baxter knew would understand the importance of his request. Baxter also knew Spano was a good investigator. Before the trial, Baxter had sent him out to see if he could find out who the other guy in the bar had been, but he'd had no luck. Seemed as if the only two who had seen the guy were Cousey and Pepper.

The courtroom was full; quite a few Negroes but mostly white men waiting to see if they'd be selected for the jury. None of the Negroes had that expectation since there hadn't been a colored man on a jury in Blanchard's Bottom in anyone's memory. At the state's table sat the prosecutor, Riley Connick, and his assistant, Jefferson Doyle. Baxter knew Connick was a bulldog in murder trials but also thought he was the most bigoted man he'd ever met. Both facts made Baxter sweat. *Lord, all I can hope for is a fair-minded set of jurors*, he prayed silently.

About the time the lawyers got settled, Judge Bishop banged his gavel and said, "Gentlemen, you may begin questionin the potential jurors."

Back and forth the two attorneys went. Connick threw out anyone who had colored people working for them. And, of course, men who disapproved of the death penalty were rejected right away. Baxter asked about the death penalty, too, but obviously, he *wanted* folks who didn't believe in it. Figuring they might have known Annie Sowards, Baxter rejected those who had ever been to Stanley's Jook Joint. Baxter also objected to anyone admitting to attending rallies where the KKK had been, even if they'd gone only out of curiosity.

By lunchtime the jury had been seated, so Baxter returned to his office to work on his opening argument. On the way, he silently thanked his considerate wife for sending him off with a sack lunch. It seemed she always knew when his day was so full he'd have no time to go out. *Bless her heart.*

As he sat there absently chewing on his roast beef sandwich, the words he'd written earlier looked stiff to him, unconvincing. *Damn, if only he'd never touched that hammer, never carried it off.* In his gut, Baxter believed Pepper's story. He could see he wasn't a bad kid, just sort of a ne'er-do-well. Steady jobs had eluded him since he dropped out of high school. He'd hung out with guys who drank their way through the day, and he wasn't real sharp. That teenage conviction for stealing a car? It had been pure joy riding. He'd gone along with another guy, but he swore he didn't know the car was stolen. Granted, it had given him a record, but that didn't make him a murderer. Baxter crumpled up the sheet of paper and decided to just go with his gut. Speaking from his heart had usually stood him well in the past, he thought.

From what Pepper'd said, he *was* treated badly by the police. Baxter thought their investigation had been sloppy, as well. From the beginning, he believed

Pepper had been a convenient collar, identified only by someone who'd seen him in the neighborhood that night. He had asked Pepper who might have had such a beef with him that they pointed out him to the cops, but no one had come to Pepper's mind. Baxter then wondered if it could it have been the white guy Leon said was in the bar. He'd certainly have had a reason to point to Pepper since he was passed out in the doorway. While he hadn't done criminal work in a long, long time, something told Baxter this kid was different, and he was determined to save his ass.

September 7, 1960
Xander

As all the mens up at the tables in front start sittin down, one of them nod and smile at Leon. I guess he the lawyer they got to defend him. *What Louie call him? Baxta? Mista Baxta? Yeah, that it.* Until he smile he look mean, like somebody you don't wanna mess with. Gray hair all slick back and parted in the middle. He had a vest on and a fat gold chain across his belly. Not real fat, but not skinny, neither. With a wad of tobacco in his cheek, he look like a lop-sided toad.

Judge Bishop bangs his gavel, "Very well, gentlemen, are you ready to select a jury?" he ax.

The two main guys say yes and start to ax the jurymen a bunch of questions. I sort of stop listenin then, but I know they tryin to decide who gonna be on the jury. I saw that on television, but I just not payin much attention to what they's sayin. Instead I'm watchin Leon. His head all bent down again and I don't see him lookin up that whole time. *Wonder if he scared. I sure would be.* I'm scared for him. I'm ashamed I didn't tell somebody what I knowed. Dr. King'd be ashamed of me, if he knowed what I knowed. Part of me want to run, leave outta here, and try not to think 'bout it. The other part want to stay. That part wins.

For the next hour or so, the lawyers call out names one by one and ax each man a couple questions. I seen some of em in Mista Feeney's buyin cigarettes or chewin tobacco. Wonder if any of em evah seen Miz Annie sneakin around with Mista Feeney? If they did, they sure didn't admit it.

All of a sudden, the guy in the uniform stands up and yells, "All rise" again. The judge musta said we could get lunch but I nevah heard him. I'm glad though, 'cause my belly growlin. I nevah told Mama where I was goin before she left out for work. I was afraid she tell me get on to school and keep my black butt outta that business. So, after she left out the door, I fix me a boloney and butter sandwich and stuff it in a paper sack. Now, I wish I made one for Louie too, but I nevah even thought 'bout it. We's walkin out the courtroom when Miz Peppa grabs Louie's hand. From the look on his face I knowed he embarrassed. But I figure she jes tryin to protect the one son she still got with her.

"Where ya'll goin, Louie?" I call.

"Chicken Little's, Mama says. Wanna come?" Louie's way down the hall so I can't hardly hear him.

"Nah, Got me a boloney sandwich. Jes gonna stay here. Later."

Louie nods as his mama pull him toward the

stairs.

I walk down behind a couple of mens that wasn't picked for the jury. One says, "I'm sure glad I ain't on that jury. I don't like hearin 'bout no murder."

Another one agrees. "All those questions… they made my head spin. Bet he's guilty as sin, though. Damn nigger. Wouldn't a minded sayin he should be electrocuted."

I hunker down on one side of that downstairs lobby hopin they hadn't seen me listenin to em. When they gets close to the front doors, I waits til they leave, then I shoves one open, hurry through, and run out past the big fountain. Run cross Tenth Street to the gas station over on Blanchard get a CoCola to go with my sandwich. The summer sun make shiny little rainbows in the oil splotches on the streets. I dodge em so they don't splash my shoes.

"Hey, Mista White," I yells over his blarin radio. I wipe my sweaty forehead on my sleeve. "Gonna get me a Coke." Mista White wave then go back to workin under the hood of this old Chevy. Feelin in my pocket for change, I wonder how long before I gotta stop mowin and get a better job. Oughta be workin today, but I jes had to be there for Leon. Had the feelin if I'd ignored Mama and said somethin back then, Leon wouldn't be up in front of that judge lookin like his life's over. *Why can't I jes call his lawyer? He don't have to know who talkin?* I worry 'bout this walkin back over to the courthouse. By the time I climbs the steps again, I know I won't call. He know it's a kid and wouldn't listen. Besides, I'm just too damn scared. If somebody found out I told, Klan be back for sure.

On the second floor, the hallway is full of mens. The noise of their voices make me wanna cover my ears. They's so loud it's like they wants everbody to hear em. "Nigger boy killed that girl sure as I'm standin here." "He gonna fry, that's for sure." Made me mad. I jerk open the courtroom doors and look for Louie and his mama. Don't see em, so I sorta tiptoe up to where we been sittin. Then, I turns to watch the doors, hopin they gonna get here soon. Finally, I see Louie and raise my hand. Louie lift his head, grab his mama hand and almost drag her where I'm sittin.

"Hey, Louie," I say as they slide in next to me. "What'd ya have at Chicken Little's?"

Before Louie can answer, that uniform guy yell, "All rise." We do. The judge comes back in and sweep to his seat, robes flowin all around him. This time, I think of the pictures of King Solomon in my book of Bible stories. *Sure hope he as fair as Solomon.* Should be wishin that 'bout the twelve men in the jury box instead, though, I reckon.

Watchin em settlin down in their seats, I can tell none of em Mista Feeney's customers, leastwise none I evah seen. Some wearin they Sunday-go-to-meetin suits, others got on bib overalls and work shoes. A few are wearin slacks, open-neck, short-sleeved shirts like they's gonna play golf later. The courtroom hotter'n the hinges of Hades. Wonder how long before them men in suits be pullin at their neckties or takin off they sweaty jackets.

The judge's boomin voice make me almost jump

when he start talkin to the jury. All twelve pair of eyes glued on him, like what he sayin's a new bunch of Ten Commandments.

Judge say, "Gentlemen, this trial is for a capital crime. Leon Peppa is accused of and has been indicted on the charge of murder. However, you must presume his innocence. The burden of proof of his guilt beyond a reasonable doubt is on the State of Georgia. There are four possible verdicts: you may find the defendant not guilty, guilty of murder, voluntary manslaughter, or involuntary manslaughter.

"Murder is when someone is killed through actual intent, or with depraved disregard for human life, or in the commission of a felony such as arson, rape, robbery, or burglary. Voluntary manslaughter is when the killin occurs with intent under sudden excitement and heat of passion and with provocation by the victim and could be considered self-defense. Involuntary manslaughter is when a person is killed, say in an automobile accident in which the defendant is found guilty of a crime, like speedin, which is not a felony. Murder is punishable by death or life in the state penitentiary at Reidsville. Voluntary manslaughter can carry a sentence of one to ten years in Reidsville. The maximum term for involuntary manslaughter is ten years, but it may also be deemed a misdemeanor and is then only punishable by less than a year in prison.

"You will also determine, if he is found guilty of murder, whether Mista Peppa should be executed or sentenced to life imprisonment. Do you all understand?" The jurymens all nod.

Lookin at Louie and his mama, I'm feelin sorta sick to my stomach. Maybe it's the boloney, but most likely, it's 'cause I jes *know* Leon isn't guilty. Can't prove it, but I sure hope that lawyer can. One of the lawyers at the other table stand up so quick I jump in my seat. He as skinny as Leon pot-bellied lawyer is fat. The seersucker suit he wearin hang from his shoulders and bag at the waist like he lost weight but didn't have a mind to buy a new one. The pants only held up by his big old red suspenders. He look like he think he a snappy dresser 'cause he got a red bowtie and red socks to match, too. He hook his fingers under his suspenders, and says, "Your Honor, I object to the addition of the manslaughter charges."

"Removed," say the judge, without lookin up. "Mista Connick, you may proceed with your openin argument."

"Thank you, Your Honor."

I look at Louie and his mama, again. Both of them are on the edge of their seats. I swallow hard. I know how much they must be dreadin what that man gonna say.

September 7, 1960

Louie watched his mother as the prosecutor gave his opening argument. He looked scared stiff as Connick strutted back and forth in front of the jury box saying he could prove Leon raped and murdered Annie Sowards. When he yelled that he could prove the hammer they found was the murder weapon, Louie nearly came off his seat. When he started talking about rape, Louie looked at his mother who looked even more scared than before. Tears brimmed in her eyes, which made Louie's stomach heave so badly he thought he might vomit. He'd never seen his mother cry, ever.

Baxter stood then. Before he began, he shifted his wad of tobacco from one cheek to the other. "Gentlemen of the jury," he said, "the defense will prove beyond a shadow of a doubt that Leon Pepper is not guilty; that the evidence against him is purely circumstantial. We will show that no one saw him inside Stanley's; that he has no history of violence of any kind; and that he was a victim of being in the wrong place at the wrong time."

His opening apparently made Louie and his mother feel better, because they sat back in their seats, looking relaxed, as Baxter continued his opening arguments. Leon, however, was still looking down at his lap, as if he could find a way out of his situation down there. Louie thought he ought not do that; it made him look guilty.

"Mista Connick, you may now call your first witness," Judge Bishop announced. Connick rose and began walking to the witness stand, thumbs in his suspenders.

"Thank you, Your Honor. The state calls Claude Stanley," Connick yelled.

Claude Stanley shuffled to the stand, dragging one leg. Louie's face registered recognition. Stanley was also a member of Louie's mother's church. He knew Stanley had gotten that bad leg in a fight with some white boys when he was young. He remembered his mother saying they had kicked him so badly they had broken his leg. Since his family couldn't afford a doctor, he had just let it heal on its own. Stanley put his hand on the Bible and was sworn in.

"State your name," Connick said.

"Claude Robert Stanley."

"And how long have you owned Stanley's Jook Joint?"

"Probably eight years. Just closed it after…" His voice trailed off as Connick interrupted him.

"How long did Annie Sowards work for you?"

"I'm thinkin it was five years, but I'm not sure.

She'd been my manager for the past two years."

"You are the person who found her body, correct?"

"Yes." He looked out the window as if he wished he could forget the sight.

"Please tell us your actions that night and the next mornin."

Stanley cleared his throat. "Well, as usual I came in about ten or eleven to pick up the money from the cash drawer. I usually come back a second time, around one, but that night I didn't. Annie had said business was light when I was there the first time, so I decided to just wait until the next mornin. Maybe if I'd come back, Annie might still be alive."

Baxter jumped up. "Speculation on the part of the witness, Your Honor."

"Strike that," Judge Bishop told the court reporter. "Gentlemen of the jury, you are to disregard the remark," he said looking at the jury box.

"I know it will be hard, but can you tell us what you found when you arrived the following mornin, sir," Connick said, trying to strike a sympathetic tone, but his lips quickly hardened into a thin line.

Stanley hesitated, swallowing several times, his Adam's apple bobbing. "I came in through the back door and went into the front room where Annie's body was lyin in a pool of blood. I nearly puked when I saw her. I immediately ran to the back room and called the police. While I was waitin for them, I checked the cash drawer and looked to see if any tools or equipment had been stolen."

Connick then asked Stanley what he discovered in his search. Stanley said the hammer he kept in the back room was gone but none of his knives. "The cash drawer was empty, although I expected it would have had *some* money in it. The front door padlock was lyin beside the drawer and all the lights were on."

Connick told Stanley he had no further questions. Then Baxter rose, spit in the nearby wastebasket, and walked to the witness stand. He smiled at Stanley and thanked him for coming. Louie frowned as if he wondered why he'd said that. He knew the man had no choice. Baxter tucked his tobacco wad in his right cheek and began.

"How did you know the drawer should still have had money in it? Do you have a way to determine if she did more business after you left?"

"Not really. She just usually has good late nights. We sorta operate on a cash basis, late nights. Don't write bar tickets then, you understand?" He winked.

Baxter grinned as if he knew the man didn't report all of his income but had no intention of exposing his subterfuge here in court. "Did any of the rooms look as if there'd been a fight?"

Connick rose. "Objection, Your Honor. Calls for a conclusion by the witness."

"Sustained," Bishop replied.

"I'll rephrase. Was anythin out of order in either room, Mista Stanley?"

"No, other than all that blood. But, the kitchen was still dirty like she'd been stopped before she could clean up like she always did."

"Does Miz Sowards usually wear a uniform?"

"Yes, usually, but she was wearin her street clothes when I arrived earlier that night, like she was fixin to leave as soon as she could close."

"No further questions at this time," Baxter said. When he returned to the table, he spat again in the wastebasket.

Connick rose again and strutted toward Stanley. "You say you don't keep sales receipts?" He sounded as if he didn't believe what Stanley had previously told Baxter.

Stanley looked away from Connick as if he thought the man was trying to get him into trouble. "Well, sometimes, late at night, we don't."

"Then, how do you know how much you sold?" Connick asked, his eyes squinting and his chin stuck out belligerently. Stanley said he counted the money each night and figured Annie didn't lie.

"After you called the police, did you call anyone else?"

"No. I just, uh, stayed in the back room so I wouldn't disturb anythin. I thought about callin Annie's husband but decided the police should do it, not me."

When Connick said he had no more questions, Stanley wiped his brow, climbed down from the witness stand, and limped back to his seat. As he went, Bishop said Connick could call his next witness. Connick yelled, "The state, uh, calls Mista Paul Sowards."

September 7, 1960

As Gerald Baxter watched Riley Connick pace back and forth in front of the jury box, he was reminded of a skinny bantam rooster his grandmother used to own. *That old feller thought he was a ladies' man, but in truth, the hens were all a bit afraid of him. Watchin the faces of the jurors, I see those hens, a bit intimidated by Connick's blusterin ways.* He decided right then that when it was his turn to examine his witnesses, he'd use a different approach.

Connick called Annie's husband to the stand. Mr. Sowards, dressed in what looked like a crisp, new suit from Victor's, came forward, his head ducked as if he really didn't want to be there. Baxter saw the look, knew it was painful for the man and sympathized with him. *Who wants to talk about his wife's murder? I hope Connick will be civil to him.*

After he was sworn in, Connick began. "Mista Sowards, are you employed at this time?" Connick's tone was casual.

"Nah, sir, I ain't. Annie makin the money these

days."

"And how late did she usually work?" Connick stuck his hands in his pants pockets and fingered the change he found.

"Oh, sometimes she don't come home till three, four, five in the mornin. Hell, sometimes she don't come home at all."

Two of the jurors tried unsuccessfully to stifle snickers. Connick whipped around and scowled at them. Then, he whirled back to face Sowards. "And didn't that bother you? Knowin she didn't come home after work?"

"No, it weren't unusual at all. Me and her had an understandin 'bout that." He grinned a sort of wolf-ish smirk like he assumed Connick understood that the two lived somewhat separate lives. Baxter made a note to ask him in depth about that.

"Mista Sowards, where were you the night of your wife's death?" Connick asked. His casual tone had evaporated.

"Out with my friends playin poker over to Por-ter's Social Club on Fourth Avenue. Come home around two but Annie weren't there. I didn't think nothin 'bout it and went on to sleep."

"I see." Connick leaned in toward his witness lookin skeptical. "Mista Sowards, your marriage sounds, shall we say, unusual. Are you married in name only or, uh, in the Biblical sense?"

"Oh, no, sir. We was truly married; in a church we was. But we jes has our own friends."

"I have no further questions for Mista Sowards.

Thank you, sir."

Sowards started to leave the witness stand, but Judge Bishop stopped him. "Mista Sowards, please stay seated. Mista Baxta has a few questions of his own, I assume?"

Baxter nodded to the judge and approached the man. "Good afternoon, Mista Sowards. I'm sorry for your loss."

"Thank you kindly, sir." Sowards smiled, looking somewhat less ill at ease.

"Sir, can you tell me how long you and your wife were married?"

"Let's see… must be 'bout fifteen years. She was 'bout twenty-five and I was twenty-eight when we was hitched."

"And did she work elsewhere in the early years of your marriage?"

"No, sir. I used to work regular. But I hurt my back. Fell off a sanitation truck. Nevah worked no more. 'Course, I nevah got no disability on account of them people always think you fakin a bad back. She got that job over to Stanley's then to help out."

"I see. Did she feel safe workin there so late? In other words, did she ever tell you she thought it might be a dangerous place to be that late?"

"Nah. Most folks comes in there we both be knowin. I mean, it's a regular hangout for folks in our neighborhood, you know? Everbody goes to Stanley's. They got great food." The same two men who had stifled snickers before did so again. Baxter wondered if they'd ever gone to Stanley's themselves, or were just amused that Mista Sowards had sounded like an advertisement for the place.

"I believe you told Mista Connick that the two of you lived somewhat separate lives. Is that right?"

"Well, not exactly. I mean we has our own friends, but we're still a couple. We do *some* thins together, too. Well, we did, before…"

"Were you ever jealous of her friends? Were there any you wished she didn't run around with?"

"Can't think of none. 'Course, I don't know em all. Like I said, we don't ax each other too many questions, if you know what I mean."

Baxter looked at him closely. Suddenly, Sowards folded his arms across his chest and sort of fidgeted in his seat like he wanted to avoid this line of questioning, like he was afraid Baxter knew exactly what he meant and was going to make him admit it. "Are you sayin the two of you were unfaithful to each other, Mista Sowards? That your wife could have had a lover?"

Sowards ducked his head slightly so that his answer was muffled. "Yeah, she coulda. But I still loved her."

"Mista Sowards, would you please speak up and repeat your answer for the jury?"

He lifted his head and repeated, "I said, 'yeah, she coulda had someone else, but I loved her anyway.'"

A murmur rippled through the crowd but died before Bishop could object.

"Thank you, Mista Sowards," Baxter said, also ignoring the audience's reaction. "Now, you said you were playin poker that night. Is that right?"

Sowards nodded.

"So, I assume your friends can vouch for you, for what time you left?"

"Sure can," he said. "Call them… they tell you. I lost big that night, so I know they'll remember."

Somebody in the audience laughed but Baxter ignored that, too, while suppressing his own smile. "Thank you, Mista Sowards. No further questions."

As Baxter returned to his seat, Connick announced that he had no redirect. Baxter hoped his questions had put some doubt in the jurors' minds about Miz Annie's morals and that he soon would have a chance to convince them she'd had a quarrel with one of her lovers and that it had gone badly, very badly.

September 7, 1960
Xander

When I hear Miz Annie husband say Miz Annie might coulda had a boyfriend, I think of Bill Feeney. Make me pretty sure I was right all along. Make me want to call Leon's lawyer even more. Tell him what I know. But, if I do, I know I'll have to testify and probably lose my job for sure. I swallow hard, knowin I can't afford to do that. I'm hopin Mista Baxta can get Leon off without me, plus, Klan might come back.

While I'm worryin 'bout this, skinny old Mista Connick call Sergeant Thad Kelly up to the stand.

"Sergeant Kelly, I'd like you to tell the court just what your activities were on the mornin of February 13," Connick says, gettin straight to the point after Kelly sworn in. I look at Kelly with that bushy red hair. Make me think of Miz Butterworth with her dyed orange hair. His look natural, though.

"Certainly. We were at the station house at the time. It was around eleven in the mornin, and a call came in…"

Connick stop Kelly before he's through answerin. "Who is 'we,' Sergeant?"

"Lieutenant Matthew Blevins and Detective Ralph Settle, sir. Like I said, we were workin together that day and the call came in. We left and went to the address given, which turned out to be Stanley's Jook Joint. We entered the buildin and viewed the body…"

Connick interrupt again. He sound sort of rude. "Do you know who made the call?"

"Yes, it was the owner, Claude Stanley. He said he'd found her when he went to work around ten that mornin. He said the front door was closed but not locked. The back door was open, too but he found her in the front room lyin on her back. Said her head was bashed in and all bloody. Made me half sick."

When he said that, Louie's mama dropped her head in her hands. She sort of made a little whimper. I look over at Leon. Now he's starin at Mista Stanley like he want to know what he sayin as bad as that lawyer. Like he's surprised to hear what he's sayin. Like it's the first time he's knowin all this.

Kelly wiggles in his seat like he pissed 'bout bein interrupted every time he tries to answer Connick's question. "Like I said," he repeats, "we viewed the scene and asked Mista Stanley several questions and then I called the station house to ask them to send the coroner over. It didn't take too long before Chief Gordon and two other detectives arrived on the scene. One of them, Detective Ballard, told us someone had called after we left to say they'd seen the accused around Stanley's 'bout one in the mornin. I don't know why they thought to call; maybe they saw our patrol car out front. We left then to go to the accused's home to question him."

Now, my imagination go wild. I can just see ol Bill Feeney in that bar talkin with Miz Annie, gettin in a fight with her, killin her, and then the next mornin callin the station hisself sayin he saw Leon there, tryin to blame him. *Lordy be, I wish I could tell somebody, anybody, what I know.*

Connick keeps axin questions. "And what happened when you approached the accused's home?"

"A lady answered the door, said she was his sister. We asked for Mista Peppa and she called him down. When he came to the door, we told him we wanted to ask him some questions about where he'd been the night before. He asked why and we told him there had been a murder and that he was a suspect but he claimed he didn't know anythin about a murder. He said he'd been out drinkin with a friend, gotten pretty drunk, and then come home and had gone to bed. We asked him if he went to Stanley's Jook Joint and he admitted goin by, but said he never went in. He told us he'd actually been by Stanley's twice that night – once with his friend, then later by himself. We told him that Miz Annie had been killed and he said again he didn't know anythin about that. Said he'd seen her, but he didn't know anythin about her bein killed. We told him he'd have to come with us to answer more questions and we left with him."

"What was his attitude, Sergeant?"

Baxta jumps up, "Objection, Your Honor. Requires an assumption on the part of the officer."

"Sustained," says Judge Bishop.

"I'll rephrase. Did the accused resist your request to go with you?"

"No, but he continued to say he didn't know anythin about a murder," Kelly admitted.

"You may continue, Sergeant." Connick walkin back and forth in front of the man, but ever once in a while, he sneak a look at the jury. Guess he wanna see how they takin what Kelly sayin.

"Well sir, when we put the accused in the car, I noticed blood on his jacket, pants cuff, and tennis shoes. When we asked him about that, he said it must have come from when he'd been haulin carcasses over at the meat market a few days earlier. Lieutenant Blevins started the car and we drove toward Stanley's. Detective Settle and I were in the back seat with the accused. He asked where we were goin, and I told him Stanley's. He wanted to know why and I said we had somethin to show him. He wanted to know what and I said, 'Miz Annie Sowards. We think you need to see her body, see what you did to her.' He got very upset then and yelled that he didn't want to go in to see the body. Said he was afraid of dead people and that he didn't want his friends to see him in handcuffs, either. I told him if he'd tell us what happened we wouldn't make him go. Told him that several times. Finally he said he was drunk but that he might have done it."

Like a shot, Leon stands up, yellin, "That ain't what I said! He lyin!" Judge Bishop start bangin his gavel on the desk and yellin hisself. I nearly jumps outta my skin, he scare me so bad. I look at Leon, but he don't look scared, not one bit. Look like he gonna come over that table and grab that cop. Baxta put his hand on Leon arm to stop him but Leon jerk it away. After the judge quits bangin and yellin, I can hear Baxta say, "Sit down, Mista Peppa. You'll get your turn later."

It take a minute before Leon sits back down, but boy, do he have a mean look on his face. He lean over whisperin to Mista Baxta and I'm wonderin what he sayin. I cut a look over at Louie. He look scared as me. But, I'm bettin he's more scared of what Leon did than of the judge. It wasn't a very smart thing to do, I gotta admit.

Once things calm down, Connick goes on and asks more questions. "And when you heard the accused confess, what did you do next?"

"We did as we had told him we would: we left the scene and went to the police station to get him to sign a sworn statement."

"And did he?"

"No, well, yes, but it wasn't a confession. After we got there, he swore he *didn't* kill her."

"Did he say why he'd changed his statement?" Connick looks like he doesn't like this answer.

"He said he was confused and that what he said was that he was drunk and didn't know what he'd done that night. He said he said he *might* have, but then after he thought about it on the way downtown, he knew he didn't."

"Thank you, Sergeant. No further questions."

Connick sits down. The judge hollers out, "Your witness, Mista Baxta."

Mista Baxta sorta ambles up to the witness stand, looks at his pocket-watch, move his tobacco wad from one side of his mouth to the other, then he look real hard at Sergeant Kelly.

"Sergeant Kelly, why did you think it was so important to take Mista Peppa inside the crime scene? For him to see the deceased? Wasn't it just to intimidate him? To get him to confess?"

"Objection!" Connick's outta his seat like he's been sittin on a couch spring that just broke.

"Sustained. Mista Baxta, watch yourself."

"Yes, Your Honor. I'll ask again — why did you feel it was necessary for Mista Peppa to see the body?"

"Well, we just thought… I thought he ought to see what he'd done. Maybe it would help him remember, you know?" Kelly's stammerin around, soundin like he doesn't want to talk about it. Like he knew he shouldn't have said it.

"Did you threaten Mista Peppa with takin him inside to *persuade* him to give what you call a confession?"

"No, sir. Only told him we'd take him inside if he didn't tell us what happened."

"And how many times did you tell him that?"

"Geez, I don't know. We were all talkin at once. Maybe three or four."

"Just one more question, Sergeant Kelly; did you question the folks at the meat market to corroborate

Mista Peppa's story of workin there?"

"We did, sir. And apparently he was tellin the truth."

Baxta smiles, "That will be all, Sergeant. Thank you."

I guess I been holdin my breath, 'cause it escapes like a big old sigh. Got a terrible feelin that sergeant just lied his ass off 'bout not *persuadin* Leon. Of course, I couldn't never prove it no more'n I could prove Mista Feeney killed Miz Annie. But I've heard plenty of stories 'bout cops' way of *persuadin* us coloreds. Hell, I seen with my own two eyes them cops in that cruiser watchin that gang of white boys threaten me and Louie. Poor Leon, I know who that jury is gonna believe. It ain't gonna be Leon.

September 7, 1960

After all the jurors had been chosen and sworn in, Judge Bishop told Denzel Pennington that being juror number one made him the foreman. He wasn't too happy about that but that's the way it was. All through Riley Connick's opening statement, Pennington had noticed that Pepper was staring at Connick, his mouth hanging open like a big old bass. It was as if he couldn't believe what was going on.

When Connick finished examining Sargent Thad Kelly, Police Chief Peter Gordon – a man Pennington had known as a schoolyard bully throughout their twelve years in school together – was sworn in. Connick walked up to the stand and, after asking him to state his name and title, asked, "What condition was the body in with respect to wounds or signs of a struggle, sir?"

"The body was layin on its back and apparently had been beaten savagely around the head. Blood was splattered all over the body, her clothin, and around the room, probably six to eight feet in radius from the body. It was on the walls, as well," Gordon said, like he'd seen this stuff every day.

"To clarify, you mean six or eight feet on each side of the body? So, the blood covered twelve to sixteen feet in total?"

Chief Gordon shook his head. "Lord no! No, I may have used the wrong word. Six or eight feet *total*, so three or four feet on each side of her body."

"And what about her clothin? What position was it in?"

"Position? Well, the dress was still on her, but it was up above her knees and her half-slip was on the floor between her legs. They were spread apart slightly. There was a garter belt with one stockin still attached, near the slip. One stockin was pulled down but still on her foot. She was still wearin both shoes, as I recall."

"Was she wearin panties?" Connick asked.

"I don't recall noticin. Perhaps the other officers or the coroner did."

"Thank you, Chief. No further questions." He snapped his suspenders as if to put an exclamation point on his inquiry.

Baxter rose as Connick returned to his chair and went up to the chief. "Afternoon, Chief Gordon. I just want to clear up a point or two. Did the room show any signs of a scuffle, a fight?" He sounded casual, as if they were havin a conversation in a bar or over coffee.

"No, sir. Other than Miz Sowards' body in the middle of the floor, everythin else was in order. Except, of course, for all that blood." Gordon's Adam's apple bobbed up and down as he swallowed a few times. He cleared his throat like he was tryin to get the taste of blood out of his own mouth.

"And, about that blood. If it was splattered so widely, wouldn't you assume it would also be all over the person who killed her? All over his or her clothes?"

"I don't see how that could be avoided, Mista Baxta."

"Were there any footprints, you know, from walkin in the blood?"

"Yes, but on examination we found they belonged to Officer Blevins."

"That's all, Chief. Thank you." Baxter walked away, but Pennington saw a little smile on his face when he turned around.

Next, Connick called the coroner, Whitney Bullard. Bullard was so fat that Pennington couldn't see how on earth he could waddle up to the witness stand. He hoisted himself up the steps and plopped into the chair with a thud. Pennington feared the chair would break under his weight. It took Bullard one whole minute to get his breath. When he did, Connick said, "You okay, Whit?"

The old man wiped his forehead with a huge white handkerchief he pulled out of his jacket pocket and said, "Yeah, I just get a little winded, time to time."

"Very well, we'll go on then. When you arrived at the scene of the crime, were Officers Kelly and Blevins, and Detective Settle still there?"

"They were not. Only Chief Gordon and another detective. I didn't catch his name, though."

"Did you question Mista Stanley after you arrived?"

"Yes, sir. He told us the same thin the police officers have testified to."

"And did you examine the victim's body at that time?"

"Only preliminarily, sir. Shortly after I arrived, Billy Jack Hoffman's fellas showed up and took the body to the morgue at Piedmont Hospital. I did my full examination there." He mopped his forehead, again.

"Would you please tell us what you found in that preliminary examination, sir?" Connick glanced at the jury as if he wanted to be sure every man heard Bullard's description.

"Well, the first thin I can say is that in all my twenty-five years as a coroner, I've never seen a more horribly mangled human head. It had been severely beaten with some sorta blunt instrument. At first, it was hard to see that because of all the blood. We washed off a bit of the blood in order to see better. Then we saw some sort of sooty mud and fine gravel or sand also smeared across her face. When we cleaned that off it looked like somethin had caused a large abrasion on her cheek. It was like someone had used sandpaper or a rasp to sideswipe her face."

When he said that, Pennington winced as if the blow had been inflicted on him.

"And did you find any object or objects that could

have inflicted those wounds?" Connick leaned in and looked closely at the coroner.

"No sir, although Mista Stanley did tell us a hammer he had in the back room was missin. Apparently the first officers on the scene had also spoken with him about that."

Connick spun on his heels, walked to his table, and picked up a plastic bag with a hammer in it. "Is this the hammer Mista Stanley said was missin?"

"Looks like it," Bullard said.

"Did you test it for blood or fingerprints?"

"We could see what looked like blood on it, but we didn't actually test it as it seemed obvious it would have been the victim's. You'd have to ask the police about fingerprints."

"Thank you. Continue tellin us about what you saw in your examination, if you please."

Bullard went on. "The lower jaw of the victim was broken on both sides allowin it to be moved around." He mopped his forehead again and then didn't say anythin for a minute. Finally, he started back up. "I hate to say it this way but it looked as if her head been stomped on by someone wearin boots. It was completely unrecognizable as that of a human bein."

Baxter jumped up from behind his table. "Objection. Calls for a conclusion by the witness."

"Sustained," said the judge.

Connick shook his head as he looked at the jury. His expression registered regret that he'd asked that question. Then, he glared at Pepper and frowned. Suddenly, it was apparent to Pennington that he *wanted* the jury to hear all the gory details. *He ain't sorry at all. That's his way of makin sure we knew just how awful her death was.* Pennington glanced over at Leon Pepper, who had his head in his hands, and then at Paul Sowards, who sat a few rows behind Connick's table. His head was in his hands, as well.

Connick turned back to his witness. "Mista Bullard, can you tell us anythin else you viewed at the scene?"

"Yes, sir, she also had a stab wound to her left chest area. That probably accounted for the large amount of blood around her body. And, as has been said before, her clothin, and her hands and face were splattered with blood. It seemed to have pooled around her head, flowed down the side of her face, and down her arms as she lay on the floor. Some of the blood on her face seemed to have dried. Her back, above her waist, was soaked in blood as well," he said.

"And, uh, what did you observe about her clothin?" Connick started jinglin the change in his pocket again as if he was nervous about something.

Bullard wiggled in his seat and mopped his face again. "Her panty girdle, actually it was a garter belt, had been pulled down… it looked like that had been done forcefully or in a hurry because it wasn't neatly arranged on her legs, you know? Her shoes were on, but her stockins were sort of inside out, like someone had tried to remove them without takin off her shoes. Understand?"

Connick nodded and looked over at us like he wanted us to nod back.

"One was almost over the shoe, the right one. The left one was still attached to the garters. Her panties, don't recall the color, were only on the left leg; they'd been pulled off the right one."

"I understand. Anythin else, sir?" Connick had stopped jinglin his change and the courtroom was still except for the drone of the fans.

"No, I believe that is all."

In the brief pause in Connick's questioning, Pennington looked toward Baxter, wondering if he planned to cross examine Bullard. His head was down, and he was scribbling notes on a yellow pad.

"Very well, now can we talk about your examination at the morgue? You've written a report as to your findins and I have it here. Could you summarize that report, particularly as to her wounds?"

"Absolutely," Bullard said. "The gist of it is this: there's three types of wounds: the ones made by a knife that pierced the left side of her chest; the scrapes on her face that I've already described; and the cuts to her head made by a blunt instrument. The scrapes could have been caused by somebody hittin her with a coal shovel or a board, or bein kicked by someone wearin dirty boots."

"Can you say with certainty, what the cause of death was?"

"Well, no sir, I can't. *Any* of those wounds could have done it."

The crowd began to murmur at that. Judge Bishop interrupted the questioning with a swift bang of his gavel. "Quiet! I'll have order in my court."

After the room fell silent again, Connick asked to have the report put in evidence as Exhibit Two. Connick then walked over to his table and picked up a piece of paper, returned to the stand, and handed it to Bullard. "I'm givin you this photograph, Mista Bullard, which we have labeled State Exhibit Three and is supposedly a picture of the victim's head. Would you look at that and tell us exactly what it is and if you were present when it was taken?"

Bullard took the picture and stared at it for a second, like he knew what it was and didn't want to see it again. "That is in fact a picture of Miz Sowards' cranium that was taken durin our autopsy. Yes, I was there when it was taken."

"And it shows what, sir?"

"The scalp has been turned back to show the broken bones, the holes in her skull, and how those broken skull bones were shoved into her brain…"

Baxter jumped up again and yelled, "Objection, Your Honor. This does not show the condition of the woman after she was injured, but after the scalp had been peeled back *durin* the medical examination. It's not a true representation of a picture of the victim's injuries. You could show a picture like that of anyone's head and it would prejudice the jury." He spat into the waste can, again.

Judge Bishop said, "Overruled, Mista Baxta."

"Exception," Baxter replied.

The judge waited a minute, cocked his head, then said, "Very well, I'll adjure the prosecution from showin it to the jury at this time. However, they may view it, if they so wish."

Baxter shook his head and returned to his seat. Pennington and the other jurors could clearly see that he wasn't happy with the ruling.

"Mista Bullard, we also have pictures of the victim taken at the scene of the crime. Would you please look at them and tell us if there is anythin else those show?" Connick walked back to the table, picked up another picture, and took it up to the witness. The room was so quiet Connick's heels clickin on the floor sounded a staccato beat against the hum of the fans.

Bullard took it, looked at it for a minute, and gave it back. "Yes, that picture was taken before the victim's body was removed to the morgue. It shows the blood pooled around the body, the disarrangement of her clothin, and the mess her head was in just like I have testified."

Connick said, "Your Honor, we ask the court to enter this into evidence as Exhibit Four and request it to be shown to the jury."

Bishop said, "Accepted. You may show it to the jury." Connick walked over and handed it to Pennington, nodding as a signal to pass it on. Pennington took one look and blanched. As it circulated through the jury, the other men turned ashen as well.

As Pennington handed the picture back to Connick, Judge Bishop said, "Mista Baxta, your witness." Pennington took a deep breath and waited to see what Baxter's questioning would produce.

SEPTEMBER 7, 1960
XANDER

When they's passin that picture of poor Miz Annie around the jury, I thank God I don't have to look at it, nor Louie or his mama, neither. Those guys look kindly sick when they see it. Now Mista Baxta's talkin to that fat guy, Mista Bullard.

He repeats what the fat guy says about bein coroner for twenty-five years then ax if that's right? Why he do that? The fat guy already said that. Anyway, he nods. Then Baxta ax if he's a real doctor.

He says, no, he's not. When he says that, Baxta looks surprised. Ax how come he's able to talk 'bout medical stuff then?

Bullard say he learned on the job. Say he used to work at some funeral parlor; say he learned lots 'bout the body there, then he just went to bein in charge of autopsies. "Been one ever since," he says, lookin sorta red-faced like he don't like to be asked 'bout that.

Sounds fishy to me. He's talkin all sorts of medical stuff, lookin at Miz Annie's brain and such. How's a guy who not a doc know 'bout that stuff? But, he say he's done tons of autopsies so, I reckon he thinks that make him an expert. Baxta frowns, but the fat guy smiles, lookin all puffed up and proud.

Then Baxta wants to know if they found anythin under Miz Annie's fingernails. The fat guy say yes; they found some dried blood and skin. Baxta ax if they tested it to see who it came from. Bullard say no, they nevah got a blood sample from Leon. Baxta jump on that like a dog on a fresh bone. Sound all excited. He says, "Then you don't have any medical evidence provin any blood at the scene or on Miz Annie belonged to Leon Peppa."

The fat guy sorta shift in his chair like he don't like answerin. "Well," he says, "I suppose not, but…" Baxta stops him. No more questions, he says. I look over to Louie and he looks sorta happy, happy as he can be, I reckon. I think Baxta done good.

Now, some short guy wearin a black suit comes up in front of the fat guy. Don't know who he is but I reckon he work for Connick. He don't look much older than me. His hair looks like straw and his suit reminds me of an undertaker's. He ax Bullard how long Miz Annie was dead when they found her. Bullard say 'bout nine or ten hours. "How do you know?" this guy ax. Bullard gets all technical, talkin 'bout how hot the buildin is, how stiff she was. He say she done peed herself, too. Says it was all over her legs. Says that happens when folks die. I didn't know that. I poke Louie in the arm and whisper, "gross." Then I cut a look at his mama; her happy look is gone. Mine too.

Turns out, it gets grosser.

He starts talkin 'bout openin up Miz Annie to see if she'd had sex. The short guy ax, "What did you find?"

Bullard says, "Well first off, we discover that she's pregnant." I hears big old gasps in the crowd, but I don't look around to see who's doin it.

"Pregnant? Miz Sowards was pregnant when she was killed?"

"Yes sir, she was."

"Could you say how long she'd been with child," ax the guy.

"I'd say, judgin by the size of the fetus, roughly three months."

"And what else did you discover?" he ax without sayin anythin more 'bout the baby.

The fat guy says they found cum in her hoohoo. Course, he used some big fancy words but I knowed what he talkin 'bout. He say that proved she'd had sex, but he can't prove when, 'cause he thinks them cells die when she did, but he got no way to prove it. Louie sorta snickered when they start talkin 'bout havin sex. Made me think back 'bout all the times me and him talked 'bout that gal that lives next door to me. How I want to do her. Then the short guy ax if the fat guy's sayin Miz Annie been raped. That's not so funny. Louie stop laughin then. But the fat guy say no, there was no sign of that, just that she'd had sex. Now his mama look like she wants to cover her ears. Bein a church-goin lady, I bet she nevah heard such talk.

Judge Bishop says, "Your witness, Mista Baxta." Baxta jumps up and goes back up to ax the fat guy more questions. This time he's not as nice as before. Say he wants to get somethin straight. He ax him if he said there was no sign of rape. Bullard says that's right. Baxta look straight at the jury men. Then, he ax him if he found anythin in Miz Annie's hand. The fat guy say yes, found black hairs in her left hand. Baxta ax if they's straight or curly. I hold my breath while he answers. Straight, he says. Whoo boy, can't be Leon's. He and Louie got hair so nappy it's like wire. I let my breath out, happy Baxta asked that.

Then, Baxta ax 'bout what hit her in the face, says did he say maybe a shovel. Bullard agrees, then Baxta ax did they find one. The fat guy say he don't know, say you gotta ax the police. Baxta tells him he done, so the fat guy pulls his big ass out the chair, and walks back to his seat, rollin side to side he's so fat. When he's gone, I look at Leon. He's taken his head out his hands and it seems like he's not mad anymore. I reckon he thinks Baxta's done a good thin. Me too.

SEPTEMBER 7, 1960

After Baxter finished cross examining the coroner, neither Connick nor his young assistant, Jefferson Doyle, asked for redirect. Baxter was surprised but took it as a good sign and decided to ask Judge Bishop if he could approach the bench. It seemed to him several earlier issues were left unresolved, things that might help Leon Pepper's case. He knew what the answers to his questions would be, but wanted the jury to hear them. First rule of trial work: *Nevah ask a question you don't know the answer to.* He repeated this to himself.

"Very well, but Mista Connick will have to come, as well." Bishop motioned for Connick to approach as well.

Connick rose and strolled up like he had all the time in the world. To Baxter, it was obvious that the prosecutor didn't want to give him any advantage. As Baxter leaned close to the well-worn bench, he could smell the furniture polish that had kept it shining these many years. "Your Honor, may I recall two of the prosecution's earlier witnesses? Sergeant Kelly and Mista Sowards? Mista Bullard raised a few points I'd like to clarify with them."

Judge Bishop looked at Connick. "Any objection, Mista Connick?"

Connick frowned, but agreed. "No, so long as I can have another shot at cross followin his questions."

"Very well," said Bishop. Then he motioned to the bailiff, who yelled, "Would Sergeant Thad Kelly please retake the stand?"

Kelly looked up, the surprise in his face telegraphing that he'd thought he was finished here. "If that's what he thought, why he'd stick around," thought Baxter. After he took the stand, the judge reminded him he was still under oath.

When Baxter approached Kelly, his mouth twisted to one side and he began chewing on the inside of his lower lip. Although Baxter realized the man was uncomfortable with being recalled, he stifled his satisfied smile.

"Sergeant Kelly," Baxter said, "the coroner, Mista Bullard, said several times durin his testimony that he couldn't answer the question bein asked, that the police would have to. So, I'm askin you as the officer on the scene and as the arrestin officer. Did you ever find a knife or any other sharp object that could have pierced Miz Sowards' chest?"

"No, and Mista Stanley said all the kitchen knives were accounted for."

"How about anythin that could've caused the abrasions he described, or that could've put the cinders or the soot on Miz Sowards' face? Did you find anythin like that?"

"No, sir. We didn't."

"And how about the shoes Mista Peppa was wearin... were they boots? Dirty boots?"

"No, sir. They were sneakers and the only dirt on them was the blood we testified to seein."

"I see. And about that blood, did you test it?" Baxter asked.

"We couldn't get a good enough sample to send to the state medical examiner. We did get a small scrapin from his pants and jacket, though."

"And did it match the blood of Mista Peppa?"

"Dunno. We never took a sample of his blood on account of we figured all the blood was Miz Annie's." He shrugs like the matter was of little consequence. His expression signals that he knew his suspect was guilty as hell, so why bother." *Sloppy, sloppy, sloppy. Never assume, kid. You'll make an ass out of you, but not out of me.*

"So, did it match Miz Annie's blood?"

"No, it didn't. Examiner said that sample was pretty small, and they couldn't tell what type it was. For all he could tell it might have been animal blood like Mista Peppa said." Again, Baxter had to hide his satisfaction.

"Okay, let's talk about somethin else." He looked down at the notes he'd carried up with him. "Did you take Mista Peppa's fingerprints?"

"Yes, we did that."

"Did you try to lift fingerprints from the hammer, once you found it?"

"No sir, it was so bloody we figured they'd be all smeared and therefore unreadable." Once more, Baxter felt he'd scored a point. He glanced at his notes again.

"How about the hair you found in Miz Sowards' hand? Did you test it against Mista Peppa's hair?"

"No, we asked him for a sample, but he said he couldn't see any reason to give us one, so we didn't force the issue. Besides, the hair was straight, so we doubted it coulda been his." As he answered, Sergeant Kelly squirmed. Evidently he could see Baxter was making the jury question his testimony.

"And one more question about Mista Peppa. Did he have any visible scratches on his face or hands when you arrested him?"

"None that we could see, sir. No, sir."

"Very well, Sergeant. Thank you. Now, let's go back to the crime scene for a moment. Did you find footprints around the deceased's body?"

"We did, but later testin showed them to be those of Officer Blevins. He apparently wasn't too careful where he walked." Kelly sort of chuckled, like he was happy to toss some blame to his partner since Baxter had shown him up on more than a few procedural mistakes.

"Thank you, Sergeant. That'll be all." Baxter walked back to the table feeling better than he had since trial started. Judge Bishop called, "Any cross, Mista Connick?"

"None, Your Honor." Connick sat slumped in his seat as if he knew the defense had scored points. Several of them.

"Mista Baxta, ready for your second witness?"

He nodded, "Yes, Your Honor."

Judge Bishop called Mr. Sowards back to the stand.

"You understand you are still under oath, don't you, Mista Sowards?" he asked. Sowards replied that he did and the judge said Baxter could proceed. He re-approached the stand.

"Mista Sowards, I know this must be difficult for you, but I have to ask. Did you and your wife have sexual relations the day before she was killed?"

"No, sir. I said I nevah saw her that day or night. I was out with my friends."

"Yes, I recall. Can you recall the last time you *did* have sexual relations, sir?"

Connick yelled, "Relevance, Your Honor?"

Judge Bishop said, "I'll allow it."

"Can you recall, sir?" Baxter asked again.

Sowards smiled sheepishly, "No, I can't really recall. Might have been last year. Like I said, we sorta has our own friends, ya know?"

Without responding to his question, Baxter asked, "Did you know your wife was pregnant, sir?"

"No, sir. I didn't. She nevah told me..." his voice trailed off.

"No further questions, Mista Sowards. Thank you."

As Baxter returned to his table, Connick sighed deeply. Baxter smiled as if he knew he'd struck yet another blow to his case. Connick rose slightly and said, "The state rests, Your Honor."

"Very well," Judge Bishop replied. "Let's take a ten-minute recess before the defense begins." He rapped his gavel twice and left the courtroom. Knowing he had to switch gears and get ready to defend Leon Pepper, Baxter stayed, however.

September 7, 1960
Xander

After Mista Judge called a recess, I stood in the aisle and watched folks up front movin around. Mista Connick was talkin to that other prosecutor, Mista Doyle. The jury folks was standin and stretchin. The bailiff was watchin the door Judge Bishop went outta. The room had exploded all over with little conversations like folk was jes dyin to talk while court was goin on, and now they could. Mista Baxta not sayin a word, though. He bent over his table so I can't see what he doin. Gettin stuffy in here but them big fans hangin off their long poles in the ceilin are turnin so slow they's barely movin the air.

Now's my chance. Baxta's so close. All I gotta do is walk up to that railin and call out his name. I'm sure he'd turn around. I'll tell him I jes got to talk to him. Tell him I know whose hair that is. Tell him I know where that skin and blood under Miz Annie fingernails came from. Tell him I know it's Feeney baby. Tell him everythin I know 'bout the day she was killed. I wait jes a second and Louie taps me on the shoulder. I lose my nerve.

"Baxta done good up there, don't you think?" Louie got a big smile on his face.

"Yeah, he made that cop look like he didn't do his job," I say as I turn to face him. Louie's mama still sittin in the pew and I can tell by her face she feelin better, too. I think maybe talkin to Baxta ain't necessary, after all. Maybe he done enough to make the prosecutor look bad. Besides, it's Baxta's turn now. The people he gonna call gonna talk in Leon's favor. If I say somethin now, Louie'll wonder why I don't say somethin when it first happened. He be mad at me forevah if he evah finds out I kept it a secret.

Louie continues. "I love how Sergeant Big Shot Kelly gots to admit he ain't done all them things he shoulda. Stupid bastard." Louie mouths the last two words so his mama won't hear him. "Me and you both knows he thought Leon guilty so he figured he don't have to do none of that stuff. But, old Baxta prove him wrong! I think he gonna get Leon off this thing."

"I hope you're right, Louie," I say. "I really do." He got no way of knowin jes how much I hope that. If he's right, keepin my mouth shut like Mama said was the right thing to do. But if he's wrong... oh brother. I don't know how I can live with myself knowin I'm a coward.

"Goin to get a drink of water, Louie. Be right back," I say, so I don't have to talk 'bout it anymore. Walkin up the aisle, I see Mista Spencer, my eighth-grade math teacher sittin in one of the back rows.

What's he doin here? Why isn't he in school? I also see Velma Arnold and Truman Rickey from the neighborhood. Then I get it; they here to testify. Oh, Lord, I hope they got good things to say 'bout Leon.

After I get my drink, I look up at the giant clock above the courtroom doors. Shit, nearly two o'clock. This last much longer, I won't make it to work. And if I don't, dependin on Mista Feeney's mood, he jes might fire my ass. I look around and spot a pay phone, so I calls the store and ax to speak to Mista Feeney. Our main cashier, Maxine, says he not there. I lie and tell her I'm sick and won't be in today and maybe not tomorrow. She don't hesitate a minute. "Fine, I'll tell him. Hope you feel better, Xander," she say. Feel bad 'bout lyin but I gotta see what happens to Leon.

I barely make it back to the courtroom before Judge Bishop start in bangin that gavel again. "Mista Baxta, you may present your case," he say. Hurryin up the aisle, I see Bill Feeney sittin on the back row near the corner. Oh crap! So that why he's not at work. Hope he don't see me. If he do, he fire me for sure since I jes lie to Maxine. Wonder if he knew Miz Annie knocked up. I turn my head hopin he won't see me or if he do, won't recognize me. I get to our row and squeeze in jes as Mista Baxta stands up.

"Thank you, Your Honor," Baxta say. "The defense calls Mista Bruce Spencer to the stand." Yep, I'm right. He gonna testify for Leon. I'm glad 'bout that but suddenly it's hard payin attention 'cause I can't stop thinkin 'bout Feeney. He been here all day? Sure nevah saw him this mornin or when I went to lunch. Why's he here, anyway? I know he hung 'round with Miz Annie, but comin to Leon's trial seem really strange. He hopin Leon's convicted? He worried somebody say he and Miz Annie knowed each other? Say it's his baby? Lordy, I sure wish I'd told somebody what I know.

SEPTEMBER 7, 1960

During the court's recess, as Bill Feeney watched the people up front milling around, his eyes landed on a Negro boy walking up the aisle toward the railing. When another Negro kid tapped him on the shoulder and he turned, Feeney saw that it was his employee, Xander Betts. Oh shit! What's that little fucker doin here? He's supposed to be in school and then at the store. I swear, I'm gonna fire his little black ass for not showin up.

Wait a minute! You don't suppose he's here to testify for that Pepper kid! If he is, I could be in deep shit. He knows Annie came to the store all the time. What if he's told that to Pepper's attorney? I should never have come down here. I should have stayed the hell as far away as possible. And who the hell is he with? I've never seen that kid or the woman with them. Reckon that's Pepper's family? Did Xander tell them about Annie and me? Fuck. Maybe he didn't see me. If I fire him for bein here instead of at work, he'll know I was here, too. And he'll wonder why. I've gotta let it slide, act like I never saw him and pray he doesn't see me.

Feeney scooched down a bit in his seat and tried to pay attention to Baxter, who had just called his first witness, but he couldn't help worrying about Xander and what he's said or done. Sweat rolled down his back. Maybe I should just leave. I need something to calm my nerves. Goddam, I wish I'd had a drink or two at lunch. After hearin that coroner talk about Annie, sayin she was pregnant, I really needed one. When I think back on that night, it gives me the willies.

That night, when Annie started talkin about lovin me, I told her I'd never leave Bertha. I mean, shit, we've got kids and everything. Annie wasn't anything to me but a piece of ass. A nice ass, but that's all. She should have known that from the beginnin. I mean, she's a nigger, for God's sake! What white man in his right mind would divorce his wife of almost twenty years to take up with some nigger gal? Oh, we had some laughs, some good times, but I never expected her to take it seriously. Just because she had a husband who didn't seem to care what she did, didn't mean my wife felt the same. She did care; or she would have, if she'd found out. She'd have cared a whole lot. Enough to leave me and take the kids!

Then Annie went and let herself get pregnant. How was I supposed to act? All along, she'd said she couldn't have kids, so, I never worried. Then, boom, she dropped this bombshell.

"Bill, I know it ain't something you want to hear,

but I'm pregnant," she said one day back in January when she was in my office. She hadn't been there long so we were just standin inside with the door closed. I could tell she had something on her mind because she didn't start in flirtin like usual.

I said, "Well, congratulations. Puddin' must be real happy about that. He's finally gonna have him a kid."

"Huh uh. Bill, it ain't his. Can't be. We ain't slept together goin on six months. It's yours," she said lookin down at her belly. "We're gonna have us a kid. You'n me." She smiled like she was really happy about that but I sure wasn't.

My face must have been as pale as death because she said, "Don't look so scared. Puddin' ain't nevah gonna know. Hell, he don't know who I been sleepin with. Don't care neither." She put her hand on my arm, but I shook it off and sat down in my desk chair. I needed to get some distance between us.

I took a deep breath. "Annie, I'll know. And no doubt some of the people I work with will figure it out quick enough. You aren't exactly a stranger here, you know. Especially that kid, Xander Betts, delivers for me? He'll figure it out in a heartbeat. And when folks get that notion in their heads, my wife will surely find out. I can't have that. You've got to get rid of it."

"But I always wanted me a baby," she whined. "Puddin' says it's my fault we nevah did, but now I know that ain't true. Don't tell me I got to get rid of it. Please! It's our baby." She came to my side of the desk and put her arms around my neck. I tried to pry them off but she held on.

"Let go, Annie. You've gotta find some way to take care of this problem. I can't do that, but you have to. And then, we've got to end this. You hear me."

She finally let go, backed up, sat down precariously on the edge of the desk, and started cryin.

"Surely, you must know some midwife, someone who can…" I said, tryin to sound firm in the face of her tears. I did feel sorry for her but I couldn't just let her have my child. My life would be over. She had to understand that.

"I'ma think 'bout it," she said. "I am," she repeated but I wasn't at all sure I believed her. She wiped her face, got down from the desk, and ran out the door, slammin it behind her.

She didn't come to the store for several weeks, so I thought she'd seen the problem she would cause me by havin this baby and taken care of it. So, one night, a few weeks later, I stopped by Stanley's just to see how she was doin. I guess I did miss her; I mean she was always good for a laugh, and, I have to admit, she was better in bed than Bertha had been lately. Anyway, it was late. I'd had a few drinks that evenin while I was playin poker with the boys, but I thought one more wouldn't hurt. And I could end the evenin with some laughs with Annie before goin home to old Bertha. Thought Annie might be up for a little mischief, too, ya know? When she looked up to see me come in the door, I think she was surprised. It must have been a slow night because I was the only one there. She'd already changed into her street clothes, so I figured she was fixin to leave early.

She put her hands on her hips, like she did sometimes, and said, "Well, looka here what the cat done drag in. What brings you in here?"

I told her I was just checkin on her. She laughed and said, "You been missin me, Bill? Been missin our, you know…?"

"Yeah, I have. You haven't been around for a while, so I thought I'd come see you for a change." She came from behind the counter, threw her arms around my neck, and kissed me like she really was glad to see me. Didn't take long for me to get a hard-on, and before you knew it, we were goin at it right there on the floor of Stanley's.

After we were done, she raised up on one elbow and looked hard at me. "You know, if I was a bettin woman, I'd say you was checkin to see if I'd gotten rid of that baby, too."

I rose to my knees and pulled my pants closed. "Well, did you?"

She sat up. "No, I nevah and I ain't gonna. I told you I want me a baby. Puddin' ain't gonna complain. And they ain't no way folks evah gonna know it's yours." She looked so defiant I went nuts.

"Goddam it, Annie! I told you that can't happen. I told you to take care of the problem. Why haven't you done it? Are you crazy?" I grabbed her shoulders and shook her so hard her head rattled back and forth. She grabbed at my face, rakin her fingernails down both cheeks and drawin thin lines of blood. She never should have done that.

"God, I gotta have me several drinks after I get outta here," Feeney muttered to himself.

SEPTEMBER 7, 1960

When Bruce Spencer took the stand, Leon smiled for the first time that day. He hadn't seen his old teacher since junior high school. Here he comes walkin up to testify for me. He's all time helpin me back then, tryin to get me to understand math but I nevah could figure out how them numbers go together. Seems like he's shorter than I recollects but maybe jes it's because I'm grown now.

Spencer didn't notice Leon's smile. Instead, he looked straight ahead like he was concentrating on what he would say in defense of Leon Pepper.

After being sworn in, Baxter asked, "Mista Spencer, how do you know Leon Peppa?"

"I been knowin him since eighth grade; I taught him math that year."

"Did Peppa ever cause trouble in school?"

"Never gave me any trouble. I'd say he wasn't much of a learner, but he was always good in class."

"Were you near Stanley's on the night of February twelfth, of this year?

Spencer nodded, "Yes, I was. I drove by about eleven-thirty. My wife and I had been to a movie downtown then we stopped for a few beers. When we saw Leon, there was another guy out front, too, but I didn't know him. He was taller and heavier than Leon."

"Are you sure it was Leon?"

"I've been seein Leon around since school so, yes, I was sure it was him."

"Were they comin or goin out of Stanley's?"

"I couldn't tell. They were jes standin there lookin in the window like they maybe were tryin to get someone's attention."

"Drawin a conclusion, Your Honor," yelled Connick as he jumped to his feet.

"Strike that last part," Judge Bishop told the court reporter. "Ignore that remark," he said, looking at the jurors.

Baxter had been pacing back and forth in front of Mr. Spencer but not looking at him while the judge spoke. When he finished, Baxter turned and asked, "Was there anyone inside? Could you see anyone?"

"No, I was drivin and couldn't really see inside. I asked my wife, but she said she couldn't either."

"Hearsay, Your Honor," Connick yelled again.

"Strike and ignore," said Bishop.

"I have no further questions for Mista Spencer, Your Honor," said Baxter.

"Mr. Connick?" said Bishop.

"No questions, Your Honor," said Connick.

The judge excused Spencer and he walked back

to where he been sitting.

Next, Baxter called Linc Cousey. Leon watched Linc slowly shuffle up to the stand like he didn't want to be there. When Baxter asked his name, Linc said, "Abraham Lincoln Cousey." Leon snickered slightly. *I nevah knowed that was his full name.*

Baxter asked, "Can you tell me what you and Leon Peppa did the night of February twelfth, 1960?"

Linc repeated almost exactly the same story Leon had told his attorney, but Baxter continued asking for details. "Did the two of you go inside Stanley's?" he asked.

Linc answered, "No."

"Was there anyone inside Stanley's when you were outside?"

Linc said, "They sure was."

"Did you know who it was?"

Linc said, "Well, I knows Miz Annie, but not the man with her."

"Mista Cousey, Mista Peppa has testified that he was drunk that night. Were you drunk, as well?"

Linc smiled until his gums showed. "No, I weren't, jes tipsy. I can hold my liquor; Leon can't."

Linc looked at Leon as he left the stand and Leon nodded at him, mouthing, "Thank you."

Next, Baxter called Velma Arnold. Oh boy, me and her dated a long time ago but now she goes with that no-account Truman Rickey. He and I had words a few years back over Velma. Hope she don't hold that against me, Leon thought.

As she was approaching the stand, Baxter put a

large map on a stand, then picked up a long wooden pointer from his table. He had turned the map so Velma could see it. Then, he asked Velma how long she had known Pepper.

Velma put her head in her hand and looked up as if the answer were on the ceiling. "I reckon it's been six or eight years. We was good friends a few years back, but we don't see each other like that no more."

Leon laughed to himself. Hell, yes, we was good friends. We slept together 'bout a year back then.

Baxter asked, "Did Mista Peppa ever act mean or get in fights that you know of?"

"Leon? Oh, no! He's a sweet, kind boy. Always nice. I never knew him to get into fights, no how."

"Would you recognize him now?

"Absolutely," she said. "He's sittin right over there." She pointed to Leon at the defense table.

"Very well. Did you see him near Stanley's Jook Joint on February twelfth?"

"I did. Me and Truman Rickey was out front of my house… it's around the corner from Stanley's. We were there when he walked by 'bout one o'clock."

Baxter pointed to a spot on the map and asked if that's where Stanley's is. Velma scrunched up her eyes and looked at the map. "Looks like it."

"And what's your address?"

She said, "610 Third Avenue."

Baxter tapped the map again. "Right there?" he asked.

Velma squinted again, and repeated, "Looks like it."

"Miz Arnold, do you wear glasses?"

"No, but that map is pretty small." Folks throughout the courtroom chuckled.

"I'm sorry about that. Would you please continue talkin about seein Mista Peppa that night?"

Velma said, "Well, I said 'hey' to him, but he nevah said 'hey' back, jes kept on goin. I don't know if he was in a hurry or jes don't want to say 'hey' to Truman or me because I'm with Truman."

"Which way was he goin, toward Stanley's or away?"

Velma pulled on her ear like it itched, then said, "Looked to me like he was headed home."

Connick yelled, "Objection. Assumption, Your Honor."

Judge Bishop said, "Sustained."

"I'll rephrase. In what direction was he goin?"

"I ain't good with directions, but he's walkin away from Stanley's goin toward the projects across Fourth Avenue."

Baxter points again. "Here?" he asked.

"Yeah."

"Did he have anythin in his hands?"

"I didn't see nothin," she said lookin quizzical as if she couldn't figure out why he would ask that.

"Do you recall what he was wearin?"

"Uh, I think he had on a jacket and dark blue pants. Might have been jeans. I think he was wearin a hat. No, wait, that ain't right. He was bareheaded."

"Thank you, Miz Arnold. That will be all." He returned to his table while the judge asked Mr. Connick if he had any questions for the witness.

"Yes, Your Honor, I do." He walked slowly up to the front and look sternly at Velma, again rattling his pocket change. He looked at that map and again asked Velma about what direction Pepper was going. She repeated what she had told Baxter, but he pressed on.

"Are you sure what street he was on?"

"Of course. I've lived near there for years. He was on Sixth Street headin toward Fourth Avenue."

"How could you see where he was goin if you weren't on the same street? It was dark, right?"

"Of course it were dark. But they's a streetlight on the corner. Easy to see Leon comin."

"And you're sure he didn't respond when you yelled at him? Wouldn't he have been able to hear you?"

She said, "I'm sure. It was like he nevah even saw that we were there."

Connick said, "No further questions," then returned to his table.

Baxter then stood and said, "Call Miz Mae Ellen Caldwell to the stand, please." The bailiff repeated his request and Leon's sister made her way through the short swinging gate and to the stand.

After Mae Ellen took her hand off the Bible, Baxter asked her name and how she knew Pepper. She gave her married name, Mae Ellen Caldwell and said she was his sister. Baxter asked her to tell what happened that night and the following morning.

She looked at her brother, smiled, and started

talking. "Well," she said, "me and my husband, Bob, and Leon, had us some dinner around six, then him and Bob got to drinkin. I had a upset stomach so I didn't join them. They's playin gin rummy when I went in the livin room to watch me some TV. Later Leon quit playin and said he was gonna watch him some TV in his room. Said he wants to watch Jack Paar later but he knew I didn't. But, then Linc Cousey came by and asked him to go out with him. Linc had a bottle so they went in his bedroom first and finished it. Then they left to go get another one. By then, Leon was pretty looped and crackin stupid jokes. I told him he didn't need to drink no more, but Linc talked him into goin out anyway.

"I went to bed but later I heard Leon stumble up the steps 'bout two-thirty. I started to get up but decided not to after he quieted down. The next mornin, he was still wearin them same nasty clothes he'd worn the day before. I guess he fell asleep in them but I'm not sure. He didn't eat anythin but he sat there awhile drinkin coffee then went back to bed. Around eleven them cops came to the door wantin to talk to Leon. They nevah told me what they wanted and they sorta pushed their way past me to get inside. When he came to the door, they told him there'd been a murder but nevah said who or why they wanted him. Then they took him away."

When she finished, Baxter asked her if Leon drank a lot. She said, "No, he don't do it much but since he don't he's not used to it, so, he gets drunk easy."

"Is your brother a violent person when he drinks?"

"Lordy, no. He's a happy sorta drunk when he does drink."

When Baxter finished, Connick rose and walked toward the stand. "Miz Caldwell, would you say Mista Peppa was drunk when he left with Linc Cousey?"

"No, but I could tell he was headed that way if he drank much more. He wasn't staggerin or weavin around. Jes happy tipsy, you know?"

"Thank you." Connick turned and walked away. When the judge excused Mae Ellen, she got down from the stand and walked past Leon smiling. He smiled back as if in approval of what she'd said.

Then Baxter called Mr. Leon Pepper. He stood, paused a moment wiping his palms on his pants. With visibly shaking knees, he made his way slowly toward the witness stand. "Lordy, I hope I does okay," he muttered in a stage whisper.

September 7, 1960

After the bailiff called his name, Leon Pepper rose very slowly. He walked to the witness stand like he'd rather turn around and leave. Everyone in the jury box leaned forward like this was the main attraction they had been waiting for. Pepper looked at the jury with an expression of sheer terror. When he took his seat in the witness box, he looked up at the judge like Bishop was what he was most scared of. When the bailiff swore him in, he responded so faintly he could barely be heard.

His attorney walked up and smiled at Leon as if he was trying to get Leon to settle down.

"Mista Peppa," Baxter said, "Would you please tell us in your own words and to the best of your recollection what happened the night of February twelfth, 1960?"

"Well, sir, I didn't have nothin to do that day, and I had me a little money, so I got me a pint of rum and did some drinkin at home. We, I mean my sister, Mae Ellen, her man, Bob, and me ate dinner and I went to my room to watch me some TV and finish off the bottle. 'Bout ten-thirty, eleven, my buddy Linc Cousey came by and ax me go out drinkin with him. First I said no, 'cause I ain't got no more money, but he say he buyin, so I go. We're walkin down to Buster's get another pint when we pass by Stanley's. We look in the window and see Miz Annie. Linc thinks Miz Annie's a looker and he wanna say hey to her. Then he changes his mind, says he want to get on down to Buster's so he wave but we nevah went in.

"When we get to Buster's, they's closed so we go on downtown to that liquor store near Polk's Corner. On the way back, we share that bottle so I got pretty drunk. Not fallin-down drunk, ya know, but pretty well-lit." He smiled sheepishly as if he was embarrassed to admit that.

"Linc headed on home after we finish it, but I weren't in the mood for no TV then, so I walk on over by Chicken Little's tryin to clear my head some, then back past Stanley's. That's when I seen Miz Annie sweepin up."

"Are you a frequent visitor to Stanley's?" Baxter asked.

"No, I nevah go there. I pass by it lots of times but I nevah did go in."

"So, then how did you know Annie Sowards?"

"Jes been knowin her from the neighborhood to say hey to, but I nevah really knowed her, ya know?" Pepper looked like he wasn't quite sure Baxter understood.

Baxter nodded. "I understand. Was there anyone

in Stanley's when you came by the second time?"

"Yeah, they's a white guy but I dunno know who he was. He's in there both times but all I seen was the side of his face and his hands on the counter."

"Did you go inside that time?"

"Started to, but then… I nevah." Pepper sounded like he wanted to set the record straight.

"Somethin told me to go in and say hey. She look tired, like she could use some cheerin up, so I opened the screen door, but I reckon I passed out before I open that other door 'cause I don't recall nothin else til I come to, sittin in the doorway."

"And, when you came to, what did you do?"

"Got up and walk on home."

"Did you see Miz Annie then, when you woke up?"

"No, I ain't seen nobody… the lights was still on, though. When I walk away, I saw I got a hammer in my hand. Don't know where it came from but I knowed it weren't mine, so I throwed it in the empty lot at the end of the block. My mama says nevah keep nothin don't belong to you, so I got rid of it."

"Did you notice whether or not the hammer had blood on it?"

"Nuh huh, it was way too dark."

"And what hand was it in?"

"Left."

"Are you left-handed, Mista Peppa?"

"No, sir. I use my right hand all the time."

"Very well. Now, tell us what you did when you got home." Baxter said.

"Went to my room. Guess I was pretty drunk because I don't remember nothin else. Musta passed out." Once more, he looked down at his lap like he was embarrassed.

"And the followin mornin. What happened then?"

"Mae Ellen waked me from a dead sleep. She screamin, 'They's cops at the door wantin talk to you.' Took me a minute to get awake but I head on downstairs and seen three cops in the doorway. They ax me step outside so I did. They start in axin me where I'd been last night. They was talkin all at once. Wantin to know did I go to Stanley's. I was tryin tell them what me and Linc done when one of them say Miz Annie dead and he thinks I know what happened. They say I got to go with em. One cop grabs my arms and cuffs me. Then they shove me toward the car and push me in."

"While you were bein questioned in the car, did you confess, Mista Peppa?" Baxter said. "No, sir, I nevah. One of them officers, Kelly, I think that his name, he says they gonna take me in Stanley's to see Miz Annie lyin there dead. I say I don't wanna see no dead people but they say they're gonna if I don't tell them I raped and killed her. He smack me a couple of times, too. I say I'll tell him everythin I done that night when we get to the station, but he says they gonna make me go in. Finally, I say I don't remember too good what I done. Maybe I done it. But I tell him I were pretty drunk so my memory ain't too good."

"Did you say Sergeant Kelly hit you?" Baxter

turned and looked at the policemen who were still in the courtroom. Two of them frowned but Sargent Kelly began turning his cap around in his hands nervously.

"Yeah, he done it a couple a times. Nevah no place you could see, though. That's what them cops do to us coloreds all the time," Leon said. His face was resigned.

"After you said you might have killed her, what happened, Mista Peppa? Did they escort you inside?" Baxter looked at the jurymen while Pepper spoke as if he wanted to see how they had taken his so-called confession.

Leon shook his head. "No, they nevah. The cop drivin pulled on out and we go down to the police station. On the way, I think back and I jes know I nevah hurt Miz Annie. I got no cause to. Besides, I recollect I nevah did go in. Jes pass out in the doorway. So, when they make me tell them again so they can write it down, I say I was wrong. I say I nevah raped or killed Miz Annie."

"Mista Peppa, let's go back to the night of the crime. Did you see anyone else that night besides Linc Cousey and the people inside Stanley's? Anyone when you were walkin over by Chicken Little's or back home? Velma Arnold has testified that she saw you and yelled to you but that you didn't respond. Is that right?"

"We saw some folks at the liquor store and downtown. But after Linc left out, I nevah saw nobody else. Reckon I was still too drunk to notice Velma."

"About when did you return home, do you recall?"

"Nevah looked at no clock, but it musta been around two."

"Thank you, Mista Peppa. I believe that will be all." Baxter looked at Riley Connick as the judge said, "Mista Connick, your witness."

Connick gathered up his papers and walked toward Pepper, jinglin the change in his pocket once again. His expression was that of a lion intent on his prey.

September 7, 1960
Xander

Prosecutor Connick is a jerk. He don't even say hello to Leon. He jes starts right in tryin to make Leon say somethin that will make the jury be against him. *Does he think he can trick Leon into confessin?* Fat chance.

"Mista Peppa, the night of Miz Sowards' death were you carryin a knife?" he ax.

"No, sir."

"Did you ever carry a knife?"

"Maybe three or four years ago, I had me a small pen knife."

"Do you still have it?"

"No, I lost it a while back."

"Have you had another knife of any kind since then?"

"No, sir."

"Let's talk about the conversation you had with the police officers the mornin after Miz Sowards' death. One of the officers has testified that you made a statement to him regardin her death. Can you tell us about that conversation?" Connick jinglin his change again.

Wish he'd stop that. Makes me nervous. I bet it makes Leon nervous, too. Maybe that's why he does it. I wonder why he ax this again. Leon jes told Baxta that stuff a few minutes ago. Is he tryin to trip Leon up?

Listenin to Leon, I see if that's what Connick's tryin to do, it ain't workin. Leon repeats, almost exactly, what he jes told his own lawyer a few minutes earlier. Connick don't look happy 'bout this, neither.

"At any time did you say you had killed Miz Sowards?"

"No sir. Nevah did." Leon sounds strong and sure.

"Did you say you might have done it?" Connick says. He's like a dog on a bone 'bout that.

"I mighta. But I said I don't recollect that night too good 'cause I was drunk. When we got to the station, I said I sure I nevah done nothin to her."

"Mista Peppa, are you sayin you might have said that or that you might have killed her?"

"I don't know. One a them cops smacked me a couple a times. I mighta said that, but I was confused. I nevah, I mean, I nevah killed her. I told them that when we was down to the station."

"Mista Peppa, if you were as drunk as you say you were, how can you be so sure you didn't rape and then kill Miz Sowards? I mean, you have admitted you woke with the bloody hammer in your hand."

"Objection," yells Mista Baxta. "Accordin to the

medical examiner, there was no evidence of rape."

Before the judge can say anythin, Connick says. "I'll restate, Your Honor. Mista Peppa, if you were as drunk as you say you were, how can you be so sure you didn't kill Miz Sowards?"

"'Cause I jes know I nevah. I guess I was all mixed up when they's yellin at me in that patrol car, but when I get a minute to think, I knowed I nevah done nothin to her. I nevah even went inside Stanley's."

"Do you have any idea where you got the hammer that was in your hand when you came to?"

"I got no idea. They say it must have come from Stanley's, but I was nevah in there, so I don't know how it come to be in my hand."

"Isn't it a fact that you *did* go in Stanley's, that you made a pass at Miz Sowards and when she rejected you, you fought with her, then killed her with that hammer because you were afraid she would report you?"

Leon look like he's gonna explode. "No sir, I nevah done any of that. I would nevah hurt nobody. I got no reason be doin nothin like that," he yells. Look like he wanna come out his seat at Connick. It's the first time I've heard Leon yell since the officers were testifyin. *Good for you, Leon.*

Baxta jumps to his feet, however. "Badgerin the witness, Your Honor."

Judge Bishop says, "Sustained. Watch yourself, Mista Connick."

"Sorry, Your Honor. Mista Peppa, how much

rum did you say you drank that day?"

"'Bout a pint."

"And that night, I believe you said you split another pint with your friend, correct?"

"That's right."

"That's not very much liquor, Mista Peppa. Maybe you weren't all that drunk after all. I mean, after all that walkin, wouldn't you have walked off the effects of what you drank? Maybe you've just *conveniently* forgotten what you did."

Baxta jumps up again. "Your Honor, he's badgerin Mista Peppa again."

"Sustained," Judge Bishop yells, his face all red. "Mista Connick, that's your second warnin. One more and I'll find you in contempt. Understand?"

"Understood, Your Honor."

Connick turns back to Leon. "I'll ask you again, Mista Peppa, didn't your late-night walk sober you up?"

"I ain't much of a drinker, sir, so I reckon it hang with me, you know?"

"Do you usually pass out when you drink, Mista Peppa?"

"I do. You can ask my sister. She seen it couple of times." Leon looks out toward the audience where Mae Ellen's sittin. I turn and see her give him a small smile.

"And when you returned home that night, did you wash up before you went to bed?"

"Don't recall. Musta peed though."

"And when you urinated, did you notice anythin

on your penis?"

"Like what?" Leon look puzzled.

"Like semen or blood, for instance."

Baxta jumps up before Connick can finish talkin. "Leadin the witness, Your Honor."

"Sustained," he says, like he tired of correctin Connick.

"Uh, no… uh, I nevah notice. Don't recollect seein nothin down there… I don't know." Leon answers, lookin very uncomfortable at hearin them ask 'bout his privates in front of his mother. He sorta squirms in his chair, lookin down at his lap like he's checkin them out now.

"Mista Peppa, did you pass out after you urinated?"

"I reckon so. Don't recollect nothin after that. When Mae Ellen call me that mornin, I was still wearin them clothes from the night before."

Connick fingers his change for a minute more, then says, "No further questions." He whip around on his heel and head for his seat. Judge Bishop says, "Mista Baxta, any redirect?"

"No, Your Honor." So, jes like that, it's over. God, I hope that jury believe Leon. I look over at em, but all twelve men got blank faces. Sorta scary, really. Wish they's smilin or frownin, somethin. They jes look like they been listenin to some interestin radio show.

Bishop tells Leon he can be excused. As he walk back to his seat, he stop and look toward his mama, then hangs his head. Wonder what goin through his mind? Do he think he hasn't got a chance in hell? Is he worried 'bout what he jes said? I would be. Make me sad to look at him 'cause I still don't think he got a chance. My stomach do that flip-flop when I'm scared. I shoulda said or done somethin, but I guess it's too late now. I'll jes have to try a little of Mama's prayin, I guess.

September 7, 1960

Following Leon Pepper's cross examination, he walked back to his seat next to Baxter. His hang-dog expression worried Baxter. He was afraid looking so defeated could sway some of the jurymen.

Connick shuffled his papers in preparation for his closing argument. After an agonizing wait, he walked toward the jury box, jingling his change again. Baxter's eyes were on the jurors as if trying to read their minds. However, their faces were blank, almost bored looking. Connick looked sternly at each of the men on the front row of the box, cleared his throat, and began.

"Gentlemen of the jury, over the course of the last few hours you've heard testimony from the police, the coroner, and the defendant himself. The words of each of them, clearly, and beyond a shadow of a doubt, convict Mista Leon Peppa of the charge of murder in the first degree. Let me enumerate."

Connick held his bony hand up in front of his chest and began to flip up one skinny finger at a time.

He was so close to the jurors they could probably see the yellow tobacco stains on it. "First, the arrestin police officers told you they found blood on Mista Peppa's clothin and shoes. They told you Mista Peppa admitted he was so drunk the night Annie Sowards was brutally murdered, that he had no idea what he did."

Next, he raised his middle finger, also deeply stained. "The coroner testified that Miz Sowards was beaten with a blunt instrument so savagely that she was very nearly unrecognizable."

With the third finger, he said, "And, Mista Peppa admits bein at the scene, not once but twice that evenin. He even admits that after passin out in the doorway of Stanley's Jook Joint, he awoke with the bloody hammer, which accordin to the coroner was one of the murder weapons, in his hand. And, furthermore, he admits attemptin to hide that evidence by tossin it into an empty lot. An empty lot, with lots of weeds where he hoped no one would ever find it."

Connick paused, then walked to the far end of the jury box. "The state believes it has proven, through the testimony of these witnesses, and the original confession of the defendant, that Mista Leon Peppa *did* enter Stanley's Jook Joint, *did* coerce Miz Sowards to have sex with him, then, followin an argument, *did* beat her with the hammer he then carried outside where he passed out. Gentlemen, he confessed, maybe not in so many words, but he said he *might have* done it, didn't he? I ask you, if you were so sure, like Mista Peppa now says he is, that you *had not* killed someone, would you say that? Certainly not! Or, if he blacked out, as he also says he did, how can he later be so sure he did not kill Miz Sowards? We believe he did kill her, but in his drunken stupor, simply does not recall his actions of the evenin. So, I urge you, gentlemen of this jury, to carefully consider all these facts, these very clear facts, and to find him guilty of the heinous murder of Miz Annie Sowards."

He walked the full length of the jury box again. When he came to the foreman, he stared at him for a long minute, before turning on his heels and returning to his seat.

It didn't take long for Baxter to take Connick's place. Just before he rose, he spit his wad of tobacco in the wastebasket beside the table. Once in front of the jury box, he smiled at each of the men with a broad sweep of his expression.

"Gentlemen, I'd like you to focus on several thins as you consider the fate of Mista Leon Peppa. I believe that the evidence given *does* point to the fact that a woman was brutally murdered on the night of February twelfth, 1960, but it does not prove that Mista Peppa was the assailant. In fact, there is no actual proof that Mista Peppa was *ever* inside Stanley's Jook Joint. The prosecution did not produce *a single witness* who could put him inside. In fact, Mista Linc Cousey testified to the contrary. As to the testimony of the police officers – they *admitted* they did not test the blood on Mista Peppa's clothin. They *admitted* they did not test the hair found in Miz Sowards hands nor did they take a hair sample from Mista Peppa.

They *admitted* they did not test the hammer for Mista Peppa's fingerprints. They *admitted* Mista Peppa was wearin tennis shoes, not hard-soled boots like those the coroner said were worn by whomever kicked her in the face.

"So how did they jump to the outrageous conclusion that Mista Peppa was the perpetrator? Circumstantial evidence, sirs. Circumstantial evidence. In fact, they have only the discovery of the hammer and Mista Peppa's confused remark that he didn't remember what he'd done that night to connect him to this crime. Remember, gentlemen, the police also *admitted* they have never recovered the knife the coroner said caused the stab wounds to her chest, which may have been the actual cause of her death.

"As for Mista Peppa havin had sex with Miz Sowards, is it reasonable to believe he coulda simply talked her into havin sex? I mean, he was a stranger to her. And she was pregnant with another man's child. So, if they *had* had intercourse, it most certainly would have to have been rape; yet the coroner said there were absolutely no signs of rape. Furthermore, Mista Peppa and Mista Cousey testified there was another man in Stanley's when they were there. Did the police look for this man? No, they did not. They simply assumed Mista Peppa was the perpetrator because someone said he was walkin past Stanley's earlier in the evenin. We have no idea who that was, nor why they would want to implicate Mista Peppa. Could it have been the actual assailant? Think on that! Someone calls the police, never identifies themselves, but suggests they should check out Mista Peppa. Don't you find that strange?

"Therefore, gentlemen, I suggest to you that Mista Peppa was simply in the wrong place at the wrong time, that he was drunk and passed out, givin the real perpetrator the convenient opportunity to place that hammer in his left hand. His *left hand*, gentlemen. Mista Peppa is right-handed, remember? As you look at Mista Leon Peppa, you, gentlemen, are lookin at an innocent man. If you make the grievous mistake of convictin him, rest assured the real murderer is still walkin around Blanchard's Bottom. I know you do not want that on your conscience. You must find Mista Leon Peppa innocent of this crime."

By the time Baxter finished, sweat had pooled under his armpits and down his back. He could feel his head pounding, signaling a spike in his blood pressure. He walked back to his seat and placed his hand on Pepper's arm. He managed a small smile, one of the few he'd exhibited all day. The audience had begun to murmur quietly as they waited for Judge Bishop's instructions to the jury.

Moments later, Bishop rapped his gavel to quiet the fidgety crowd and the room fell silent. Before he could speak Baxter stood and said, "Judge Bishop, I move for a directed verdict for the defendant."

"Overruled," Bishop responded so automatically it was as if he knew the request was coming and was prepared for it. Baxter returned to his seat with no further comment.

"Gentlemen of the jury," Bishop began. "Your

solemn deliberative duty starts now. You are charged with considerin all you've heard here today in makin your decision. Let me remind you of your options." He clears his throat and glances down at his desk. "Mista Leon Peppa, the defendant, is charged with murder in the first degree. Accordin to Georgia law, murder in the first degree is when someone is killed in the commission of arson, rape, robbery, or burglary. All other murders are second degree. You must unanimously decide that the evidence supports your verdict beyond a shadow of a doubt. You will also determine, if he is found guilty of first-degree murder, whether or not Mista Peppa deserves to be executed or sentenced to life imprisonment. Do you understand?"

As if it were a Greek chorus, the entire jury answered, "We do."

Baxter stood again. "I object, Your Honor. You have not included the possibility of manslaughter in the charges. I know Mista Connick objected to its inclusion earlier and you removed it, but based on the testimony given, I believe it must be added."

"I'm sorry, Mista Baxta. My previous rulin stands. The charge of manslaughter is not to be considered. Gentlemen, you may, however, consider that the defendant's drunken state could be enough for him to be incapable of deliberation and premeditation."

Connick looked at Baxter with a smug expression as he returned to his seat. Just as Baxter turned to sit down, he heard the judge say, "Very well. Mista Foreman, you and your fella jurymen are excused to deliberate this case. Court is adjourned." Bishop rapped his gavel sending echoes around the quiet room.

Almost as one, the twelve men stood, stretched, and began to leave their seats. Before they could get very far, Judge Bishop rapped the gavel again. "Gentlemen, I just noticed the time and my growlin belly. Considerin the late hour, I suggest we recess until nine o'clock tomorrow mornin. You may begin your deliberation then. Until then, you will be sequestered at the Blanchard Hotel and provided dinner and breakfast. Durin that time, you are to refrain from discussin this case or havin any contact with others about it. Bailiff, escort these gentlemen out."

September 8, 1960

After a night at the Blanchard Hotel, Deputy Philip Mason escorted the twelve jurors back to the courthouse and into the jury room to begin their deliberation. Old as the ancient courthouse itself, but used less often, it had a musty stink. The twelve had barely arranged themselves around the big oval table when one of the jurors, Jimmy Mayes, started talking. "We heard enough yesterday. I say we take a vote right now," he blurted out. Some of the others muttered agreement until the room was buzzing.

Denzel Pennington had to yell to get them settled down. "Hold on now... hey! I said hold on. We can't just vote. We got to talk about it. You guys know that. Now, settle down."

The muttering continued, with Mayes still complaining about having to spend more time making a decision he apparently had already made. "Looka here," he said. "We got to at least go over the testimony, Jimmy. Tain't fair to Mista Peppa if we don't."

Mayes scratched the stubble on his chin and

mumbled something. As if Pennington didn't hear him clearly and didn't want to stir him up again, he took a deep breath and tried one more time.

"Damn it! I'm the foreman of this thing. I got to go over what we know, so lemme do that, okay, fellas?" Finally quiet descended.

"One, Mista Peppa says he's at Stanley's but says he passed out before he could go in, right? And, two, he admits he woke up with a hammer in his hand, right?" Pennington said, trying to put what they'd heard from the defendant in simple words.

"Right! In my book that makes that nigger boy guilty as hell," interrupted Ralph Martin. "Hell, I mean, he had all kinds of time to rape that woman and then kill her."

"Now hold on there, Ralph," Pennington said. "The coroner said she wasn't raped, remember? You can't say that's what happened. It don't match what the coroner said. Remember, you gotta go with that. Now, let me finish, hear?"

Ralph said, "I reckon," reaching in his jacket pocket for his cigarettes. Soon, blue smoke encircled his head.

Before Pennington could continue, another voice chimed in. "Look, I been drunk plenty a times, but I never couldn't remember what I done when I was." It was Lou King, a man who worked at the mill in the same department as Pennington, although he didn't know him well. "I think the boy's lyin. He knows what he did," he said down at the far end of the long table.

"Yeah," said Jimmy. "He's just tryin to save his

ass. I would be too, but you can't lie about it."

"Come on, guys, lemme finish." They settled down again and Pennington continued. "Let's look at Baxta's closin argument: he said the evidence was circumstances. That means it don't necessarily prove he's guilty. If Peppa is right-handed, why'd he have that there hammer in his left hand? If he killed her, and they's blood everywhere, why ain't he got none on him? She's got skin under her fingernails, so why ain't he all scratched up the next mornin? They said she been kicked by someone wearin boots but Peppa's wearin tennis shoes. Don't add up. Baxta's right; it's all circumstances, don't you think?" Pennington said, trying to get them to think about *all* the facts, not just those ones that made Pepper sound guilty.

Jimmy jumped in with both feet. "I can't answer all them questions, Denzel, but what about that confession? Why would anybody say they 'might have' done a killin if they ain't? Who the hell changes their mind about such a thin? Geez!" He shook his head like Peppa's whole denial was unbelievable.

"Yeah, that's sorta fishy, I agree," said Lou. "I think a guy would know if he killed someone or not. And he sure ain't gonna confess if he hadn't. Wouldn't even say he might have, would he? I mean, shit. I sure as hell wouldn't."

"Well, remember, Mista Peppa said the police beat him up and threatened to take him in to see her dead body. If that was you, you might have said anythin to get them to stop," Pennington said.

"Aw hell, do you really believe that bullshit about

bein scared of a dead person? I mean, it ain't gonna be pretty to look at, but scared of seein it? I say that's a giant load of crap."

Stacy Hendricks stood up and started pacing the room. "Come on guys, the cops just said what they had to say to get him to confess. You heard 'em; they swore on the Bible they ain't never laid a hand on Peppa. Who you gonna believe, our boys in blue or some outta-work nigger?"

All around the table the others agreed.

"You takin his side, Pennington? You ain't said a word yet about what old Connick said. What the hell?" said Jimmy.

A chorus of "Yeahs," came from around the table.

"What about the blood on his clothes? Didn't them police say they ain't tested it?" It was a small older man, whose name Pennington couldn't recall.

"That's right. They said it wasn't enough to test. Lemme look over the testimony, just to be sure." Pennington flipped through the papers 'til he found Baxter's questions to the coroner. "Says right here," he tapped the page and read, 'So, did it match Miz Annie's blood? No, it didn't. Examiner said that sample was pretty small too, and they couldn't tell what type it was. For all he could tell it might have been animal blood like Mista Peppa said.' So, they never drew no conclusion on that blood. Any more questions?"

"Why don't you read the prosecutor's closin statement, too, just to be fair?" said Stacy.

"Okay, gimme a minute." Pennington flipped on through the papers again. "OK, here's what he said at the end:

> The state believes it has proven, through the testimony of these witnesses, and the original confession of the defendant, that Mista Leon Peppa did enter Stanley's Jook Joint, did coerce Miz Sowards to have sex with him, then, followin an argument, did beat her with the hammer he then carried outside where he passed out. Gentlemen, he confessed, maybe not in so many words, but he said he might have done it, didn't he? I ask you, if you were so sure, like Mista Peppa now says he is, that you had not killed someone, would you say that? Certainly not! Or, if he blacked out, as he says he did, how can he later be so sure he did not kill Miz Sowards? We believe he did kill her, but in his drunken stupor, simply does not recall his actions of the evenin.

Jimmy repeated his earlier opinion. "See, Connick pointed out that bullshit about the confession, too. Just like I said, ain't nobody confesses then takes it back."

Lou jumped in, "Yeah, he also says Peppa first says he don't remember what he done, then all of a sudden, he ups and says he *clearly* remembers he ain't killed her. *That's* what don't add up."

Ralph said, "I agree. Seems like a load of crap that Peppa would confess just 'cause they threatened to take him in to see her body. I say we take a vote."

Pennington looked around the table and saw a table full of nodding heads even though most of them hadn't asked a single question. He asked, "Are you sure? Nobody wants to hear any more of the testimony? What about Peppa's statement about someone else in the bar? About who called the police but never said who he was? Coulda been the real killer, you know? Shouldn't we think on that? Remember, Baxta pointed out their sloppy police work. We got to think on that, too."

Ralph spoke up. "Looka hear, the judge said our verdict had to be based only on what was given to us, ain't he? Well, Baxta didn't really do shit. I mean, he talk a good story in his closin, but he never disprove nothing Connick said. I mean, that boy coulda had a better lawyer, but he didn't. And yeah, maybe the police shoulds looked for that guy, but they didn't. We only can use what was said to make a decision. Right? In my mind, that's a confession by someone who claims he was too drunk to remember what he did. Besides, the biggest piece of evidence that proves for me it is that damn hammer. I mean, come on. You want us to believe it just jumped in his hand like magic without him knowin a thin about it? Seriously? How hard can this be? He's guilty as hell." His voice rose with each sentence as his cheeks and forehead bloomed as red as a poppy.

"Yeah," Lou chimed in. "Let's us vote."

Pennington sighed and began to pass out the ballots. Most of the men filled out their ballots immediately and folded them in half. The other men, the quiet ones, took their own sweet time. One, a short guy going bald and wearing a suit that looked like he'd slept in it, stared out the filthy window as if 'guilty' or 'not guilty' might be written in the grime. Finally, he took a deep breath and started marking his vote.

Pennington looked around the room. Everyone was staring at him and the blank ballot in front of him. After a few minutes, Lou said, "Aw, come on, Pennington. Whatta ya waitin on? The damn boy's guilty. You just can't ignore that hammer or his confession."

Finally, Pennington leaned over and made his mark. Two minutes later, he gathered up all the ballots, opened them, and said, "We got us a verdict, fellas." He stood, and as if the other jurors where all hooked together, they joined him and they filed out to the courtroom. As he glanced up at the clock over the door, he could see they had been deliberating for just a bit over an hour. He sighed, shook his head, and continued down the hall.

September 8, 1960
Xander

When the jury left out the courtroom, I did too. I didn't have any way of knowin how long they be gone, so I told Louie I was leavin for a minute. I ax him to go with me, but he look at his mama and shook his head. I could tell he didn't want to leave her, so I took off for the gas station and a Coke. Plus, I need to pee bad, and I knowed Mista White wouldn't care if I was to use his. He was sittin in his office with his feet on his desk drinkin a cup of coffee.

"Hey, Mista White. You finish up that car you was workin on yesterday?" I say.

"Yeah, it was just a carburetor adjustment. What you doin back here again? Aren't you supposed to be in school? You didn't drop out, did you?" He look serious but I knew he was jes kiddin.

"You caught me," I say, grinnin at him. I pop the top on my Coke. "I didn't drop out, but I did skip school. Please don't tell my mama, though; she shoot me. Been at a friend's brother's trial. They say he killed that woman worked at Stanley's, but I don't think he did. They finished all the testifyin yesterday. Jury's out now, so I took me a break." *I don't jes think he's innocent, I pretty much know he is; but I can't tell Mista White that.*

"Oh yeah, I read about that. You know this guy?"

I nod. "His brother my best friend. I don't know how he gonna take it if things go bad, you know?"

"I know that's right," says Mista White, slowly shakin his head.

I chat with Mista White for a few more minutes then go pee before I head back. *Maybe I can catch Mista Baxta. Tell him what I think before the jury comes back. Surely he gotta tell em what I said.* I start in runnin, then, after a minute, I slows down. *He'll nevah believe me. Like Mama said, 'Who gonna believe some Negro kid?'* I walk the rest of the way, not sure I even want to be there when they come back with their verdict.

I pull open one of the double doors real quiet-like in case court's already goin on. Don't want that judge yellin at me. The place quiet as a grave, though. Judge Bishop's bench still empty. The lawyers still gone, and so's Leon. Folks in the audience are talkin in whispers, if at all. If I had me some paper I could put a note on Baxta's table but then Louie's gonna ax what I'm doin. Can't tell him 'cause I kept it a secret all this time, so I jes take my seat by Louie and give him what I hope's an encouragin smile. His mama's got her hands folded like she prayin. "Anythin happen while I'm gone?" I ax.

"Nothin. Only guy walkin around is that bailiff

guy. Reckon we jes gotta wait."

"Where's Leon?"

"Took him back. Wish I could see him. Be there with him."

"I know. I know," I said, pattin him on the leg. I nevah do that to anyone before but he look like he really need a hug and I sure wasn't gonna do that. *My belly feel like somebody's grabbin it, like it's full of ice. Maybe I shouldn't had me that Coke. Or maybe I'm jes plain scared, too.* I know I shoulda said somethin to Baxta, or Louie, or somebody. *If they convict him, it gonna be my fault.* I turn away. Can't look at Louie and his mama another minute.

All of a sudden, that bailiff come back in through a side door, walks across the room, and goes back out where the judge had gone yesterday. A few minutes later, the judge and the bailiff come back. Judge Bishop settle hisself behind the bench, and the bailiff yell. "All rise. Superior Court is now in session, Judge Michael Bishop presidin."

We all stand up; Bishop rap that gavel and says, "You may be seated. The jury has indicated they have reached a verdict. Bailiff, will you please bring them in and tell the attorneys to return?"

He nod and goes toward the jury room. While we're waitin for the lawyers and jury to come back, and for the deputy to bring Leon back from jail, I'm watchin Louie's mama. She twistin a handkerchief and starin toward the door like she tryin to catch Leon's eye. But when he does come back in, he look straight ahead; nevah even glances at her. I try to swallow, but my mouth is dry. *What a coward you are, Xander Betts. You chicken shit. You shoulda done somethin! Coulda mailed that note long before this. Now, it too late.*

After the jury seated, Judge Bishop ax if they reached a verdict. One guy on the front row stand up and say, "We have, Your Honor."

The bailiff walks over, takes a piece of paper from him, goes back to the bench, and hands it to Judge Bishop. I'm holdin my breath. I look over at Louie. He starin straight ahead. He and his mama look like they holdin their breath, too. Bishop opens the folded note, reads it, and closes it back up. He says to the jury guy. "Is your verdict unanimous?"

"Yes, sir. It is," he say and sits down. He don't say it very strong; that worries me. His face don't tell me nothin, neither. Now I'm startin to sweat.

Judge Bishop says, "Would the defendant please stand for the verdict?"

Baxta takes Leon's elbow, tellin him to stand up like the judge said. Baxta's assistant stands next to him. The three of em face the bench. I can't see anythin but the side of Leon's face, but he standin up strong, like he ready for whatevah they gonna say. *If that was me, I'd nevah be that strong.*

"Leon Peppa, the jury has rendered its decision," says the judge. I sucks in my breath, again. He unfolds that small note he closed a second before like he wants to be sure he got it right. He reads, "We the jury find the defendant, Leon Peppa, guilty of murder in the first degree. Further, we recommend that Leon Peppa be executed for this crime."

Leon drop like he been sucker-punched. Baxta grabs ahold of him and lowers him to a chair. He sits there, his head so far down that his chin is almost touchin his chest. At the same time, I hear a loud cry from Miz Peppa and see Louie wrap her up in his skinny little arms like he her daddy. She sobbin so loud I can't hardly hear Baxta, who's still standin, tryin to get the judge's attention. Her cryin reminds me of my friend's mama at that funeral I went to when I was 'bout twelve. I'll nevah forget it. Mama made me go even though I hate funerals. That boy's mama throwed herself on the casket and cried so hard she fainted. She had to be revived with smellin salts. Now I'm afraid Miz Peppa gonna faint like that. *I nevah shoulda listened to Mama.* I wants to cry, too.

People are yellin all over the room after the verdict was read. Somebody shouted, "Serves him right. I knew that damn nigger was guilty." A couple of reporters jump up and rush out the doors.

Bishop pound his gavel, yellin, "Order. I will have order in my courtroom." He bang it several more times.

Once the noise quiet down, Baxta says, "Your Honor, I would like to have the jury polled."

"Very well, Mista Baxta," he says, rappin on the bench again. The men in the jury box already started pickin up their jackets. When he raps, they sit back down. "Gentlemen of the jury, I will ask you one by one, if you agree with the verdict handed me by the foreman, Mista Pennington."

One by one, he ax the same question. Juror

number two, three, four, and so forth, do you agree with the verdict?

Each time a man answer "yes," I flinch. It's like a nail bein driven in my heart. Like they sayin I'm guilty, too. And I know I am. *If I jes stood up; jes opened my big dumb mouth and not been such a coward.*

When all the questions are over, Baxta thanks the judge and says, "Your Honor, I move the verdict be set aside on the grounds to be assigned, as contrary to the law and the evidence and other grounds to be assigned at the bar." I don't know what that mean but it sound good for Leon, and I finally feel like I can breathe.

"Denied, Mista Baxta. However, you have thirty days in which to file your appeal, should you choose to do so, but, in the meantime, I am settin the sentencin date for September thirtieth, 1960." He bangs the gavel and I feel sick to my stomach again. Feel like it's not as good as I thought. "Gentlemen, thank you for your service. This jury is dismissed. Court is adjourned until September thirtieth." He raps the gavel one more time, gets up, goes down from behind the bench, and disappears out the side door.

Up front, Baxta leanin over, talkin to Leon. He still sittin there with his head down. Baxta talks, and Leon keeps shakin his head. I'm stunned. Don't know what to do. Wanna say somethin make Louie feel better, but he busy huggin his mama. Wanna rush up and tell Baxta what I know. It's my last chance, I know. I look around see if Miz Annie's husband still in court, but I don't see him. I see Bill Feeney sittin there in the corner. He got the oddest look on his face. Like the kind of smile my sister get when she gets away with somethin she been told not to do. Sorta smug, you know? Maybe I'm imaginin things but it make me want to go up there even more, and tell Baxta everthin. I stand up, start to move out of the pew. I look at Feeney again, and lose my nerve. I fall back on the hard pew. I sit, not movin, not talkin, not doin anythin while Louie and his mama push past me out into the aisle. They leave without sayin a word. She still leanin on Louie and cryin. I stay there like I'm glued to the bench. I nevah felt so terrible in my whole life. *It's all my fault. I know it is. My fault. All my fault.*

September 30, 1960

The morning of Leon's sentencing the sky was a brilliant blue. To Gerald Baxter it still felt like summer, never mind that it was the last day of September. Even before nine o'clock, as he walked over to the courthouse, he was starting to sweat. Inside the courtroom, as if they'd been left on since the day of the trial, the fans still labored, with little success, to move the thick air. As Baxter walked up the aisle, he noticed a handful of reporters toward the front of the seating area, but aside from them, the benches were nearly empty. There was no sign of Pepper's family. As he swung open the gate that separated spectators from the court, Connick turned and nodded. "Counselor," he said, his smirk broad. Baxter nodded in return but did not reply. Despite the jury's death-sentence recommendation, Baxter knew the judge had the option of overriding the recommendation and sentencing Leon Pepper to life, but he also knew Bishop was a tough judge, and therefore, wasn't optimistic.

The door at the left front of the courtroom

opened and Pepper came shuffling in with a guard behind him. He seemed thinner, more haggard, than he had at his trial less than a month earlier. Baxter nodded and smiled at Leon when he took his seat, but Pepper's return smile made only a straight line on his face. Baxter leaned toward him and said, "Try not to worry, son. We've got the option to appeal, remember. Today isn't the end of the road." Pepper's smile broadened slightly but he still looked anxious. A moment later, Judge Bishop took his place at the bench and the bailiff called the court to order.

Bishop wasted no time. "Mista Peppa, we're here today to pass sentence on you. Before I do, do you have anythin further to add to what you said previously?" Baxter looked at Pepper. He shook his head but didn't say a word.

"Very well, then," Bishop said. "Accordin to the law and the unanimous verdict of the jury, you are to be taken to the Georgia State Prison and held there until January sixteenth, 1961, when you will be electrocuted." He banged his gavel and stood as if he was ready to be done with the whole distasteful matter. From the audience, a woman wailed. When Baxter turned to look, he saw Mrs. Pepper standing about two rows from the front, her head thrown back, crying loudly, "No, no, not my boy." Beside her, a teenage boy grabbed her around the waist and got her to sit down. He put her head on his shoulder as if trying to muffle her cries.

The bailiff yelled, "Order, we'll have order in this courtroom."

Before the judge could leave, Baxter yelled, "Your Honor." Bishop turned and retook his seat. "I do plan an appeal," he said.

"Fine, sir. Remember, you have thirty days… thirty days *only* to file." Bishop said emphatically as if he assumed Baxter didn't remember that since criminal work was no longer his field.

Bishop banged his gavel again, turned and left the bench, reaching the door to his chambers almost before the bailiff could pronounce that court was adjourned.

Reporters scrambled for the door. Baxter put his arm around Pepper's shoulder. "Don't give up, son. We'll have another chance. You heard him. He gave me some time to work on your appeal."

"Thank you, Mista Baxta, I know you doin what you can," he said, but his eyes were on his mother, not his attorney.

"I'll go talk to your mother, if you think that would help," he said.

"Don't know if it will or won't but can't hurt to try. Thank you."

The guard took Pepper's arm, forcing him to stand. "This way, Mista Peppa," he said.

"Take care of yourself, son," Baxter called as he turned to try and catch Pepper's family, but the courtroom was completely empty.

OCTOBER 7, 1960
XANDER

After the trial, I started skippin school like Louie had done. I jes couldn't keep my mind on my classes. I kept thinkin 'bout Leon and how I'd helped send him to the chair. On the days I skip, I leave out for school like I always done; then, after I know Mama done left out for the café, I come back home. One day I'm down in our buildin's laundry room and I meet that girl live next door, you know, the one always playin her record player up loud. She told me her name was Phyllis. I told her I liked her music. She say she'll bring it over sometime and we can dance. She real good lookin, so, ever day after lunch, I bang on the wall to let Phyllis know I'm home, and she come over.

Sometimes, after dancin, we neck, but I'm always afraid Ladonna'll come in from school and catch us, so we don't do anything else. I'd already given Ladonna candy not to tell Mama I was skippin, but catchin me with Phyllis woulda been too much. She'd snitch, no matter how much candy I gave her. Being with Phyllis took my mind off Leon, that's for sure.

Wasn't like me to skip school, so after I missed about a week, my social studies teacher, Miz Johnson, came to the house. Phyllis wasn't there, thank goodness. Miz Johnson's a friend of Mama's from church but she also my favorite teacher. When I see her, I know I'm 'bout to be in big trouble. Knowin her, Miz Johnson would tell on me 'bout Phyllis, for sure, and that would have made everthin a whole lot worse. When she knock on the door, it scares me half to death. I thought it might be the truant officer. I look out the window and there she stands on our stoop, hands on her hips like she gonna lecture me right there and I haven't even opened the door. I wasn't gonna, but when I look out the window she catches my eye. The feathers on top of her maroon-colored hat wavin like a peacock's tail when she shook her head back and forth like she was fed up with me. No use hidin. I been caught.

I open the door. Before I can say a word, she blurts out, "Alexander Betts, what are you doin home on a Thursday? You haven't been to school for at least a week. Are you sick?"

"Come in, Miz Johnson. Nice to see you," I say in my most polite voice. She steps across the door sill, and I look around be sure the place isn't a mess. Don't want her fussin at me 'bout that, too. And, she woulda.

"Have a seat," I say, pointin to the sofa.

"I'll stand right here, if you don't mind, because I don't plan to stay long. I've been worried about you.

Why in the world are you skippin school? You've never done that before. Don't you realize you're about to ruin your chances for grades good enough to get into college?" She's shakin her finger in my face. Remind me of Mama when she's mad.

"Hadn't thought 'bout it that way, Miz Johnson. I'm not sick but I guess you could say I been upset. You know Louie's brother, Leon? Got accused of murder?" She nods, so I continue. "Well, first, I skipped school to go to his trial but after he got convicted, I was so upset I jes couldn't concentrate on schoolwork, you know? So, I jes stayed away."

"I heard about that and I know Louie is your friend, so I'm sorry. Looks like he dropped out of school recently. I hope you aren't plannin on joinin him." She look hard at me from under them feathers.

"No, ma'am. I'm jes tryin to get over Leon bein sent to the chair. See, I, uh, I know what... uh, nevah mind," I say. *I wants so much to tell someone, get this guilty feelin off my chest.* From the look on her face I think she might understand, but then I get scared. If Mama wouldn't listen, Miz Johnson might not either. Thinkin 'bout it is wearin me out, so I decide to take a chance.

"What do you know, Alexander?"

"Miz Johnson, if I tell you somethin terrible, somethin awful I did, you promise to keep it a secret? I mean, don't tell anyone. Not the principal, not my mama, not anyone." I look her straight in the eyes hopin to see trust in them.

"Certainly, Alexander. Come over here. Let's sit down." She walks to the sofa like she in her own house and pats the cushion next to her. I'm embarrassed because dust clouds rise up, but I sit. She leans over to look in my eyes but I can't look at her.

"Miz Johnson, it's my fault Leon's gonna be electrocuted," I say, starin at the floor.

"I don't understand, Alexander. How is that possible? From what I read in the papers, you couldn't have had anything to do with that."

"Well, yeah, I did. See, I'm pretty sure I know who really did it. It wasn't Leon but I nevah got up the nerve to tell what I knew. I did tell Mama right when he was first arrested but she told me to keep quiet. Now I wish she'd nevah said that 'cause I minded her. I wish I hadn't listened to her. Now he gonna die all because of me."

Miz Johnson puts her arm around my shoulders and pulls me toward her. "Alexander, I'm sure you think it's your fault, but didn't he admit to waking up in front of the place where she was killed with the murder weapon in his hand? That's what convicted him, not your lack of testimony. Why don't you tell me the whole story and why you think it's your fault?"

I do. When I'm through, I look up. Her forehead has a deep frown in it. She says, "Alexander, sadly, I think your mother was right. They wouldn't have listened to you. I know you feel bad, but I really don't think anything you could have said would have changed those men's minds. They'd have found him guilty no matter what. You know how it is. Negroes are always guilty in the white man's eyes." Her expression look angry but I know she's not angry at me.

164

"But maybe…" I start to argue, but realize there's nothin else to say. I sniff and wipe my face with the side of my hand, suddenly aware I been cryin. "Maybe, maybe you're right," I say. "When the trial started, I felt like he couldn't win, but Mista Baxta do such a good job, I thought he convinced the jury. I shouldn'ta gotten my hopes up, I guess."

"I am right. I know I haven't kept you from feeling guilty, but here's how I think you should make up for not saying anything. Get yourself back in school. Study as hard as you can. Make something of yourself. Maybe become a lawyer so you can help other Negro boys fight our rotten system. You're smart enough. And since I've heard you argue a point or two in class, I know you'll make a good one. You hear me?" She winks at me.

"Yes, ma'am," I say, as she gets up to leave.

"And, if you do that, no one will ever know what we talked about here today. Deal?"

"Deal," I say, puttin out my hand. She takes it, but doesn't shake it. She jes hold it in both her hands and look at me with shimmery eyes like she might could cry, too.

"Think about what I've said over the weekend and then I'll see you on Monday, Alexander." She turns, walks to the door, and leaves without another word.

After she left, I felt like I been standin in a warm shower for the longest time and was cleaner than I evah been. It was a good feelin. Talkin to her had been the right thing even if I nevah planned on it.

OCTOBER 10, 1960

Monday morning an unusual fall drizzle set in; not quite enough rain for an umbrella, but uncomfortable all the same. As Deputy Philip Mason entered the Blanchard Hotel lobby, he brushed off his uniform jacket and smacked his cap against his legs. The desk clerk looked up like he wished the man hadn't gotten his carpet wet.

Inside, Gerald Baxter sat at one of the small tables along the wall. Mason told the hostess he knew where he was going and headed toward the lawyer.

"'Mornin, Deputy," Baxter said, half standing.

"Sit, sit," Mason said as he took his seat. "Good mornin, sir."

Baxter didn't waste time with niceties. "Deputy Mason, I wanted to meet with you to discuss the sequestration of the jury in the Leon Peppa trial last month. Why don't you order and then we'll talk?"

"Okay," Mason said, motioning the waitress over. "You not eatin?" he asked.

"No, just havin coffee. I'm not much of a breakfast man."

"I see," he said then placed his order. While the waitress poured their coffees, Mason was quiet, as if trying to remember the details of that night.

Baxter stirred his coffee deliberately, then cleared his throat. "Deputy, I wondered if you could tell me how the men were sequestered that night? Did they have separate rooms? Do you know if anyone used a telephone, read a newspaper, or watched TV, thins like that? I want to see if we have any grounds in that area for an appeal. You see, I think the man is innocent but my only chance to argue that again is in an appeal. So, what can you tell me?"

"Mista Baxta, I gotta tell you, I didn't have anyone else with me that night, so it was pretty damn hard to keep an eye on those twelve guys. And I gotta admit I was pretty pissed at Bishop for not assignin another man to go with me. Pardon my language, but it's the truth. So, if I didn't keep a close enough eye on them, it's not my fault; well, not entirely. Can't be everywhere at once, you know."

"I understand, Mason. Just tell me how it went. First, where were the men sleepin? Room arrangements, that sort of thing." He blew into his coffee cup then took a big swallow.

"Well, as I recall, the hotel had to put them on two floors, most of them two to a room. I had words with the clerk over it, but there wasn't anythin he could do. Hotel was nearly full up." The waitress put a plate of French toast and bacon in front of Mason.

"What floor were you on?" Baxter asked, seemingly oblivious to the aroma of the hot food.

"Two, I think. I shared a room with the foreman, Pennington. He was asleep long before I came to bed, so I'm pretty sure he didn't break any of the rules." Mason took a bite of his bacon.

"Did you instruct them as to what they could and couldn't do?"

"I did. Told them not to watch TV or listen to the radio. I did let them call home to get toothbrushes, clean underwear, that sort of thing," Mason said, cutting up his French toast.

"What about other calls? Did you monitor those? Or tell the hotel operator not to put them through?"

Baxter didn't seem to notice the man he'd questioned had food in his mouth, so Mason held up his hand to get him to wait a minute. He swallowed, then said, "No, I meant to, but it slipped my mind. You know, I thought if I listened to their calls, it would be okay. But I guess since I couldn't be in every room all the time, I should have, huh?"

"Yeah, you probably should have," Baxter said, as he made notes on his lined yellow pad.

"So, tell me how the evenin went, if you can remember. Like, were you with them at all times when they were out of their rooms? Did you all eat together? That sort of thing." He sat back and signaled for the waitress to refill his coffee.

In between bites, Mason told him what he could remember: about having to split up the group to ride the elevator, the two meals they had, the poker game, and checking on them around ten or ten-thirty. He also told him the TV was on in the poker room but that he'd told them to turn it off before the news came on. He had to admit to Baxter that he wasn't sure they did, though, because he had left the room. He said one guy even asked for a beer, but that he thought he was really joking. Baxter remained grim-faced at that detail.

"So, you're sayin they could have watched the eleven o'clock news and you wouldn't have known it?"

"Well, I suppose you could say that," Mason said, a flush rising on his face.

"So, you didn't see those men who were playin poker after the time you checked on them in that room?" Bishop wrote furiously as Mason talked.

"No, like I said, I told them what to do and then I went off to check on the others. I guess they did what I told them – went back to their rooms and went to bed – but I can't swear to it."

"And the next mornin, did you gather up the men to go to breakfast?" He took another swallow of the coffee.

"No, I met them in the lobby. I'd told them to be there at seven-thirty sharp so I went down a few minutes early to be sure we could get tables together. When I left, Pennington was just gettin out of the shower."

Baxter cleared his throat. "So, again, they were by themselves and you can't say if they had their radios on or if they talked to each other. Am I gettin this right?"

"I suppose you are. Like I said, I couldn't be in more than one place at a time. I did the best I could,

Mr. Baxter. Sorry if I made a mess of it."

"On the contrary, Deputy. You've been a big help. Hell, for my purposes, you've given me several grounds for appeal just based on the jury's sequestration. I appreciate your comin. Enjoy the rest of your breakfast." He grabbed his raincoat and left.

Mason grinned as he watched Baxter head toward the door as if he was relieved by the lawyer's parting remark. He picked up his fork and devoured every bite of the rest of his breakfast.

When he returned to his office Baxter called the local television stations to find out if they had shown anything about the trial that night. Channel Eight said they'd shown comments at both six and eleven. The Channel Four folks said they had a piece on it as well.

Next, he called the jury foreman, Denzel Pennington. He confirmed that he'd gone to bed early and had no idea what the others had done. Ralph Martin, the guy who had the poker game in his room, couldn't remember the names of the other guys but he did recall that the television set was on. He did say that the sound was down and that they weren't paying any attention to it.

That afternoon, Baxter added 'misconduct on the part of the jury' to the other things he thought had been done wrong at trial in order to make his case for an appeal. Knowing he had a short time to submit it, he began to formulate his case.

OCTOBER 15, 1960
XANDER

I nevah saw Louie again till the middle of October. He was on his stoop when I came home from mowin one Saturday and he hollered at me. Scared me some to talk to him, but I waved and went over. He'd dropped outta school after the trial to get a job. I hated that, but I knew his mama needed the money. He nevah liked school anyway, so I bet he wasn't too upset 'bout havin to quit. I heard he was workin down to the meat market where Leon used to work. Maybe they felt sorry for him, for the family. I'd been missin Louie, but after I read in the paper that Leon had been sentenced to the chair, I nevah knew what to say to Louie, so I jes stay clear of him. Thought 'bout goin to the courthouse the day Leon was sentenced, but I didn't. I jes didn't wanna hear the judge say it.

"Hey buddy; how you doin?" I hear my voice start in shakin, so I clears my throat.

"Aww, you know, I'm doin, I reckon," he says, lookin down at the steps.

"How's Leon? He doin okay? I think 'bout him all the time. Man, I'm sure sorry the way things turned out." *I really want to tell Louie how bad I feel. Tell him I coulda made a difference. But Miz Johnson was right: it's too late, now. Tellin Louie now would jes make things worse. And he'd hate me for bein such a chicken shit.*

Louie's voice rises and sound mad. "How the fuck you think he's doin in there waitin to be electrocuted? He scared shitless. Unless that Baxta can work some kinda magic, he gonna be a dead man in three months."

I can't look at Louie. I duck my head and put my hand on his knee. I'm afraid if I say anythin, it'll be wrong. "I know. Sorry man. I jes can't help worryin 'bout him, ya know? Baxta's a good man. I heard he's gonna appeal. Maybe he can convince the new judge to change Leon's sentence."

"Sure hope so. Mama tore all to pieces. Can't even imagine what she be like if they kill Leon. Hey, you hear anythin down to the store 'bout Feeney? Somebody told me he went to the police sayin it was all his fault Miz Annie's dead. Said he was talkin so crazy they throwed his ass out. Why the hell he do that? Heard anythin like that?"

My face flushes and I stammer. "No… I nevah… ain't heard nothin like that but he ain't been in the store for… oh, least a week, either. Somebody said they saw him drunk in the middle of the day. First time I evah seen him miss work for more than a day. Maybe he all broken up 'bout Miz Annie."

"What the fuck you mean? Why'd he care if she's

dead?" Louie says.

Oh, God. Now I've done it. Why didn't I jes leave before I said somethin. Shit.

"I dunno. Maybe he jes knew her from the store."

"You know somethin you ain't sayin?" Louie said, givin me the stink eye.

"Nah, I shouldn'ta said anythin. She used to come in the store, that's all."

"If you knowed somethin coulda helped Leon, you'da told me, right?"

I didn't answer.

Louie jumped off the stoop and grabbed my shirt. "You little shit. Thought you was my friend. What you know 'bout Miz Annie and Feeney?" He starts shakin me, snappin my head back and forth.

"Stop it, Louie. What the fuck?" I said, my teeth clackin together as my head shook. "Leggo, you sonofabitch," I yelled. But he didn't. I swung at him, and he ducked. I struggled to get free, but his grip was too strong. He kept on shakin me.

"Lemme go, dammit. I'll tell you." I was breathin hard and my head ached.

Louie turn loose of my shirt but didn't move outta my face.

"Miz Annie used to come in the store all time to see Feeney. I think they had somethin goin on." I ducked my head, ashamed I hadn't told him long ago.

When I looked up, Louie hocked a loogie in my face. "I don't nevah want to see your ugly ass again," he said, then turned and went in his house.

Stunned, I sat down on the stoop and wiped my

face. Unwanted tears began. I nevah cried in public before but I couldn't stop. *Lord, I didn't mean to say anythin. It jes slipped out. Now I lost my best friend. Serves me right. Louie's right… I shoulda said somethin back then.* I wipe my face with my sleeve, get on my bike, and leave outta there. Can't get away quick enough.

Back home, I think 'bout what Miz Johnson said and I think 'bout Louie. Now, tears flow for real. *Damn it. I knew I shoulda told him and Baxta. Now, I've lost my best friend since we was little. Wish I nevah listen to Mama. Wish I weren't such a chicken shit. Maybe she was right, but look what it caused. Can't go back, though. Gotta try and make it right, somehow. Miz Johnson's right. Gotta find a way to make up for what I did, or, what I didn't do. I owe Louie and Leon that much.*

MAY 17, 1961

The day was cool when Gerald Baxter got up to drive to Atlanta, but as the morning wore on, the heat had begun to build. By the time he parked and got to the Supreme Court Building, his shirt was beginning to stick to him, whether from the heat or a case of the nervous flop-sweats, he wasn't sure. He had waited more than six months from the day he first had filed with the court to give his oral argument. And all that time, Leon Pepper had been sitting in prison in Reidsville not knowing what his future held. Now, that future hung on this presentation. If Baxter couldn't convince this panel of judges, Pepper would be heading for the electric chair, and soon.

Chief Justice Everett Stevenson had a nasty reputation for being a hard-nosed justice with an unusual talent: he swore he could tell a criminal by the space between his eyes – the wider, the greater the criminal tendency. Some lawyers believed this was a bad joke. But the many others who repeated it registered the disgust that said they knew he'd said that and had acted on it. This story had made Gerald Baxter very nervous since it was clear that Stevenson was a racist.

The whole setting around the government buildings intimidated him as well. He felt out of his element as he gazed at the impressive supreme court building with its tall pillars soaring to the sky and the sun glinting off the gold capitol dome across the street. He was nearly overwhelmed by the sense of austerity he imagined would be inside. Back home in Blanchard's Bottom, the courthouse felt comfortable to him because he was in and out of it on a weekly basis. It was home for Gerald Baxter; this was a stranger's house. He glanced at his watch and realized he was half an hour early. Grateful for the chance to orient himself, he consulted the wall directory and headed to the elevators for the ride to the sixth floor.

When he pulled open the courtroom's double doors, it was quiet as a deserted house. The long judicial bench was empty. A lone bailiff stood beside the door that led to the justices' chambers. He gave Baxter a short nod. Baxter took that to mean the man knew he was supposed to be in that hallowed hall, which made him feel more at ease. He took a seat on one of the well-polished pews. He wanted to look over his notes, but there wasn't any place to put them, so he simply balanced his briefcase on his knees and waited.

A few minutes later, a familiar voice sounded behind Baxter. "'Mornin, Baxta," it said. "You ready for this?" It was Riley Connick.

Baxter turned. "Absolutely," he said, in a voice that sounded more confident than he felt. "You?"

"Yeah. There may be seven of them up there behind that bench, but they put their pants on same as I do."

Soon, others began to fill the rows behind the two rivals, men who were bringing other cases on appeal. Pepper's case had been given an early slot on the docket so they would be among the first to be heard. Baxter wished that wasn't the case, since being later on the docket would have given him a chance to study how the justices might question him. He sat there getting more and more nervous and wishing he had a good plug of tobacco in his cheek, when the bailiff stepped in front of the bench and announced, "All rise; the Supreme Court of Georgia is now in session."

Seven black-robed and very serious-looking men filed in and took their seats. Chief Justice Stevenson was a florid man who looked a bit like Colonel Sanders, including the goatee, but without the colonel's beneficent smile. He rapped his gavel and said, "Gentlemen, let me remind you that you have a set time limit on your oral argument, depending on the type of case you're bringing. Following the appellant's argument, the appellee may present his cross appeal. At any time, any of us may ask you questions for clarification. Is that clear?"

No one spoke. "Very well," Stevenson continued. "It's a full docket, so let's get started. The court first calls the case of the State of Georgia vs. Leon Peppa. The attorneys may take their places."

Connick and Baxter rose, pushed through the

short swinging gates and headed for separate tables on either side of the aisle. Baxter took out his notes, studied them briefly and stepped forward to stand in front of the bench. "Your Honors, I come before you to present facts of error in this case that I believe are contrary to the verdict, facts that should have been taken into consideration at trial but were not, or facts I have subsequently discovered.

"As stated in my appeal brief, I believe Judge Bishop erred in not allowin manslaughter as a possible verdict because of the un-disputed and admitted state of drunkenness of the defendant the evenin of the murder of Annie Sowards. To my mind, the state did not prove deliberate intent as required by the definition of murder. Nor, should they have found for first degree since there was no rape or theft. Instead, the jury should have been allowed to consider the charge of manslaughter. As you know, accordin to Georgia law…"

Before he could say another word, one of the justices interrupted. Red-faced, the portly judge banged his fist on the bench and boomed, "Mista Baxta, we have no need to be lectured to on Georgia law. Remember to whom you are talking."

"Yes, sir. Sorry, Your Honor. May I continue?"

"Very well," the justice said, leaning back in his chair.

"Thank you, Your Honor. Although we do not believe Mista Peppa killed Miz Sowards, we also believe that *if*, I say, *if*, he did so, it was due to his careless actions. In this case, the careless actions bein his state of drunkenness. Therefore, I believe manslaughter would have been the proper verdict."

Connick rose, "Your Honors, this was ruled on at trial."

"Mista Connick, return to your seat," said Stevenson. "You'll have your opportunity to rebut after Mista Baxta presents his case."

Connick did as he was told, and Baxter continued. "I also believe Mista Peppa's coerced confession should not have been allowed. He testified under oath that he was both struck and threatened with bein shown the dead body if he did not confess right there in the police car. If you know the old superstitions of the colored race and some folks' long-held fears of the dead, you know Mista Peppa would have gone to any extreme to avoid scenes such as he would imagine existed in the bar. The court should have taken this into consideration and thrown out the confession, especially since Mista Peppa denounced it once he was at the police station and no longer under duress."

"Mista Baxta, did the police admit to strikin Mista Peppa?" It was the justice on the far-right end of the bench.

"No, Your Honor. In fact, they denied it."

The justice made a note on a pad in front of him. "Thank you. Please continue," he said.

"Secondly, a number of facts in this case do not point to this man, Leon Peppa, as bein the assailant. In fact, they are completely contrary to that conclusion. Let me enumerate. One, the police stated that there were straight hairs about an inch long in the victim's hand. Mista Peppa has the kinky type of hair typical of the colored race. Therefore, they could not have been his. Furthermore, the police did not take a sample of Mista Peppa's hair and thus could not have compared the two even if they had been inclined to do so.

"Two, the coroner testified that any person committin such a crime would have to be splattered with blood. The police officers also testified as to the large amount of blood on both the floor and the walls of the room where the body was found. However, the only blood found on the defendant, who was wearin the same clothes the mornin he was arrested, was a slight trace on the cuffs of his pants, which he stated was animal blood from the meat market where he had worked a few days earlier. Again, no tests were made to dispute this claim; the lab merely concluded that it was blood."

"But it also could have been human blood, correct?" The Chief Justice narrowed his eyes as he spoke. His piercing gaze made Baxter nervous.

"Yes, but that was not proven," he replied.

"Continue, Mista Baxta," he said.

"Thank you. Furthermore, as it regards blood, the victim had dried blood and skin under her fingernails, which neither the police nor the lab tested. Again, the police did not obtain a sample of Mista Peppa's blood in order to perform such a comparative test. Moreover, the defendant had absolutely no scratches of any kind on his person when he was arrested the followin mornin. It's unrealistic to believe if he had such scratches, they coulda miraculously healed overnight, gentlemen."

That same justice who had asked about the beating said, "Are you suggestin criminal misconduct on the part of the crime lab, Mista Baxta?"

"No, sir. I'm simply sayin certain tests, which might have exonerated my client, were not performed. I don't know if that rises to the level of criminality, but it does, in my opinion, show incompetence and/or neglect." Baxter wiped his brow where sweat had begun to appear. The justice waved his hand dismissively as he made another note, so Baxter continued.

"Additionally, the coroner stated there were absolutely no signs of forcible rape, one of the possible felony conditions for a verdict of first-degree murder. He did testify that the victim had had intercourse, but it is unreasonable to believe she would agree to such an act with a man she barely knew. Further, Mista Peppa said he did not notice any signs of semen or blood on his penis when he returned home that night. And, in my opinion, a man would know if he'd had intercourse, no matter how drunk he'd been." When Baxter said that a half-muffled snicker could be heard from the judge to the left of the chief justice. He, however, remained stone-faced.

Now solemn again, the previously-smiling justice said, "Excuse me for the interruption, Mista Baxta, but did your man know this woman at all?"

"Mista Peppa testified that he knew her only to speak to her and that he'd never been inside the establishment where she worked. Shall I continue?"

"Yes, thank you," the justice replied.

"Very well. Next, I'd like to bring to the justices' attention two other contradictions of fact. Despite the evidence of a grimy or oily substance on the victim's face, the substance was not analyzed, nor was any such substance found on Mista Peppa's shoes. Furthermore, the evidence indicated she had been kicked by a person wearin boots. Mista Peppa does not own any boots and was wearin tennis shoes both that night and the followin mornin. Additionally, the coroner testified she could have died from the severe knife wound to the chest, yet no knife was found, and none was missin from the bar, which indicates, to me, that the assailant had it with him and subsequently took the murder weapon when he left. Yet, no such knife was found at Mista Peppa's home."

It was the judge on the end again. "Did they search his home?"

"It's my understandin that they did, although not at the time they arrested him."

"Was there testimony as to the result of the search?"

"No, sir. I assume the evidence report was included in the state's evidence, however. The jury must've seen it."

"Thank you; please continue." Baxter watched him make another note and wondered if he was leaning his way.

"As to testimony that either should've been investigated or was ignored, Mista Peppa stated that when he returned to the bar, he saw a man inside. Although he could not identify him, he testified that it was a white man. Yet, at no point did the police ever ask others if they had seen anyone else inside the bar that night. Nor did they go lookin for possible witnesses who might have. Mista Peppa further testified that he never entered the front door of Stanley's Jook Joint but that he passed out in the doorway. However, accordin to the owner, Mista Stanley, the back door to the establishment was unlocked, which could've allowed the actual assailant to enter from the alley completely undetected. To my knowledge, this was never investigated at all, Your Honors.

"Lastly, I have statements from both the deputy in charge and the night auditor at the hotel in which the jury was sequestered that improprieties occurred that night. Their statements are included in my brief. Deputy Philip Mason, the only man assigned to supervise the twelve jurors says they were housed on two separate floors of the hotel, renderin his close scrutiny of all of them quite impossible. Statements from both Mista Mason and at least one of the jurors corroborates that the television set in at least one room was on. Evidence from two station managers indicates that the case was discussed on both evenin news broadcasts. Further, the hotel's night auditor admits that no telephone conversations were monitored, suggestin that calls made could've involved discussions of the case. Since Mista Mason was unable to be in all the rooms all the time, I believe this possible mishandlin of the jurors constitutes improper jury sequestration, a condition that requires this panel to consider overturnin the verdict."

"Mista Baxta, did you interview all those men and are their statements also available?" It was the fat justice who had yelled at Baxter earlier.

"Yes, sir. I can make them available. I have copies with me." He walked back to his table and rummaged through his briefcase for a moment. Finding the file, Baxter handed them to the Chief Justice.

"Thank you, Mista Baxta. You may continue."

"Gentlemen, in conclusion, Mista Leon Peppa had no motive to kill Miz Annie Sowards. He has never been arrested for a violent crime, and accordin to those who knew him, never lost his temper, even when he was drinkin. Given the facts I have presented, the lack of testin done by the police lab to corroborate their circumstantial evidence, and the improprieties allowed at trial, I move that this verdict be overturned."

Baxter walked back to the table without looking at Connick and took his seat. His palms were wet and so was his shirt. He knew he'd given it his best shot but had no idea if it would be enough.

The Chief Justice was speaking as Baxter sat down. "Thank you, Mista Baxta. Mista Connick, do you wish to make an oral reply?"

"Yes, sir. I do," Connick said as he hopped up and approached the front of the courtroom.

"Your Honors, Mista Baxta can claim exculpatory evidence was either suppressed, omitted, or disallowed all he wants, but the truth of the matter is this: Mista Leon Peppa admitted he awoke from a drunken stupor on the doorstep of the murder scene with a bloody hammer in his hand. And he admits to disposin of the weapon that night. This evidence alone was enough to convict him, in the state's opinion, even if the other evidence had been presented. Furthermore, he admitted to the arrestin officers that he didn't recall what he'd done that night.

"Secondly, I find it hard to believe, and I suspect you will too, that a man would confess to murder just because he was afraid to look at the deceased's body. Unless, of course, he knew what horrible condition it was in and didn't want to face what he'd done. I'll say no more on that count."

As he reached in his pocket and began playing with the coins there, he turned and gave Baxter a smug grin. Baxter frowned as if wondering how the justices would take that. After all, Connick was supposed to be presenting his case to them, not to Baxter. Connick turned back and continued.

"As to the manslaughter charge, based on the facts of the case, the state believes the superior court judge was correct in omittin that as a possible verdict. Such a verdict as Mista Baxta wants is reserved for a homicide done unwilfully, as in a fatal automobile accident in which the defendant was, let's say, speedin and the person he hit died as a result of his carelessness. The magnitude of Miz Sowards' injuries hardly indicate an unwilful killin. In fact, it's clear the perpetrator wanted her good and dead. Accordin to the coroner, any of the three types of injuries could have killed her. The evidence clearly pointed to either premeditation or a struggle of enormous proportions. And it certainly rises to the level of depraved disregard for human life."

Connick turned and looked at Baxter again. His sneer registered both condescension and disgust that Baxter had even suggested Pepper had been railroaded. Connick returned his gaze to the bench.

"Your Honors, my brief cites the relevant case precedents, so I won't take your time to repeat them here. If you don't have any questions, then that's all I have to say. It's clear to the state that the correct verdict was reached in this case. Thank you, gentlemen."

Not a single justice spoke. No questions; no comments. Finally, Chief Justice Stevenson said, "Very well. Thank you both for your time. The court will study the submitted briefs, the proffered statements, and the arguments presented here today. When we have rendered our opinion, you will both be notified. That is all. You are dismissed."

Baxter gathered up his papers and sighed as if he felt he should have been able to do more, but he didn't know what. Connick grabbed his briefcase and gave Baxter a jaunty salute. "See you back at the ranch, Baxta." From his smug expression, Baxter knew he thought he'd won. Sadly, Baxter did too.

OCTOBER 27, 1961

At Reidsville Prison, a guard yelled, "Hey, Peppa, you got a visitor," It was mid-morning and Leon Pepper was lying on his bunk staring at the calendar on the wall near his bed. Each day, until this one, crossed off with a red X, marking the days since he'd been in prison. He jumped off his bunk and went to the front of his cell. Doors clanged and heels clicked on the tile floor. It wasn't visitin day, so he knew it couldn't be his mother. He shivered as a cold chill of apprehension passed through him.

The guard pulled out his massive ring of a keys and unlocked Leon's cell door.

"Gotta cuff you. Leon. Turn around," he said.

Pepper obeyed and the two walked down the hall. Other men in the cells yelled. "Hey, Peppa, you ain't leavin us, is you?" "Ain't visitin day. Where you goin? Who you gonna see?"

"Don't know but I'm fixin to find out," he hollered back as the guard unlocked the next door.

Unlike the visitor's room, this one was no bigger

than a cell. At the small table in the middle, sat Gerald Baxter, a big wad of tobacco in his jaw. Despite the puffed-out right cheek, his face seemed thinner, more deeply lined. His lips were drawn into a straight line.

"Afternoon, Mista Peppa," Baxter said as he rose and stuck out his hand. Then he realized Pepper was cuffed and couldn't shake hands, so he apologized. "They didn't need to do that, Leon. I'm sorry." He pointed to the chair on the other side of the table and Pepper sat down. "How you doin?" Baxter asked.

"I'm tolerable, I reckon. So far, ain't nobody givin me grief. Food's terrible, though. Wish I could get me some honest-to-goodness fried chicken like Chicken Little's."

Baxter laughed. "I know what you mean. That's some fine fried chicken."

Baxter cleared his throat, looked down, then finally focused on Pepper's face. "Leon, I didn't come here to talk about the food. Do you remember how I said the state supreme court might take a while to decide on my appeal?"

Leon nodded. "I remember." Suddenly sweaty, he tried to wipe his palms on his pants legs, but the handcuffs stopped him.

Baxter looked down at the floor, moved his tobacco wad to the other side of his mouth, and cleared his throat a couple times. Finally, he looked up. "Son, I'm afraid I have bad news. They turned down our appeal."

Leon licked his lips several times but said nothing.

"They decided the jury did nothin wrong when

they were sequestered at the hotel. And they believed the evidence Connick presented was enough to convict you." Baxter's face twisted as if he was tryin to keep from cryin. "I'm so sorry. So, so sorry. Leon, I tried my best. I'm sorry."

"What's that mean? Does it mean they're gonna electrocute me? They ain't believed me sayin I nevah done it?" Now Leon's face mirrored Baxter's.

Baxter shook his head. "No, that's not it. It doesn't work that way. I couldn't try the case all over again. All I could do was tell them what I thought the court had done wrong."

Leon looked down. "Reckon now all I got to do is wait until they decide to fire up that chair." He looked back up at Baxter as if he hoped his attorney would assure him that wasn't the case, but Leon's tears distorted Baxter's face. He'd tried hard to be stoic, but the tears came anyway.

"No, no. I can appeal to the United States Supreme Court, but I've got to get permission from them. That could take a while. The state won't carry out your sentence until I get the word from them. Don't worry, son, it's not over yet."

"How in the hell can I keep from worryin? I'm facin dyin. And I ain't done nothing neither." He wiped his face on his sleeve.

"Son, I believe you didn't do it, but it's not up to me. If it were, you'd be back home right now."

Baxter stood and called for the guard. While they were waiting, Baxter put his arms around Leon's shoulders, gave him a deep hug and said, "Wish I could have done better, son."

Leon looked stunned. No white man had ever hugged him before, not even when he was a child. "Thank you, sir. Wish I could hug you back."

MAY 12, 1962
XANDER

The year I graduated high school was the worst year of my life. Leon got executed the day before commencement, and it was all I could think about. I knew it was gonna happen sooner or later. After Mista Baxta lost his appeal last year, he couldn't get the supreme court to hear Leon's case. I know he tried hard; but the court had to give a lawyer permission to appeal, and they hadn't. Baxta had done all he could. It just wasn't enough. On the other hand, I hadn't done a damn thing and I was sorry as hell I'd listened to Mama or Miz Johnson back when it might have made a difference. I knew they were right – nobody was gonna believe me – but I knew I'd done wrong. I betrayed my best friend and his brother. And for that matter, all Negroes.

Gettin dressed in the new suit Mama scrimped and saved to buy for graduation, I knew I should be excited. I'd been lookin forward to no more lazy teachers who didn't give a crap about us; no more stupid, pointless assignments, no more algebra or geometry I was never gonna use. I'd even been celebratin because Miz Johnson had gotten me a little scholarship from her sorority, Alpha Kappa Alpha, to get me started in college. But that last day I realized I was gonna miss Miz Johnson's social studies class a bunch... and Miz Humphreys' talkin 'bout novels in English class. She really made me think. But none those things crossed my mind on graduation day; all I was thinkin about was Leon.

I was almost cryin walkin across that stage. Not because I was happy about graduatin, but because I knew I was a failure. A miserable failure. Miz Johnson saw me standin outside with Mama and Ladonna afterward and she came over. She hugged me before I could blink. "I'm so proud of you, Alexander," she said. "Livvie Betts, you should be very proud of your son. He's a fine boy and he'll go far."

Mama grinned, shifted her purse from her hand to her arm, and gave Miz Johnson a little hug. "Thank you, Mable. I *am* proud of him. He done real good in school and ya know, he worked whole time too?" She beamed.

"Thank you, Miz Johnson," I say, tryin to sound happy, but Miz Johnson read me like a book.

"You don't look very excited to be graduating, Alexander. What's the matter?"

"You remember Louie, my friend that dropped outta school? His brother Leon was executed yesterday."

Mama said, "Xander, you can't let that ruin

your special day. Ain't nothin you could have done would've changed it."

I glowered at her. "Yeah, Mama, they're was. Remember what I told you about that?" I knew people were lookin at me because my voice had gone up several notches, but I didn't care. "I told you somethin I knew but you told me to keep quiet. I nevah should have done that. Now Leon's dead and it's my fault." I stormed away, afraid I'd say somethin worse.

Mama stood there lookin like I slapped her but Miz Johnson followed me. "Xander. Xander. Stop," she called. I did.

She took my shoulders and turned me around toward her. "First of all, your mama didn't deserve being yelled at, today of all days. She's got a right to celebrate." I ducked my head, ashamed of how I acted. She put her finger under my chin, lifted up my head, and made me look at her. "I know you feel terrible about this. I remember our conversation about what happened quite well, but maybe you don't. Do you?"

"Yes, ma'am, I do. But now, I'm not so sure you and Mama was right."

"'Were' right, Xander. You don't say 'was right' if you want to be respected. Say 'were.' But I'm not talking about that part. I'm talking about what you can do to make up for it. You take that scholarship I got you, go to college, and become someone who matters, someone who can change things. It looks like things might be changing for the Negroes, for us. I believe you'll be part of making it happen, at least in your corner of the world. I know you know about Rosa Parks. If that little lady can make a difference, so can you. And if the Reverend Martin Luther King, Jr. has anything to do with it, change *will* happen. You know what I'm talking about. Pay close attention to him. You may not be able or want to do what he's doing, but in your way, you can be just as effective if you put your mind to it."

I nod, too stunned to answer her. She gave me a pat on the shoulder. "Now go back over there and apologize to your mother. And keep in touch with me. I'll be paying attention to you, Xander Betts. Take care." She smiled, patted me again, and walked over to another group of kids who had been in her class with me.

After she left, I stood there a minute, thinkin 'bout what she'd said. *She's right. Somehow, I gotta make up for what I didn't do for Leon.* I walked back over to my family, hugged Mama and told her I was sorry, then told Ladonna we were gonna celebrate. "Ice cream on me."

JULY 5, 1962
XANDER

The next bad thing happened the day after the Fourth of July. I biked to work just like I did the last three years, but a sign on the door said CLOSED. I figured Mista Feeney forgot to change it from being closed the day before, so I rattled the door trying to get somebody's attention. No answer. I looked in the front window but the lights were off and the store was plain smack empty. I rode around to the back. *Maybe Feeney's in his office. Maybe he'll hear the back doorbell.* I rang it a few times, but I never heard anything but its echo. *I bet he laid out drunk last night.* I heard Mista Feeney'd been drinking a lot since Miz Annie died, but he'd never not opened the store when he was supposed to. I mean, he came on in to work, even if he did stink of booze. After a couple more rings, I gave up.

I sat there on my bike a few more minutes, worrying. *If I leave and he comes in late, I'll get fired for not coming to work. But, I can't see sitting here all day, either.* So, I rode over to the café to tell Mama why I was heading back home. I didn't want to be in trouble with her, either.

The place was full of people. Every counter seat was full and most of the tables and booths. I caught Mama's eye through the open window into the kitchen and waved at her. She wrinkled up her brow like "What the hell you doing here?" I nodded and she held up her hand like, "Wait a minute." While I was standing at the end of the counter, waiting, I heard somebody say Feeney's name. I didn't want to look like I was eavesdropping, but I wanted to hear what they were saying, so I sorta leaned on the counter hoping to hear them without being noticed.

A woman in a denim dress said, "Poor woman. Bad enough he took to drink, but to kill himself, and her findin him like that makes it even worse." *What? Bill Feeney killed himself?* I couldn't believe my ears. Before I could hear what else they were saying, Mama was standing next to my elbow.

"What you doin here, son? Ain't you supposed to be at work?"

"That's exactly why I'm here, Mama," I said, as low as I could. I didn't want the two women to hear me.

"What'cha whisperin 'bout, Xander?" Mama looked pissed that I'd bothered her.

I put my finger to my lips, then said. "Went to work, but the store's all locked up. Tried the door; rattled it hard, rang the alley doorbell, but it was dark as pitch inside. Couldn't figure out why Feeney closed. But I jes heard that woman right there say he killed himself." I jerked my head to show Mama who I meant. "You suppose it's true?"

"I got no idea, Xander. I heard it too, but I ain't heard no details. If it's true, I reckon that means you ain't got a job. So, what are we gonna do without your pay?"

"God, Mama, is that all you can think about?" I hissed, still trying to keep the counter folks from hearing me. "Don't you worry. I'll get another job. But don't you get it? If he *did* kill himself, it's probably because *he* killed Miz Annie Sowards jes like I said. Now I think I caused his death, too."

I storm out, leaving Mama just standing there. I'm angry all over, but more at myself than Mama. Riding home, I nearly wreck, thinking about Mista Feeney and all. I almost run smack dab into a car when the light turns red. *What'd they mean, finding him like that? Did he leave a note? I told Mama I'd find another job, but that might not be easy as I made it sound. What if I can't? How am I gonna get enough money for college? Geez, what a mess.*

Didn't take long for the rumors to start up. Some folks in the projects say they heard from somebody who was cleaning white ladies' homes that Mista Feeney *did* leave a note. They say he admitted to killing Miz Annie. Of course, I've got no way of knowing if that's true, but it wouldn't surprise me any. It's a terrible thing to think, but if he'd killed himself sooner, maybe Leon would still be alive.

That night, Mama said she heard something about it down to the café. Said she was serving two women who said they knew the Feeneys. They were saying Miz Feeney found him in a bathtub full of water with his wrists cut. Said the water was pink on account of his blood. *Poor lady. What an awful thing.* She heard them say he left her a note apologizing for taking up with Miz Annie and ruining their lives. They never said Feeney wrote that he did the murder, but I can put two and two together.

After she told me, she said she was sorry about making me keep my mouth shut. "I reckon you was right. Now I sees why you was so mad the other day. All this time, you was thinkin you coulda kept Leon from the chair, right? Well, maybe so, but maybe not. You knows how it is for Negro kids."

"Yeah, Mama. I do. Look, I'm sorry for yelling at you, again."

"That's okay, son. I understand." Then she said almost the same thing Miz Johnson said on graduation day. "Xander," she said, "You go on get your education and make somethin of yourself. Might make a difference for other boys caught up like Leon. You hear me?"

"I hear you, Mama." And that's what I mean to do. But without a full-time summer job, I wasn't feeling so good as I been before.

The rest of summer dragged by like a funeral procession heading for the graveyard. Because I couldn't find a steady job, most days I mowed grass of a morning then piddled around in the sweaty afternoon. I never saw Louie. He'd cut me out of his life for sure. He'd found new friends; the kind that liked to play penny-ante poker and drink beer all day. Wasn't my style. I was afraid he was headed for trouble, but I didn't want to stick my nose in where I knew it wasn't wanted. I was sure he still hated me for not saying something. And, I wasn't gonna risk him spitting on me again.

AUGUST 13, 1962
XANDER

People say bad news and deaths come in threes. I never believed that crap until I picked up the paper one day in August. I don't know why I was reading the obituary page, but there, big as life, was Mista Baxta's picture. *Shit!* I folded the paper over and read the whole thing.

> **Local attorney Gerald Scott Baxter, II, 59, died Thursday, August 10, at his home**. *The unexpected death was the result of a massive heart attack, according to Martha Anderson Baxter, his wife of thirty-one years.* It talked about his education, his career, and who was still living in his family. Even mentioned Leon's case. They called it a "fool's errand" him trying to get the United States Supreme Court to hear a Negro's case. They *said* he was a good church-going man. Said he always stood up for justice for the little guy. According to the obituary, he was a real estate lawyer, not a criminal

defender. *Poor guy. If I was a betting person, I'd say Leon's trial and not being able to save him had something to do with that heart attack.*

I lower the paper and stare out the window. *Shit! That does it. If I'm gonna make a difference like Mama and Miz Johnson say, then I gotta get my ass in college. I might not believe in myself, but they do. Look at Mista Baxta. He did something he probably didn't feel qualified to do either, but he did it. I want to do that. Be a lawyer. Help kids like Leon. Like me. But I've got to get out of Blanchard's Bottom. Get my shit together. Maybe go to Atlanta – to Morehouse, or Georgia State. With that scholarship and what I've saved, I can pay for at least one semester. Morehouse must have some way to help students pay for tuition. After that, who knows.*

The paper hits the floor as I jump off the sofa, run to the door, and across the courtyard to the pay phone. I put in my dime and ask the operator get me Morehouse College. While I'm waiting, I pull out all my change and lay it on the shelf where the phone book used to hang.

"Hello," I say to the lady who answered. "I want to apply to Morehouse starting this September." She said, "You do, huh?" like she wasn't sure I'm serious.

"Yes, ma'am," I said. "I'm gonna be a lawyer."

OCTOBER 5, 1962

The first time Charlene Merrick heard Xander Betts question the professor in the Historical Implications of the Civil War class she was taking at Morehouse, she knew she wanted to get to know him. He seemed willing to challenge Professor DeSantis, to ask hard questions about "why" rather than just taking things he discussed at face value. One day, during a discussion about Reconstruction, Xander asked why, if so many Negroes had gotten elected to state legislatures in the South, they didn't make changes that could have improved the lives of their race. He argued that they should have done more. He wasn't confrontational, just eager to discuss the issue.

Charlene caught up to him in the hall after their class. She put her hand on his arm, stopping him in his tracks beside the bulletin board outside the social studies suite of offices. "Mr. Betts, have you got a minute?" she asked.

"I've got another class in a few minutes, but we can talk as we walk." He smiled, then started walking again.

"I'm Charlene Merrick," she said, putting out her hand. "Sometime, I'd like to further discuss what you and Professor DeSantis were talking about. If you have time, that is." When Xander took it, his touch warmed more than Charlene's hand.

"Sure. I've got a lot more questions about it too. But you've got to call me Xander or I won't talk to you." He laughed. "Maybe we could get a Coke later. There's a drugstore over on Wellborn. Want to meet there about four? Or I can just get us some Cokes and we can sit on the grass in front of Graves Hall. Might be easier to talk there."

"Yeah, probably so. See you then," Charlene said, waving goodbye as he rushed off.

While he was gone, she went back to her dorm room on Spelman's campus, grabbed her granny's patchwork quilt off the end of the bed, and went back to the lawn of Graves Hall. She chose a spot where she'd be visible from any direction and spread out the quilt. Then, she waited, her philosophy textbook open in her lap, enjoying the soft breeze that rustled the nearby magnolia tree. Although it was October, fall hadn't nipped the air or colored the trees yet. Remembering fall back home in Ohio, she longed for it, but knowing Georgia's weather, knew it was a long way off.

She spotted Xander before he saw her. She'd noticed Xander since school began but had just now gotten up the nerve to approach him. To her, he seemed confident, self-assured in his stride. Although he was tall enough to play basketball, she thought he looked like someone who spent more time with his nose in a book than with his hands around a ball. While lots of guys had started wearing their hair in an Afro, his was still shaved short, like a little boy's. She smiled as he came closer.

When he saw Charlene, he raised his arm in recognition. She could see the bright red Coke cans in his hands. His face was split into a broad but lopsided smile. "Hey," he said, settling on the quilt beside her. "Here's your Coke. I hope it's still cold."

She grinned at him as she opened the top and took a drink. "Hey, yourself. Thanks. It's good and cold."

"So, what did you want to talk about? You said you had questions about our class discussion," he said.

"I do. Why do you think those elected to public office didn't make changes? I know the professor said only sixteen Negroes were in Congress, but over six-hundred were in state legislative offices. Couldn't they have done more?" She took a sip of Coke and looked up at him.

"Well, sixteen men obviously can't make a difference, but the others? I think they were intimidated by those still willing and ready to refight the war. I think there just weren't enough of them in government for long enough. And the Klan got real active, too. Remember? My great-granddaddy was in the Georgia legislature back then and he got lynched." He sighed and raised his hand in greeting as a classmate walked past. "Sorry, that was my roommate," Xander said as he refocused on Charlene.

"No problem," she said. "I've never known anyone who had family lynched. I'm sorry. But I suppose you're right. Something sure did stop them. We don't have a Negro congressman to this day. And until we do, nothing is going to change." She took another drink of Coke and watched his face.

"Sounds as if you're becoming an activist." He looked concerned. "I've been listening to Dr. King, but do you think things will ever change, really? I've seen first-hand how things are rigged against us." He started ticking things off on his fingers. "I mean, they make it as hard as possible for us to register to vote, despite the law; we can't buy houses in decent neighborhoods; there are still segregated schools; and in most places we can't eat or go to movies like every white person in this country. Look what happened when those kids tried to sit in in Greensboro. They all got arrested. Do you really believe his way will work?"

"I think it's the *only* way it will work. It worked here. A couple of years ago, Dr. King joined the student sit-ins here and they changed the law. Now nearly every place serves us. Besides, violence will only create more violence. You watch; eventually, things will change everywhere," she said. "What do you think? Have you ever protested?"

"No, I haven't. I want to be an attorney so I can defend colored kids who get railroaded. I saw that back home. Actually, I think trying to work within the system is better than fighting against it."

Charlene scoffed but didn't argue with him. "Well, until we get full voting rights, that system is going to stay rigged against you and those boys you want to help."

"Maybe you're right. So, you go protest, and I'll do the studying." He grinned.

"Hey, I'm studying too. I'm not just in school to waste time or my parents' money." She frowned and swatted at his arm, as if offended by his remark. "Besides, I haven't actually joined a protest – yet, although our president is cool with it. I just wish I'd joined the Freedom Riders but…"

"I didn't mean to imply… I just can't see me getting involved. I've got to study, hard. Seems that's the way I can make a difference. It's not that I'm not interested or concerned. I just have to concentrate on one thing only. Besides, if I don't keep up my grades, I'll lose my scholarship. And Vietnam will be right around the corner."

"I hear you. So, where are you from, Mr. Xander Betts?" She grinned at him, trying to steer the conversation in a more personal direction.

"A little Georgia town I guarantee you've never heard of: Blanchard's Bottom. It's in the southwest part of the state, almost to Alabama. How about you?" He finished his Coke then crumpled the empty can as if it were made of tinfoil.

"Columbus, Ohio. My dad owns a barbershop there. As long as I can remember, Mama has cleaned office buildings. She said it was to save money for me to come here. It always made me feel bad, especially when she'd come home so tired at the end of the day." Her eyes looked off into the distance as if she could see her mother, exhausted, crumpled in her chair. "But I'm glad I'm here now," she said, smiling at him again.

"Yeah, me too. But, like I said... if it weren't for that scholarship. My dad died when I was little and my mom's a cook at a restaurant. I had to work all through high school to help out. Still, I managed to save a little bit to pay for books and things, but I have to be careful, so it will last. Things in Atlanta are a lot more expensive than in Blanchard's Bottom." Now, he looked away as if he might be ashamed to have admitted he didn't have the same advantages Charlene did.

"Don't get me wrong. I scrimp too. Coming from Columbus it may sound like I'm well off but there's Columbus and then there's colored Columbus. Know what I mean?"

"Absolutely!" His smile returned. "So, what are you studying?"

"I'd like to be a teacher. Seems to me that giving colored kids a good education is one of the most important things we can do for our future. Back home, after they integrated, the white teachers in the school I went to ignored us almost completely. None of the Negro teachers in my old school got hired there. Said their education wasn't good enough. We've got to become well educated so we can get hired in the inte-grated schools and pass a good education on to the next generation."

"That's some lofty goals there, girl. Good for you. I hope we both succeed. But I won't if I don't go do some studying." He started getting to his feet. "I've enjoyed talking to you. Maybe we can do it again sometime. Watch yourself joining those protests, Miss Charlene. Ya'll take care now," he said as he picked up his books and began to walk away.

"I'd like that. You take care, too, Mr. Betts." She grinned up at him, knowing she'd broken the rule he'd laid out. But he just laughed.

December 22, 1962
Xander

Long before Charlene grabbed my arm in the hall that day in October, I'd noticed her in class. I'd never seen an Afro on anyone in Blanchard's Bottom, but she had the beginnings of one. Back home, the girls either had their hair crimped, braided, or straightened. On her, the Afro seemed natural, as if that was the only way a Black girl should wear it. I couldn't take my eyes off of her. Every day, she wore several gold bracelets and the biggest hoop earrings I'd ever seen. But because her clothes made her look like she had more money than I did, I was afraid to approach her. So when she said she wanted to talk to me, I was thrilled.

I'll never forget that day we sat on the grass in front of Graves Hall. I can't recall what we talked about, but I sure remember her smile and her determination to make things better for us, for the Negroes. Before the first semester ended, I knew I wanted this gal in my life forever. I wasn't sure she felt the same way, but I'd had a few hints that she did. Not that she'd said as much, but she'd confided things in me that she said she'd never told anyone else: that her older brother had tried to molest her when they were young; that she had run away to live with her grand-mother until he was out of the house on his own; and that her father had nearly disowned her because she'd left and refused to tell him why.

I'd told her about Leon and how guilty I still felt about not doing anything to try to save him. She'd said the same thing my mother and Mrs. Johnson had said – that I needed to do something to make up for it and that she would support me in whatever that turned out to be. That was a big clue that she *did* care for me like I cared for her.

Charlene decided not to go home to Columbus for Christmas break, so I told Mama I couldn't afford the bus ticket back home, and I stayed too. Truthfully, we just didn't want to be apart. The weather had been beautiful the day we decided to go downtown to see Rich's giant Christmas tree. By the time we arrived, the sun had gone down, and it was getting chilly. For-tunately, I'd worn a jacket and Charlene had on a heavy cable-knit sweater. The huge tree was on top of the glassed-in walkway between the old store and the new addition. I watched Charlene as we turned the corner and she first saw it. Her eyes grew big as hubcaps and just as bright. She was like a little kid.

"Oh, my goodness," she said as she looked upward at all those lights. "I've never seen anything so grand. It's enormous."

"It is, isn't it? When I was little there was a big tree in the middle of the projects, but it only had lights on it. We always had a little one at home, too. Mama decorated it with the ornaments we made in school. You know – like paper chains, stars with glitter on them, things we made for our parents. Real corny looking, but we thought it was beautiful."

"We always had one too. Granny used to make popcorn strings to put on it. But Christmas wasn't the best time for me, until I went to Granny's that is. Bruce used to dress up like Santa and try to get me to sit on his lap. I knew it was just a way for him to try to feel me up and I hated it. Daddy always insisted, though. He didn't know any better." Her face had fallen from a big grin to a look so sad, I hugged her right there in front of everyone.

"Come on," I said. "Let's go see the decorations on Peachtree." I grabbed her hand and turned, running smack dab into a guy standing behind me. He had been holding a small boy by the hand but when we collided, his grip broke. The boy started crying and the man yelled, "Watch where you're going, boy. You nearly ran my ass down. And you made my boy cry."

"I'm so sorry, sir. I didn't see you. Honestly," I said leaning over to pat the boy on the head in an effort to console him as well. "I'm sorry, kiddo. I didn't see you."

Suddenly, the man grabbed my shoulder and pulled me upright, almost jerking me off my feet. "Take your nigger hands off my boy, you sonofabitch."

"Watch your mouth," I said, my face screwed up in an angry scowl. Then, I stepped back, remembering Dr. King. "I'm really sorry, sir. I was just trying to calm your son."

Charlene grabbed my hand. "Come on Xander. Let's go to Peachtree. We don't need this shit."

April 1963
Xander

Spring was here to stay and in fact, it felt almost like summer. The ancient magnolia in front of Graves Hall was in bloom and its heady scent filled the air. As I stood at the top of the steps and breathed in its perfume, it reminded me of the ones in Satterwhite Cemetery back home where Louie and I used to play. As I stood there, Charlene caught up.

"Hey baby, what brings you over here?" I said, leaning over to kiss her.

Without answering my question, she said, "Xander, let's go to Birmingham next week. A bunch of folks are gonna march and demonstrate for civil rights. They're gonna sit in at lunch counters and all kinds of other stuff." A wide smile dominated her face and her earrings seemed to shimmer with the excitement she radiated.

She'd wanted to do this for a long time. Although she'd wanted to be a Freedom Rider when she was in high school, she never went because her father was vehemently against that kind of protesting. It was more her thing than mine. I had my head in my books while she read every newspaper she could, following the civil rights movement every step of the way.

"Stuff's been going on there since the first of the year. You heard about the bombing last month, right?" I nodded. "Well, now the Southern Christian Leadership Conference has started a whole campaign. They want people to join marches, sit-ins, protests, a boycott, all sorts of stuff. Some of my classmates are going. You said you'd go with me if we ever had a chance. Dr. King's speaking, too. Now's the perfect time. It'll be spring break and we've got nowhere else to be, right?"

"Wow, I don't know. I've still got a lot to do over the break… my English lit term paper's due… but, if Dr. King's gonna be there, that would be awesome, wouldn't it?"

I had to admit, the idea did intrigue me. After just a semester I'd gotten a lot more knowledgeable about the civil rights struggles. So many of my class-mates had told stories similar to Leon's that I could see being involved, trying to change things, was our only option; I just wasn't quite ready to jump on the protest bandwagon yet.

"Come on, Xander. We'll only be gone one day. It's an easy drive. We'll get on the road early Wednes-day and can be home that night, won't even have to stay over." She tugged on my arm like a kid at the zoo wanting to go to see the monkeys.

I smiled back. How could I deny this gal anything she asked? I'd fallen in love with her almost on the first day we met. "Okay," I said. "I'll get my term paper finished this weekend and then we can go. You got gas?" I didn't have a car then, so we had to rely on hers.

Her smile became even broader when I said yes. "I'll fill it this weekend," she said. "Gotta run. Love you!" She gave me a quick peck on the cheek, then took off.

"Love you, too." I yelled at her back as she ran toward her next class, her maxi-dress billowing behind her and her Afro bouncing with each step.

By the time we arrived in Birmingham on Wednesday, April 10, boycotts, sit-ins, and demonstrations had been going on for a month, just like she'd said. Now even more Black students and adults had volunteered to join the protests. In front of the imposing Sixteenth Street Baptist Church where Dr. King was scheduled to give a speech later that week, Charlene found someone who seemed to be directing others and asked her what was planned for that day. The girl, who introduced herself as Millie, said groups were going to sit-in at various lunch counters around town. She then pointed to a group of about a dozen people standing down the block and suggested we go with them. We thanked her and rushed off, eager to take part. I was stunned by the size of the church. Back home, no church was even half that size, and none had that many steps. It looked as if they wanted you to think you were climbing the stairs to heaven.

"Hey," Charlene said to a girl wearing huge sun-glasses and a scarf on her head. "I'm Charlene and this is Xander. Can we join your sit-in?"

"Pleased to meet you. The more the merrier. I'm Ruby. We're headed to Lane's and then to Tutwiler's lunch counters. Some of us sat in last week and got arrested. We're gonna test them again."

I was stunned at how casually she spoke of being arrested. In my book, it would be a traumatic event. As we began walking, I noticed we were moving closer to the center of town and out of the Negro neighborhood. The area was unremarkable, though, except that fewer Negroes were on the streets. White ladies and their children were coming in and out of the brick-front stores, instead. When they saw us, they pulled their children closer as if we might soil them.

Charlene couldn't stop asking Ruby questions. How'd she get involved? Had she demonstrated in other cities? Was she arrested there, too? Had she been a Freedom Rider? Did she expect the police to be at the lunch counters this time? I just listened, amazed at how quickly she became a part of the group. I went along but I felt a bit like a cur in a pack of purebreds. When we arrived at Lane's, the place was dark, closed. A sign on the door said CLOSED UNTIL FURTHER NOTICE.

Ruby peered in the plate-glass window but couldn't see anyone moving about. She turned back to us and shrugged.

"Shoot," Charlene said to me. "Came all this way for nothing."

Then she turned to Ruby. "Now what?"

Ruby said, "Let's try Tutwiler's. It's only a few blocks over." The group started walking again. We passed a five and dime and I wondered if they had a lunch counter. I remembered that some boys had sat in at one in a Woolworth's in Greensboro a few months earlier.

Charlene grabbed my hand. "Come on; we'll try this one." I smiled and we followed the others. Tutwiler's had put up the same sign. Inside, only a dim night-light shone from the kitchen doorway.

"Well, shit," said Ruby. "There's a few more we can try, "You coming, Charlene, Xander?"

Charlene looked at me.

"Might as well," I said. "That's why we came." She reached up and kissed me.

Around the corner on Twentieth Street, we found another group with signs standing in the middle of the street, chanting and singing "We Shall Overcome." Hand-lettered signs read: WE DEMAND VOTING RIGHTS; END SEGREGATION, and ALL MEN ARE CREATED EQUAL. Charlene punched me on the arm and pointed to the last one. "Unh, unh unh, it should say all *people*, not all *men*. What about me? I'm equal, too."

I said, "You sure are, gal. You're more than equal," I said with a big smile. Here, a small band of white people were on the sidewalk yelling at the singers. Their Confederate flags outnumbered our protest signs. Screams of "Nigger go home," "Get back over the tracks," and George Wallace's favorite, "Segregation now, segregation tomorrow, segregation forever" overlapped the singing.

We blended in with the protestors and added our voices to the chorus. Charlene's pure soprano rang loud and clear while I kept my voice low; I knew I couldn't carry a tune if I'd put it in a bucket. Now, we far outnumbered the white crowd, but our added presence seemed to enrage them even more. One man came off the sidewalk and spat at a pair of sign carriers. True to Dr. King's teachings, they didn't return their vitriol; instead, they just sang louder.

It wasn't long before we heard police sirens approaching. We stopped singing for a moment then continued. Determined to stand our ground, we drew a bit closer together. Three patrol cars pulled up and cops poured from each side, billy clubs in hand.

"This demonstration is illegal," one cop yelled as he walked toward us. "Disperse now."

"Go home," screamed another, trying to be heard over the singing. Behind them the yelling from the sidewalk changed to, "Yeah, get them all. Arrest all them niggers." We didn't stop despite the closing approach of the police. Then, two of the cops grabbed the signs of the couple at the front of the group, wrestling them out of the protestors' hands, and stomping on the signs. "You don't have a permit for this demonstration. Put down those signs. If you don't stop and disperse, you'll be arrested," another yelled through a bullhorn.

Nothing changed. We sang. The sidewalk group screamed at us. Frustrated, the nearby cop who had grabbed the signs, yelled, "You're all under arrest."

Two guys broke from the crowd and started to run, but the cops caught them almost immediately. Another guy shoved the sign-snatching cop and yelled, "We've got a right to protest. It's our first amendment right, you asshole." Suddenly, all six cops charged into the crowd and began handcuffing people. Since we weren't chanting or carrying signs, I naively wasn't worried about Charlene or myself until I saw one cop go back to his patrol car and pick up his radio. At that moment, my gut said he was calling for help. Within minutes, a paddy-wagon pulled up and I knew we were all headed for jail.

As the cops began to herd us toward the vehicle's open doors, a scuffle erupted between two male protestors and a cop. When I heard one man cry out in pain, I turned. The cop had his billy club raised and was hitting him on the shoulder. "Get your ass in there," he yelled, grabbing the guy's wrist and twisting it behind him. Another cop shoved Charlene just as she was about to step on the first step, and she nearly fell. "Hey, that's not necessary," I yelled, reaching for Charlene's arm to steady her. "She's going."

Inside, we crowded together, sitting on each other because there were so many of us. Charlene and I ended up on the floor, huddled together. "I'm scared, Xander," she whispered.

"Me, too," I confessed, thoughts of Leon flitting through my memory. I remembered how the frightened look on his face at his trial had made me wonder if they'd beaten him. Now, I wondered if that was about to happen to us. "Don't worry, babe. We'll get outta this. We really didn't do anything but sing. We didn't have anything to do with organizing that march."

Charlene seemed to know I was only trying to make her feel better because she said, "Xander, I'm sorry I got you into this mess. I know you only came because I begged you to. I'm so, so sorry."

"It's okay, baby. I'm a big boy. I could have said no. We'll be fine."

"Oh, yeah? Then who we gonna call to get us outta here?" she asked. "My daddy'll probably tell me to get myself outta my own mess, because he don't hold with these protests. And I know your mama can't afford bail. Any bright ideas?"

"Not right off." I shook my head. "Lemme think about it." We went silent as the paddy wagon bounced along the streets.

At the station, the cops pulled us out and marched us into the brick building two at a time. Since we were on the floor, we were among the first inside. A surly-looking cop, wearing several ribbons on his broad chest, stood behind the desk and yelled, "Alright, stay quiet and don't approach the desk until you're brought up. I'll need to see your ID when you get here." Each time a new group crowded into the small lobby, he repeated himself.

At the desk, I started explaining. "I'm Alexander Betts and this is Charlene Merrick. We're both from Atlanta, from Morehouse and Spelman Colleges. We just drove down here today to join a sit-in, but we never did... we just..."

"Got ID?" he said, abruptly.

"Yes sir," I said, motioning to Charlene as I pulled out my wallet. She fumbled in her purse as I put my driver's license on the desk. He copied down the information, then turned toward her.

"You got ID?" he said.

"Yes, sir. Here." She put hers on the desk beside mine.

"Okay, you two. You're charged with protesting without a permit. It's a misdemeanor but until you can post bail, you're gonna spend a little time here courtesy of the Birmingham City Police." He smirked as if he was delighted with our predicament.

"Fulton, here's two more for you," he yelled at a short, squatty cop standing nearby. "Go with him," he said, motioning toward the man.

After a short walk down the hall, we were ushered roughly into a holding cell with about six others. I looked around for a bench or someplace to sit, but only the grimy floor was available. Several people sat around the edges of the cell, backs against the wall, knees pulled up in front of them, their heads resting on their kneecaps. The cell smelled faintly of Clorox but underneath their attempts to sanitize it, the unmistakable stench of urine and sweat still lingered. *No way am I letting Charlene sit down there. Nor me, either. Uck.* Each time the door opened, another few protestors joined our ranks. "They gotta let us make a phone call, don't they?" Charlene asked when she saw Ruby come through the door. "You've done this before, right? Aren't we guaranteed at least one call?"

"Yeah, they do. But you can bet your ass they'll take their sweet time about letting us. Last time, when we were sitting-in at Lane's, I didn't get to the phone until evening. You might as well get used to it, honey," Ruby said, patting Charlene's arm.

By the time our names were called to go make a phone call, we'd met nearly everyone in the cell and heard their stories of why they felt compelled to protest. Not all were students, not by a long shot. Some were married couples who wanted a better education for their kids, and several had been denied the right to register to vote. I kept my mouth shut, feeling insanely lucky to have no personal grievance to claim. Still, I felt their outrage, felt it more for Leon than for myself or Charlene. Since I'd met her our freshman year, I'd heard her life story and knew she had no personal experience to discuss, either. Her gripe was more principled, assimilated from what she'd read or heard the civil rights leaders, like King and Abernathy, preach about. While we'd both suffered the white man's version of 'separate but equal' with dual water fountains, movie entrances, and lack of places to eat, it had been what we'd grown up with, what we'd come to expect. She'd just become outraged faster than I had.

While we were waiting, Charlene said, "You think President Manley would bail us out? He's pretty attuned to protesting. I know he supported the civil rights manifesto our students wrote a few years ago and he's a big fan of Dr. King's."

"You got the president of Spelman's number? Wow! Call him. It's a long shot but we gotta call somebody. I don't want to accept Birmingham's hospitality any longer than we have to. Besides, what about our car? They could tow it, then we'd have another problem on our hands."

"I've only got his office number, so he probably won't get the message until morning. I think we're gonna have to sleep here." She looked so forlorn I took her in my arms.

"It's okay. We'll live. Just call him." I gave her a tight hug and she managed a weak smile.

The next morning, a guard yelled, "Charlene Merrick, you've got a phone call." He appeared at the cell door, a wad of keys in his hand. "Come with me," he said as the door swung open. She turned and looked at me.

"Go. I'll bet it's Dr. Manley," I said.

Ten minutes later she was back with the same guard who said, "Come with me Betts. You're free to go."

"Where's my friend, Charlene? I'm not leaving without her."

"She's already free. She's waiting for you in the lobby."

When Charlene saw me coming, she ran and threw her arms around my neck. "The president's office wired the money right after they got the message. Someone from there called to say that. We can go," she said, the relief showing in her voice. We may have to come back for court, but they don't think so. Ready to get outta here?"

"Let's go," I said, grabbing her hand and rushing

toward the door. "That's it for protesting for me. I can say I've done it but I've seen the last of jail cells, haven't you?"

"We'll see," she said. "We'll see."

MAY 2, 1963
XANDER

I heard someone yelling, "Hey, Xander. Phone's for you. Xander. Hey, Xander, you got a phone call." I was in my room studying for a poly-sci test and didn't hear him the first two times he yelled.

"Keep your shirt on. I'm coming," I yelled back.

I took the receiver from a guy I didn't know and said, "Thanks." Before I could say hello, Charlene said, "Xander, my God, you've gotta come to the Morehead student center. It's Birmingham. It's all over the news. You've got to see what those damn cops are doing."

"I'm studying, babe... can I..."

She interrupted, "No, you've got to come. Now! It's terrible. Please."

She sounded as if she were crying, so I said, "Ok, I'll be right there."

I ran across campus and into the student center. Kids were packed around the only television set in the building. They were staring at the screen with expressions that looked like their mamas had died. I found Charlene and went to her.

"Hey baby, what are you doing over here? What's going on?" I said, as I squatted on the floor beside her.

"Just watch," she said almost mechanically. She was so mesmerized by what she was seeing that she didn't even look at me.

I turned to face the small screen just as two huge German Shepherds lunged at a boy marching peacefully along the street. The policeman at the other end of the dog's leash didn't restrain him; he let that snarling dog grab the boy's arm, ripping away a piece of his shirt. Beside them, two more dogs jumped and lunged, growling at another pair of Negro boys. Kids, teenagers, and younger were scattering all across the streets trying to avoid the same fate. I looked over at Charlene who had tears in her eyes.

The reporter was saying that the marchers were children who had joined the Birmingham protest to end segregation there. He said, the police chief, "Bull" Connor, had seen so many children flooding the streets of downtown in protest the day before that he decided to "restore" law and order. His method was to call out the dogs. Charlene turned to me, her face twisted in pain. "Xander, those are just young kids. That man is evil. How could he do that?"

All around us other students looked as stunned as she did. One yelled, "Fucking cops." Another slammed his fist into the back of a metal chair, sending it flying. His friend grabbed his arm, saying, "Hey, you're gonna get us thrown out. Settle down."

"Hell, he doesn't think of us as human beings," Xander said. "If he did, he couldn't. It's like sending dogs to catch slaves."

"He doesn't; you're right," the chair hitter said.

I couldn't tell where this was happening. The reporter said the children had started at the Sixteenth Street Baptist Church right where we'd been, but I didn't see any of the shops we'd passed the previous month. One or two of the stores had bars across the entrances like they hadn't opened yet, or had closed because they knew what was coming. I saw signs for Irene's Beauty Shop and the Twentieth Street Barber Shop, so it must have been nearby because Tutwiler's was on Twentieth, too.

As we watched, the cameras pivoted to show firemen on the other side of the street with hoses trained on more groups of young people peacefully walking down the street in pairs, some carrying signs. When the water hit them, the force threw their bodies against buildings and knocked them off their feet. "Oh my God, what the hell? They're not doing a damn thing. Look, that kid's pants are hanging in shreds," I said, jumping to my feet. "Damn those sonsabitches. Look, they're still spraying them… they're down on the sidewalk. That one guy's bare back is showing through the hole in his shirt." I wanted to turn away, but I couldn't. We watched as wave after wave of children were grabbed by the police, attacked by those horrible dogs, and knocked down by the force of the firemen's hoses.

More students had surrounded us and were yelling, cussing at the television. I saw several girls sobbing into the shoulders of their boyfriends. Finally, I looked over at Charlene expecting tears, but her face had contorted into a hardened frown. "Dammit, Xander, some of them are just little kids. What the hell are they doing there? They're letting the police dogs attack children."

Too stunned by what I was watching, I didn't have an answer. I was as outraged as Charlene, but what struck me the hardest was the courage these children were showing. I'd been a reluctant protestor, only going with Charlene because she begged me to. And I'd sworn not to do it again. But here were hundreds of kids, some looked like elementary age, marching and being attacked. And probably facing arrest. I was ashamed.

I had a chance to do what was right once but I was a chicken shit. These kids are braver than me. Right then, I made up my mind.

"Charlene, next time we have a chance, we're gonna march," I said, my voice cracking.

September 5, 1963
Xander

Dear Mrs. Johnson,
So here I am beginning my second year at Morehouse. I still can't believe it. If it hadn't been for you, I wouldn't be here. This summer I had a mail clerk's job at the law firm of Alston, Miller & Gaines, thanks to one of my professors. I was able to save enough, along with my work-study job during school, to afford this semester. We'll have to see about the next one, though.

If you saw me now, you might not recognize me. I've let my hair grow out into an Afro. You probably wouldn't approve of that, would you? It's what the guys are all wearing, though, and Charlene likes it. That's good enough for me.

Believe me, that first year was quite an education. Not so much what I learned in class, although that was a lot; but what I learned from Charlene. She's a girl at Spelman I met when

I first got here. Her name is Charlene Merrick and she's the kind of civil rights activist you'd approve of. Here in Atlanta things are pretty open, but I know they aren't in other places. Charlene had wanted to join the Freedom Riders a few years ago but I'm glad she didn't. Some of those folks were beaten pretty badly.

We both were devastated by the church bombing last week in Birmingham. Those poor innocent little girls. Charlene wants to go protest there but since classes have started, we probably can't. We went to one protest there in April and were arrested. It scared me to death, but it didn't seem to bother her until we were actually in the holding cell. In a way, though, I think she was sort of glad. Made her feel like we'd made a difference.

It made me determined to never protest again, but after they sprayed those kids with fire hoses and turned the dogs on them, I felt terrible. They were no older than I was when Leon was on trial, but they had the courage to confront the police. And look what it changed. Back then, I didn't even stand up for my best friend's brother. Made me realize, again, what a coward I'd been. And it made me re-think my stand against demonstrating.

We just got back from Washington, D.C. where we were in that huge crowd listening to Dr. King at his March on Washington. I've never seen so many people! They say it was a quarter of a million! They stretched from the Washington Monument all the way to the Lincoln Memorial where the stage was. Not just Negroes either; I saw a lot of white folks. People also surrounded the Lincoln Memorial – standing on the plaza, sitting around the outside pillars, everywhere. There were old people, people our age, and kids, lots of them carrying signs and chanting. Some people had their feet in the reflecting pool. The atmosphere in that crowd was electric.

We heard Joan Baez and Bob Dylan, although we couldn't see them, we were so far back in the throng. Mahalia Jackson sang two hymns, but I didn't know either one of them. Still, the crowd was so quiet you could have heard the splash if someone had kicked the pool's water. After the hymns she sang "Stand By Me," which brought cheers from the crowd. Just hearing her and watching the crowd sway to her music was so inspiring.

There were lots of other speakers before Dr. King took the stage. Charlene was getting hot and tired of standing but she refused to leave before he spoke. And, wow, am I glad we stayed. His speech gave me goosebumps and made Charlene cry. He made all of us feel like we could take over the world, so we'd have our freedom at last. You know me; I never liked confrontation. But listening to Dr. King made me realize even more that if I don't do something, it will be just like when I was too scared to stand up for Leon. I still don't know when that will happen, but now I'm committed to doing my part.

I hope everything is good in Blanchard's Bottom and that you are well. I'll write again when I can.

Sincerely,

Xander

Summer 1964
Xander

In mid-May, during finals week, a couple of organizers from the Student Nonviolent Coordinating Committee came to Morehead to recruit volunteers. I'd read about them in the *Atlanta Daily World*, the Black newspaper distributed on campus. I went looking for their table in the student center.

The center room was full. At some tables, guys had their heads bowed over their books. Others were gathered around the television set watching the Atlanta Braves. Apparently their finals were over. As I passed, a cheer went up from that group.

"Hey," I said, as I approached a table with a large SNCC banner behind it. "Tell me about SNCC," I said, pointing to their logo. "I heard you got some stuff going on this summer."

"Hi there," said the mustachioed young man behind the table. Beside him sat a girl wearing cornrows and a mile-wide smile. "What's your name? You a student here at Morehouse?"

"Yeah, I'm Xander Betts. I'm a junior here… well, I will be in the fall. Just finished my sophomore year, finals and all… almost finished, that is. Grades aren't in yet." I laughed although I was pretty sure I'd done well in all my classes. "And you are?"

"I'm Dexter, Dexter Britton, and this is Zalia Bowles. Are you familiar with SNCC?"

I reached across the table and shook both their hands. "Sorta. I've read about it, what you're trying to do, uh, you know, registering people to vote. You doing that here? In Atlanta? I could help, you know, if it's here."

"Unfortunately, we're not. We're focusing on Mississippi this summer. Our leaders say it's the most segregated state in the union. Only five percent of eligible Black voters are registered there. We're fixing to change that," Dexter said. "We're recruiting all over the country, north, south, all over. We for sure could use you."

"If you don't have summer plans, we'd love to have you," Zalia said. "Folks are opening up their homes to the volunteers so it wouldn't cost you much. Just gas, really," the girl smiled like she was inviting me to a party. "Why don't you join us?"

"Well, I'd like to help, but I have a summer job. I'd have to see if I could get some time off. And, I'd, uh, want to talk to my girlfriend… see if she'd go. You gonna be here a while?"

"Be here the rest of the week. Here, take this," Dexter said, handing me a mimeographed one-page flyer. "It'll tell you all about our plans. Come on back after you talk to your gal. We'll sign you both up."

I thanked them and walked away reading the sheet as I went. Another cheer echoed behind me as I left the room. The flyer explained how they were organizing voter registration events in various Mississippi cities and gave the dates for each city. Folks would also be passing out leaflets in the Black neighborhoods urging people to come register. It sounded like something that needed to be done and I was ready to go. I rushed across the Spelman campus to Charlene's dorm to see if she'd go, too.

Guys weren't allowed upstairs in the dorms, so I called her from the parlor. "Hey, Char. I'm downstairs. Can you come down? Got something to tell you."

"Sure, babe. Be there in a minute," she said.

I sat on the long floral print sofa under the windows and waited. Two girls walked through with what looked like a plate of cookies and cartons of milk. "Looking for someone?" one of the girls said.

"No, my girl knows I'm here. I'm just waiting until she comes down."

"Groovy," one said as they disappeared into a back room.

Charlene yelled as she came down the stairs, "Hey, Xander. What's up?" Her smile brought a matching one to my face. As she reached me, I looked around to be sure those girls hadn't returned. When I saw we were alone, I grabbed her by the shoulders, pulled her toward me, and kissed her.

"Hey, I'll get in trouble if anyone sees us," she

said, pulling back.

"Relax, I checked," I said, leaning over to kiss her again. This time, she kissed me back.

"So, what's up," she said as we walked to the couch. "What's so exciting?"

I pulled the flyer from my hip pocket and showed it to her. "I want to volunteer, and I thought you would, too." As she read, I continued. "If I can get some time off... or maybe we could go before my job starts. It sounds important and not as dangerous as protesting. What do you think?"

She looked up at me. "Not dangerous? Are you kidding? Remember what happened to Medgar Evers last year? Those segregationists aren't gonna just stand by and watch us march in there and get people registered. Why you think so few are registered now?"

I laughed at her. "Seriously? Look who's reluctant to protest now. Before, it was me. And now I'm ready to do my part, you acting all scared."

"Hell, no, I'm not scared. I just know it could get bad. Didn't say I wouldn't go. Just want you to be ready for what we might get into. Staying in folks' homes. That might be fun. Meet some others who think like we do."

"I'll check with the guys at work to see when I have to be there. If I can wait until the middle of June, we could go." She grinned and gave me a big hug. "Since you're here, let's go get something to eat. How about The Varsity?"

"Mmmmmm, love their chili dogs and onion rings. Let's go," she said, jumping up and grabbing my hand to pull me up.

Two weeks later, we drove to Cleveland, Mississippi, where SNCC had planned a voter registration in front of the courthouse. First, we went to a training session at Amzie Moore's gas station on Highway 61. It was an innocuous brick building that also housed a restaurant and a beauty shop, Mr. Moore's establishment had become the headquarters for the voter registration project. There, among a stack of rolled up sleeping bags, Robert Moses, the organizer of the Mississippi Project, explained what we were to do and what might happen. "You may face intimidation, jeers, spitting, things thrown at you. Whatever you do, remember this is a non-violent action. We don't want you hurt and we don't want to start a riot. Just pass out the leaflets, if that's your job, or do the registrations, but do not engage with anyone who tries to rile you up. Understand?"

The group answered, "Yeah!" I looked around at those sitting behind us on rickety metal chairs and was surprised to see more whites than Blacks. That surprised me. Most looked our age and were probably college students. I spotted a few familiar faces from Morehouse, but the rest were strangers. Charlene recognized two girls from her dorm but said she didn't know their names. Many of the white girls were well dressed in crisp sundresses as if they were heading to a sorority picnic. Some of the guys even wore ties. "Where do you suppose they came from?" I whispered to Charlene. She shrugged her shoulders.

"Dunno. But I aim to find out."

Following his talk, Moses held a practice session where one group of volunteers screamed at the other to see how we would react. I tried to hold my temper, but after being called "dirty niggers" by the white boys, several of us reacted, screaming back at them, ready to fight. Moses laughed because he knew that's probably what would happen, but he told us we couldn't ever do that unless we wanted a riot.

Once everyone calmed down, Moses gave each of us a small bundle of leaflets to pass out urging folks to come the next day to register. He said, "You also may encounter resistance going door to door, especially those of you who are white. Remember, white folks being in the Negro neighborhoods poses a threat to those families as well as to yourselves." I looked at Charlene, remembering what she'd said about this being dangerous work. She smiled, as if she could read my mind.

Finally, one of the organizers gave us a card on which was written the name of the family we'd be staying with, and directions to their home. Fortunately, she told us, the Williams family had two rooms, so we both could stay in the same place. What she didn't say was that they lived in the poorest section of town. We drove the mile there passing from newly paved streets to those with so many potholes we couldn't avoid them. Charlene said, "Think how generous it is that this family is willing to share their home with us, even though they must not have much. I mean, look at this neighborhood. Obviously, the city ignores the broken sidewalks, the potholes in the streets. Can't be bothered with Negro folks' problems, I guess. Unh, unh unh." She shook her head in disgust.

Despite the obvious poverty, Ervin and Eula Williams' home was the best one on the block. The couple, who looked to be in their seventies, hugged us both tightly in greeting. "We're so glad you've come," said Mr. Williams. "Let me help you with your bag."

"No, sir. I've got it," I said, surveying the neat-as-a-pin living room. The overstuffed gold tweed sofa and matching chairs had seen better days, but were clean looking and free of worn spots, unlike the one we'd had at Booker T. Feeling good about our accommodations, I turned to Charlene and smiled.

"Let me show you to your rooms," Mrs. Williams said, walking down the hall. "Then, we'll have us some supper. I'll bet you're hungry."

Charlene and I looked at each other, then nodded in unison. "Yes, ma'am. That would be wonderful. Been a spell since we've had a homecooked meal. You know, cafeteria food isn't the greatest," Charlene said, then laughed.

Over a Formica table laden with a chipped platter of country-fried steak and mismatched bowls of green beans, mashed potatoes, wilted lettuce salad, and biscuits as big as my fist, we chatted about the movement. "What you kids are doing is so important. We've never been able to vote, and Eula here wants to before she dies," said Mr. Williams, his face registering hope.

I handed him one of the leaflets. "You'll come

register, then?" I said, hoping to secure our first success.

He studied it briefly, then said, "Well, don't know about this time, but, like I said, Eula sure wants to vote just once before she go up. If there's no trouble tomorrow, maybe we'll do it next time." He smiled broadly, showing a missing eye tooth.

"Well, we hope we don't let you down," Charlene said as Mrs. Williams stood.

"All you can do is do your best," she said, patting Charlene on the shoulder. "Now who'd like some apple cobbler?"

The next morning, we rose early to the smell of coffee and frying sausage. Although we'd loved to have lingered over breakfast to visit further with the kindly couple, we ate hastily, said our thanks and goodbyes, and walked around the neighborhood passing out leaflets with Mr. Moses' words in our heads. Sadly, most of those we spoke to echoed the comment of Mr. Williams. "Don't know about that," one man said. "Tried before and got beat for my troubles. What makes you think it'll be different now?"

As I smiled at the little one peeking around his legs, I tried to explain, told him if we didn't keep trying, we'd never have the vote, and neither would his boy. He kept the leaflet, but I knew we wouldn't see him at the registration site.

Returning to the Williams' house, we picked up our car and drove to SNCC headquarters. From Mr. Moore's we drove to the Bolivar County courthouse, where SNCC had set up tables on the front lawn for us to register voters. It was an imposing buff-colored building with tall columns fronting the center section, though not as imposing as the Sixteenth Street Baptist Church had been. Nearby, we saw signs announcing the registration drive, however, several had been defaced with a big, red, sloppily-painted X that obliterated most of the words. One or two signs lay beside the road.

Behind the table, on the courthouse steps, six troopers stood, nightsticks in their hands, which were crossed in front of them. Clearly, potential registrants weren't getting past them. My stomach clinched at the matching scowls on their faces. I remembered what Charlene had said about trouble. Across the street from the registration site, a small crowd was beginning to gather, as well. White men in khaki pants and white helmets stared menacingly at us. The gleaming helmets made them look like they were expecting trouble, but I didn't see any weapons in their hands, so that made me feel a little better. Charlene smiled, saying, "You okay? They ain't scaring me."

"Yeah, I'm okay," I said, smiling back.

The first person to register didn't appear until eleven. A man, about forty, walked up with a young boy about eight or nine. "Come to register. Want my boy here to see me do it," he said, his hand on the boy's plaid-shirted shoulder. Before I could respond, yelling began from across the street. "Take your nigger ass back home, boy. You ain't got the vote. Ain't never gonna get it." Then they began to chant. "No vote for no niggers. No vote for no niggers."

I watched his face, waiting for the fear to set in. It didn't. He didn't even flinch. It was if the taunts steeled his resolve. "I said I'd like to register to vote. Can you help me?" I stammered, "Uh, I… uh, absolutely. Sorry, sir. I just got distracted."

"Son, I been listening to that shit all my life. You can't let it get to you."

"I know. I'm sorry. Here, fill out these papers and we'll get you registered."

He did as we asked, writing in letters that looked bold and proud. "That all?" He asked.

"Yes, sir. Congratulations. We'll register this at the courthouse, and they'll mail your registration card to you," I said, reaching to shake his hand.

He clapped the boy on the back. "See, son, you can do that yourself someday." The boy smiled up at his father proudly.

After he left, we were alone until two of the men in khaki crossed the street and came toward us. I felt Charlene stiffen. "Uh oh," she said.

"Who you think you are, comin' down here messing in our affairs? Registering niggers to vote. We don't want your kind here. Got enough trouble with our own niggers. Don't need no more of you," the shorter of the two yelled as they came closer. I didn't say a word, just stood there.

"I'm talking to you, *boy*," he yelled emphasizing 'boy.'

"We have every right to help these folks register to vote," I said as calmly as I could. "I'm registered and believe others should be allowed to be as well."

At that, the taller of the two spat a huge spray of spit in my face. "You got no rights here," he screamed before his buddy could pull him back. "Enough, Ernie," he said. "Enough."

The two returned to the other side of the street to the others who were clapping and cheering at their behavior. I slowly wiped my face, remembering the last time I'd been spit at. Then, it had been my best friend who was furious at me for being a coward. I remembered how guilty I felt after that. I'd let my best friend down. This time it was a complete stranger, furious because I'd been brave. I liked the second reason much better. Maybe it helped make up for what I didn't do back then.

March 5-7, 1965
Xander

"Did you read about SNCC's plan to march from Selma, Alabama to Montgomery for voting rights?" Charlene had asked me Friday evening while we were eating dinner at a seafood place near campus. The restaurant was one of those that both sold raw seafood and served it for dining there. You could smell the fried fish before you stepped inside. The tables had holes in them so you could dispose of shrimp tails and oyster shells.

I hadn't read about the march, so she gave me the details. "They claim the Civil Rights Act didn't do enough. It didn't even mention the right to vote. Just made restaurants and other businesses integrate. King wasn't in favor of the march at first, but SNCC got him to support it. They're gonna start on Sunday and march all the way to the capitol."

"I knew they weren't satisfied, but why Selma?" I asked.

"Several reasons, apparently. SNCC had been

trying to get folks registered there for almost a year... you know, like they did in Mississippi? And then when the cops killed Jimmie Lee Jackson last month, that really infuriated them. But, in the county... I forget its name... that Selma's in... less than two percent of the Black voters are registered. They only open the damn registrar's office two days a month but won't say when that is. A group of guys recently went to register and were met on the steps by troopers. They beat them back with their nightsticks. So, I guess SNCC chose to make a point there," she said with one raised eyebrow as if she'd asked a question. I knew that expression well.

"So, let me guess. You want us to go."

"Well, yeah. We could go tomorrow. The march isn't until Sunday. Or we could go really early that morning. Obviously, we can't do the whole thing. I think it's over fifty miles to Montgomery so it will take a few days. But we could march a while and then come home." Now she looked like a little girl begging to stay out past her bedtime.

Char was still the one who followed every story of the Civil Rights Movement. She read the Negro newspaper and the *Journal Constitution* whenever she could find them on her campus. I was still studying hard so I relied on her to tell me what was going on. But, after the children's march I *had* become much more invested in doing my part, so I didn't hesitate. "Okay," I said with a grin. "Talked me right into it." She reached across the table and kissed me on the cheek.

She sat down and grinned back at me. "Sunday morning at six? Can you be ready that early? I don't know what time it starts so we need to get there early."

"If I go to bed right now. Just kidding. Yeah, I'll be ready."

I was waiting out in front of my dorm when Charlene pulled up on Sunday morning. It was unusually cold, so I was glad to see she'd worn a coat over her heavy green sweater. "Hey, babe," I said as I leaned over to kiss her. "You excited?"

"Like Christmas morning," she said and kissed me back. "Let's go."

Three hours later we found ourselves on the outskirts of Selma. We pulled into the first gas station we saw, and I went in to ask for directions to Brown Chapel AME Church. As soon as I saw the white guy behind the counter, I knew I'd made a big mistake. The scowl on his face was intimidating, but I went in anyway. "Morning, sir, I wonder, could you give me directions to the Brown Chapel AME Church?" I asked.

"Never heard of it," he replied almost before I could finish asking.

"It's a Negro church near the middle of town, from what I hear," I said, trying to be helpful.

"I got no reason to know about no nigger church, boy. You just get on outta here and ask one of your own kind." He turned his back on me and began fiddling with the cigarette display behind him.

"Thank you, sir," I said, as politely as possible

although I was seething inside.

Back in the car I told Charlene we were on our own. "Let's just head on into town. Maybe we'll get lucky. We've got some time. Surely they won't start this early."

Without asking what had happened, she sighed knowingly and put the car in gear. There was almost no traffic, so we crept along looking for the church. As we drove, it was clear that we'd entered the Negro section of town. Back where the gas station had been, the streets were well paved, the sidewalks pristine, but as we went, both slowly deteriorated. Potholes threatened our tires. Sidewalks suddenly disappeared. But the lawns, tiny as they were, were neatly mowed. The white clapboard houses, however, had sagging eaves, chipped paint, and broken porch railings. Still, the towering trees gave the area the feel of a solid neighborhood. The houses didn't look abandoned; just that the owners couldn't afford to keep them up. I'd seen this happen in the neighborhoods near the projects in Blanchard's Bottom.

Charlene said, "I think we're in the right part of town. This looks the way my neighborhood in Columbus does now. Keep looking for the church. It's on Sylvan Street."

As we crept along, we drew closer to the business district. Shop signs for a bicycle shop and a barber hung in the distance. We passed a brick housing development where I noticed the George Washington Carver Homes sign. "This reminds me of the projects I lived in back home," I said.

"Whoa, I think we just passed the church," shouted Charlene. "I'll go around the block. I missed the sign but there's a bunch of people milling around in front of that church next to the projects. That must be it."

We turned left on St. John's Street, then left again on the next street. It didn't go where Charlene thought it would. Instead, it led away from where she had seen a church. After a few minutes, we made our way back, found a place to park, and joined the crowd huddled in their overcoats on the sidewalk.

Char approached a woman near the steps who was leaning on a sign she rested on the sidewalk. "Hi, what's your sign say?" Charlene asked, cocking her head to try to read it. The woman held it up and read, "We Want to Vote!" Then she said, "You from around here?"

"No, we just drove here from Atlanta. You?"

"Oh, yeah. We sick of the way they treats us down here. I tried to register, me and my husband, but they never open or they closes up early, or troopers tell us we can't go inside. A friend of mine, they told him he got to explain part of the constitution before he can register. You think that right? Hell, no. Ain't no white man have to do that." She pulled the scarf on her head tighter around her chin.

"I hear you," Charlene said. "You right. It's wrong. Just plain wrong. That's why we came."

"They say Dr. King and them others inside. Say he gonna speak before we march. I ain't never heard him, so I'm waiting right here until I does." She blew on her ungloved hands.

"Any idea when he'll speak?" I asked.

"Nah, just say before we go."

I turned to Charlene. "Let's go inside for a while and warm up." She nodded, told the woman she'd enjoyed talking to her, and we went up the steps. Inside, there must have been a hundred people scattered across the pews. We took a seat near the back and watched men milling back and forth on the dais.

"Look, Xander. There's John Lewis. And I think the man on the far left is Abernathy, but I'm not sure. I don't see Dr. King, though. Do you?" Char said taking off her gloves.

I scrutinized the faces but didn't see King. "No, I don't. Maybe he's in the back somewhere." We sat there in silence for a while, letting the fact that we were actually here sink in. With the warmth of the sanctuary, Char began to nod, so I gently pulled her head onto my shoulder, and she slept. My mind drifted back to Blanchard's Bottom as I thought about what Mama would think of where I was. I knew without a doubt. She'd be saying, "Keep your mouth shut," just like she did back then. She never wanted me or Ladonna to cross the white man. But this time, I had no intention of listening to that voice. It was time to do some serious confronting. I hadn't done it back then, hadn't had the guts to approach Leon's lawyer when I could have and regretted it; now I was determined to do the right thing.

About eleven, the men on the dais began to assemble into a line with Lewis at the pulpit. I shook

Charlene. "What's happening?" she said, her voice full of sleep. "I must have dozed off."

I laughed. "You sure did… for about an hour. What time did you get up?"

"About four. I made us some sandwiches. Want one?"

I realized I was hungry, so I nodded. "That would be great." As she handed me a bologna and mustard sandwich from her bag and unwrapped one for herself, I thought, *Mama would wear me out for eating in the sanctuary.* I looked around and saw others doing the same, so I went ahead and took a bite. *Must be making an exception for today.*

"I think Lewis is fixing to speak," Charlene said motioning toward the front.

"Folks, if I could have your attention… ladies and gentlemen… quiet please," Lewis said. "We're going to assemble out front, then have a short prayer by Brother Hosea Williams before we begin our march. Remember, this is a peaceful protest. If you are jeered at, spit on, or have things thrown at you, do not respond. Our way is to show the world we can demand our rights, peacefully." He continued talking for a few minutes, telling us exactly what route we would take, but I had begun to worry at his comments about being confronted. I looked at Charlene, but she seemed calm and strong in the face of possible trouble.

"We okay with this?" I asked her.

"I am if you are," she responded with a smile while stuffing the sandwich wrappers back in her bag.

"I'm not real okay but I'm determined. Let's go," I said, more strongly than I felt.

We followed the others outside and stood quietly while Williams prayed a lot longer than Lewis had promised. After the crowd's 'Amen,' I asked the man next to me, "What happened to Dr. King? I thought he was coming."

"Naw, I heard he wasn't in favor of this here march. It's a SNCC thing. I heard he ain't too happy with them." He shrugged as if it didn't matter. I thanked him and turned to tell Charlene what he'd said. She shrugged, too. "Oh well, we're here now."

As we started down tree-lined Sylvan Street folks locked arms, walking two by two, so we did the same. Up ahead, I could see signs above our heads, but the crowd was as silent as if they were in church. Neither of us said a word, either.

Three blocks later we turned right onto Alabama Avenue. At the end of the first block, I pointed to a Coca Cola sign that proclaimed, "Selma: Progressive & Friendly." I turned to Charlene. "I hope that's right."

She laughed. "Doubt it," she said. "Or else we wouldn't have to do this."

Folks along the sidewalks stared at us but said nothing. I took that as a good sign and relaxed a bit. Three blocks later we turned again onto Broad Street where we passed a drug store and loan office. There, in front of us was the Edmund Pettus Bridge, its tall metal arches gleaming in the sun. The marchers at the front were already making their way up the incline. We were about halfway back, so we couldn't see across to the other side. But when we crested the top, there they were. A massive phalanx of troopers blocking the way, helmeted, with gas canisters hooked to their belts, and nightsticks drawn. Behind them, I saw troopers mounted on horseback. In front of a mattress store a large group of white folks stood jeering at the marchers. Confederate flags waved in the air. Suddenly, my stomach clenched as if I'd been sucker-punched. I looked over at Char. Her mouth hung open in shock. *This is worse than being arrested.* I took a deep breath.

Still, the leaders kept on going. About half a block off the end of the bridge they stopped. We could hear the trooper's bullhorn. "This is an unlawful assembly. You have two minutes to disperse. Go home or go to your church. This march will not continue." My jaw clenched and I pulled Charlene tight to my side. I wanted to ask her if she wanted to turn back but the resolve in her face stopped me. Hosea Williams said something, then the lead trooper yelled, "I got no more to say to you." Suddenly, I saw the troopers put on their gas masks. Now, I was really scared but we stood our ground.

"Troopers, advance," yelled the leader.

A shot rang out and the massive line of troopers stormed the marchers, swinging nightsticks and shoving them to the ground. I felt stuck to the sidewalk, but Char grabbed my hand and pulled. "Oh, my God, Xander! Run, run," she yelled. Before we could move, I saw people shoved to the street, laying on the sidewalk, heads bloodied. Screams filled the air as people ran toward us, bumping into us.

We turned and ran hand in hand. People behind us kept shoving, running us over, trying to get past. All around us people fell. We jumped over them and kept going. As we ran, I could hear the cheers from the white folks we'd seen at the foot of the bridge. Suddenly, mounted troopers swooped past with whips lashing at all of us as we ran. A man nearby screamed as the whip hit him on the legs and he fell. I stopped to pick him up and nearly got knocked down myself.

Charlene yelled, "Come on."

I got the man to his feet then continued to run just as another trooper rode by, whip swinging. He lashed at us but missed. Charlene screamed and took in a huge swallow of the tear gas that filled the air because she began coughing, pulling on my hand as if she needed to stop to catch her breath.

"Char," I yelled. "Come on." I could hardly see. The white, burning mist covered everything.

"I can't see. Can't breathe," she yelled back between coughs. "You go on. I gotta stop."

"Oh, hell no, you don't. Don't turn loose my hand." She began running again, still coughing. Now, I was coughing, too, gasping for air.

At the foot of the bridge, I felt her hand jerk loose. "Char," I yelled, then began coughing again. I could barely see her on the ground next to the woman she'd stumbled into. I tugged both of them out of the path of the other runners and crouched down to check on Charlene. "What the hell happened?"

She coughed so hard I thought she might puke, then she took a ragged breath, and wiped her eyes with her coat sleeve. "Don't know. Tripped, I guess. I'm okay. What about the lady I ran into? See how she is." She began coughing again. "Xander, my eyes burn like hell."

"Mine too, baby. I can hardly see." I wiped my eyes and turned to look for the other woman, but she'd already gotten up to continue running. "Let's get back to the church. Maybe they can help us." The crowd of runners had thinned, taking different streets away from the mayhem, but I could see several limping along in the burning fog, holding each other up. I'd never seen anything like it.

The scene at the church was chaotic as well. Men were loading someone on a stretcher into an ambulance, others were sitting on the steps holding their heads. Moans and cries filled the air. One man's pants were ripped, and his leg was bleeding, drenching his pants' leg. "Let's go inside. Maybe someone knows how to treat tear gas."

As we entered the sanctuary, I was stunned to see people laid out on pews and in the aisles. It looked like an overcrowded emergency room. "Stay here," I said to Charlene, pointing to a seat at the end of one pew. "I'll find someone." I coughed, got my breath, and wiped my eyes again. When she sat down, Charlene's dress rode up over her knees and I saw that they were scraped and bleeding. "Char, your knees are bleeding. You need to get them cleaned up and bandaged."

She looked down. "They're not that bad. Don't

worry about it. Look at these other people. They're lots worse off."

I shrugged, but still intended to ask someone for help with both things. At the front of the church, I found someone who looked like they were sort of in charge. "Excuse me, I know you've got some serious injuries to attend to but my girl back there, she skinned her knees. Can you help her? And we both took a bunch of tear gas." I pointed toward the back where I could see Charlene coughing again.

"Give me a minute," the man said, "and I'll send someone to you with some soda water. You should drink that to neutralize the tear gas.

"And you should wash your hands and face real good, too, and wash those clothes as soon as you can. That smell can stay for days," he said before turning to answer another man's questions.

I walked back to Charlene and told her what he'd said, then sat down to wait with her. After a minute, she said, "Well, I sure never expected that. Yelling, and spitting, yeah, but geez. It was whole lot worse than any of the other marches. Did you see that guy's leg? And that kid on the steps holding his head? He was bleeding like crazy. We could have been killed in that mob. Or by the cops."

"Yeah, but I saw a TV helicopter overhead. If the whole world saw that, things *will* change. Folks gotta be outraged. If they are, we did our part." I smiled and gave her a hug. "To tell the truth, I'm glad we came. Are you?" I said, then coughed.

She nodded. "Yeah, we can say that now, but

would we feel the same if we'd been seriously hurt?"

I chuckled, "That's a whole 'nother question, isn't it?"

Twenty minutes later, we'd been treated, had stopped coughing, and were walking back to our car. "We'll sure have a story to tell our kids, won't we?" I said.

"You proposing to me, Mr. Betts?" she said with a shocked look on her face.

"Listen, after all we've been through together, I can't imagine spending my life with anyone else. You're fearless, smart, considerate, and adorable. I love you, gal. So, yes, I'm proposing."

"I love you, too, Mr. Betts, and I'd be honored to be your wife." She turned and threw her arms around my neck. As we kissed, a couple who had been walking behind us hooted and applauded. "Yeah! That's cool, man. Way to go." I saluted the man and kissed Charlene again.

MARCH 15, 1965

The Morehead student center was surprisingly empty when Charlene and Xander arrived around 8:30 p.m. Perhaps it was too late, or maybe some were studying, or partying, or just didn't care, but the two of them couldn't wait to hear what President Johnson would say to Congress. Charlene, as usual, had kept up with the news and knew his speech was being broadcast to the nation at nine. The scuttlebutt was it would be about voting rights. They spotted a small group seated around the television set and went over to join them.

"You gonna watch Johnson's speech?" Charlene asked the group, afraid they were glued to some sitcom or sports event.

"Yeah, but it doesn't start for a while," a light-skinned boy with an Afro and mutton chops said.

"We know. We were afraid we wouldn't get a seat if we didn't come early," Xander said. "But it looks like we didn't need to worry."

"Grab a chair. Yeah, seems most folks don't care.

That surprises me. You?" another kid said. This one had the scraggly beginnings of a beard, but his head was closely shaved.

"Yeah," Xander said. "Everybody oughta be watching this. I mean, I hate to say it, but some Black folks don't seem to give a good damn about their own rights. How can they be so complacent? Don't they see it?"

"Guess not. You think King finally got to him?" Afro said.

"No, I think Bloody Sunday did," said Charlene before Xander could answer. "Or, rather knowing that the whole world saw what happened then. We were there, me and Xander. And, believe me, it was as bad as it looked on television. Worse, actually."

The bearded kid looked at them with awe. "Really? You went? Were you hurt? I heard they fractured John Lewis's skull. Gave him a concussion. He okay, do you know?"

Xander said, "Well, he's still in the hospital, but I think he's gonna be. We were lucky; but we were tear gassed. Man, we saw some stuff. I never thought it would be like that. It was a peaceful march." He snorted derisively. "Charlene warned me it could get dangerous, but... well, she sure was right. Damn."

"It was terrifying. Those guys on horseback had whips. I mean, it was scary as hell. I sure hope Johnson does what we marched for. Giving us the vote. If not, I'm gonna be really pissed," Charlene said, angry at the possibility Johnson might waffle. Word was he'd told King several times that this wasn't the right time.

While the television announcer talked about what to expect, the couple continued to talk to the boy with the Afro. But as the screen flipped to a view of congressmen beginning to take their seats, their conversation died down. With the announcement, "Mr. Speaker, the President of the United States," the members of Congress jumped to their feet and began applauding. Near the group gathered around the television, another group burst into laughter. Charlene hissed, "Shhhhh. We're trying to listen to the damn president. You oughta be too."

Xander put his hand on her arm. "Babe, it's okay. We can hear him."

At President Johnson's opening remark, "I speak tonight for the dignity of man and the destiny of democracy," Charlene grabbed for Xander's hand. She turned to him with an expectant look on her face. He smiled back at her.

They sat rapt with attention as he continued. "So it was last week in Selma, Alabama. There, long-suffering men and women peacefully protested the denial of their rights as Americans. Many were brutally assaulted. One good man, a man of God, was killed," he said with a solemn expression. Charlene turned to Xander and whispered, "Did you know that?"

He shook his head as Johnson continued. "There is no cause for pride in what has happened in Selma. There is no cause for self-satisfaction in the long denial of equal rights of millions of Americans." Xander said, "Damn right."

He continued, "But, there is cause for hope and

for faith in our democracy in what is happening here tonight." Charlene said, "Better be."

Afro hissed, "Shhh," just as Charlene had done earlier. Both Charlene and Xander mouthed, "Sorry."

They continued to listen intently. "There is no Negro problem. There is no southern problem. There is no northern problem. There is only an American problem. And we are met here tonight as Americans – not as Democrats or Republicans – we are met here as Americans to solve that problem," Johnson said to thunderous applause. Xander looked at Charlene and saw tears brimming in her eyes. He squeezed her hand.

"Yet the harsh fact is that in many places in this country men and women are kept from voting simply because they are Negroes. Every device of which human ingenuity is capable has been used to deny this right. The Negro citizen may go to register only to be told that the day is wrong, or the hour is late, or the official in charge is absent. And if he persists, and if he manages to present himself to the registrar, he may be disqualified because he did not spell out his middle name or because he abbreviated a word on the application. And, if he manages to fill out an application, he is given a test. The registrar is the sole judge of whether he passes this test. He may be asked to recite the entire Constitution or explain the most complex provisions of state law. And even a college degree cannot be used to prove that he can read and write. For the fact is that the only way to pass these barriers is to show a white skin." As Johnson described this situation, one she and Xander had witnessed in Mississippi, the tears rolled down her cheeks. Charlene wiped her eyes and gave Xander a small smile.

"On Wednesday I will send to Congress a law designed to eliminate illegal barriers to the right to vote," Johnson said. At that, Charlene yelled, "Amen! Preach it, brother!" as if she were in church. Xander pumped his fist in agreement, then shushed her so they could hear the rest.

As the president continued, outlining what he proposed to the lawmakers: striking down restrictions to voting in all elections; establishing a simple, uniform registration form; providing for officials of the federal government to register voters if the states refused to do so; eliminating tedious, unnecessary lawsuits that delay the right to vote; and ensuring that properly registered individuals are not prohibited from voting. Throughout, he was interrupted over and over with applause from both sides of the aisle.

As he exhorted congress to pass the bill immediately, Johnson said, "But even if we pass this bill, the battle will not be over. What happened in Selma is part of a far larger movement which reaches into every section and state of America. It is the effort of American Negroes to secure for themselves the full blessings of American life. Their cause must be our cause too. Because it is not just Negroes, but really it is all of us, who must overcome the crippling legacy of bigotry and injustice. And we shall overcome."

At that, Charlene lost what little composure she'd managed to maintain. She jumped to her feet

and shouted, "Amen!" as if she were about to witness in church. Xander and the others broke into loud
applause and cheers. "Yes!" "Alright." "Way to go."
"Hallelujah!"

Xander was on his feet. He turned and hugged
Charlene. "Oh, my god, baby. We did it! We did it!"

MAY 14, 1966

Clouds hung over the Morehouse quadrangle as Xander arrived, fully gowned, for the commencement ceremony. Charlene, who had graduated from Spelman the day before, walked beside him. Other graduates milled around the edges of the seating area chatting with parents, fellow students, and friends. The rows of white folding chairs reminded Xander of the pecan groves he'd passed on the bus ride from Blanchard's Bottom to Atlanta four years earlier. No matter whether you looked at them vertically, horizontally, or diagonally, the rows were perfect. He wished his future, and Charlene's, were so easily mapped out.

In front, robed school administrators and faculty milled about on the draped podium. Morehouse banners and the flags of Georgia and the United States flanked the sides. Xander frowned as the Georgia flag rustled, revealing the large, starred X that had been added to it a while back in honor of the Confederacy's centennial. He and Charlene had discussed it, and both vehemently hated the message they believed it sent.

"I hope it doesn't rain on us," Charlene said, looking at the sky. "That'd be a mess." She hugged her mother then turned to her father, squeezed his arm, and smiled. "I'm so glad you both stayed for Xander's graduation."

His eyes sparkled as if tears were brimming, but his huge smile radiated pride. "Wouldn't have missed yours for nothing," he said, then kissed Charlene's forehead, his disapproval of his daughter long forgotten. "You looked beautiful yesterday, baby. All tricked out in that fancy robe."

"Thanks. I like your new beard, Daddy, except it hides your dimples." She poked him on the cheek, like she was trying to find them, and laughed.

George Merrick laughed. "I always hated those things. Made me look like a kid. And, when I was one, old ladies used to pinch my cheeks. Beard makes a good camouflage. Your mother likes it though, don't you, Helen?"

"You know I do." She smiled as if tolerating her husband's remark but said no more. Charlene had told Xander that she was a shy woman, ashamed of her position as a domestic, and not comfortable in settings like this one. Charlene had said it had taken much coaxing on her father's part to get her to attend her daughter's graduation, let alone that of Charlene's boyfriend.

The two women who flanked Xander wore similar smiles to Mr. Merrick's. The shorter of the two, bedecked in a red cloche with a huge faux jewel, grabbed her son's arm. "I'd have rode that bus all night if that's what it took," said Livvie Betts. "I spent four years waiting on this day, worrying he might not make it. But here we is." Her smile broadened as she looked up at Xander, now over a foot taller than his mother. She looked shorter than he remembered, with a stoop to her shoulders he'd not noticed before. "I'm sorry Ladonna couldn't get off school. She wanted to come but she had them final tests," she said quietly. Understanding, Xander nodded.

"Well, I never doubted him," said the taller woman. Mrs. Johnson's hat was straw, with a wide brim that nearly hid her face. With both hands she clutched an enormous straw purse as if it contained the crown jewels. She still was as upright as Xander remembered from the classroom. It gave her an air of authority he'd always admired.

Xander smiled at his old teacher. "I wouldn't be here if it hadn't been for you. That scholarship made it possible! I'll never be able to repay you."

"Oh, yes, you will. Just remember our bargain and get that law degree. You'll more than repay me if you do that."

"What bargain?" Livvie Betts asked.

"Oh, it's a promise I made to Xander back in high school. I thought he had what it took to go to college, and I promised I'd help if he'd do something good with it. He's still got to make that happen, don't you Xander?" She gave him a conspiratorial wink.

"Yes, ma'am. And I will. Just haven't figured that

part out yet."

A breeze kicked up, fluttering Xander's gown and the brim of Mrs. Johnson's hat. She grabbed at it, nearly dropping her purse. "You will. I've no doubt on that score either."

Charlene tugged on Xander's sleeve. "You better go get seated. They're gathering up front." She turned to her father and said, "Why don't we sit with Xander's family and then catch up with him afterward?" He nodded, took his wife and Livvie Betts by their arms, and turned to escort them to find seats. Mrs. Johnson marched along behind the trio. Charlene grinned. "Such a gentleman," she said to Xander.

The two parted with a kiss and the agreement to meet afterwards back where they'd been standing. As he took his seat, Xander recalled his high school graduation day. *My life sure has changed. Back then, I thought it was the worst day of my life. Leon had died the day before and would never have a life. Now, I'm a college graduate engaged to the best gal in the world. It's the best day of my life, so far. I've still got things to do, though. I've still got to make it up to Leon, and Louie.*

His thoughts were interrupted by the university president's welcome to the students and their families. Xander tried to listen intently to the speakers, but the clouds had cleared, and the sun was warming him into a state of drowsiness and his head drooped.

At the first notes of "Pomp and Circumstance," Xander snapped awake. The front row of students was standing, ready to cross the stage. Suddenly, graduation felt real. As he crossed the stage and received his diploma, the president announced, "Alexander Lee Betts, Bachelor of Arts, *magna cum laude.*" He could hear clapping from the back rows. Yesterday, he'd been the one who stood and cheered as they watched Charlene accept her *cum laude* diploma. Now the hoots from the back-row chorus were for him. *Mama said she never thought she'd see this day. I'm so glad I proved her wrong. Me, a kid from the projects, graduating from Morehouse with honors.* With a huge smile on his face, he thanked the president and returned to his seat.

After the closing strains of the recessional had faded away, Xander made his way back to the spot where they'd agreed to meet. Once there, it was obvious how proud of their children Livvie Betts and the Merricks were. Their faces radiated; Mr. Merrick's grin apparently left over from yesterday. Livvie Betts took her son's arm just as Mr. Merrick grabbed his daughter. It was as if they had choreographed the scene.

As congratulations and hugs overlapped, an exuberant young man bounded over to Xander. "Hey, buddy, way to go! We made it!" he yelled as he approached the group.

"Hey Arn," Xander said as the man drew near. "Yeah, some classes were touch and go, but we made it." The two hugged, clapping each other on the back.

Charlene broke into their conversation, "Guys, come on!" She laughed at their self-deprecation. "You both graduated with high honors. Nothing was touch and go for you two!"

"You either," Arnie said to her. "You didn't do

so bad." As the three laughed, Xander said, "Let me introduce you. "Mom, this is Arnie Bruce. He was in most of my classes. Arn, this is my mother, Livvie Betts."

Arnie reached for Livvie's hand, "Pleased to meet you, Mrs. Betts. You must be very proud of Xander. He's been outstanding both in class and out."

Charlene chimed in, "And these are my mom and dad, Helen and George Merrick." Mr. Merrick extended his hand, but her mother just smiled. "Nice to meet you, Arnold. It is Arnold, isn't it? These nicknames... I prefer proper names."

"Yes sir, it's Arnold, but I've been Arnie all my life." Mr. Merrick looked a bit ashamed he'd cast aspersions on the kid's name. "You should be quite proud of Charlene, sir," said Arnie, apparently unfazed by her dad's chiding. "Besides graduating with honors, she's been quite a champion for civil rights; Xander, too."

Both George and Livvie looked surprised. "What you mean?" said Livvie. "What'd they do?"

Now it was Arnie's turn to be shocked. "You folks don't know how they marched, sat in, protested, and tried to get folks registered to vote? They even marched at Selma and were tear-gassed!" He sounded proud, as if the experiences of his friends somehow added status to his own standing.

Livvie looked at her son with an expression that moved from fear to exasperation to anger. "No, he nevah mentioned it. Why didn't you tell me, Xander? You ain't the kind to keep stuff from me. I even recollects us talking about them protestors. But you nevah said a word."

"Mama, I… I'm sorry… I knew you'd worry yourself to death so…"

"And you knew I'd try to stop you, didn't you?" she said, her hands on her hips.

"I reckon I did. I figured if you didn't know we wouldn't argue about it because I was gonna go no matter what."

"So, in a way you lied, too." Her voice had taken on the sometimes-hard edge Xander remembered from childhood. "That's like the time you was playing with matches and caught the wastebasket on fire. When I asked you about it, you lied. Remember? I punished you for the lie, not the matches. You've done the same thing this time."

"Come on, Mama. Don't fuss at me," Xander said in a low voice. Charlene could see that he was embarrassed to have his mother chastising him in public. "I'm fine, now. I just didn't want you all upset and worried."

Livvie huffed and crossed her arms over her bosom as if to indicate that she'd say no more but wasn't at all happy.

Beside Livvie and Xander, George Merrick was saying to Charlene, "And I thought you'd given up all that crap after high school. Thought I'd talked you outta being a Freedom Rider. Now you go off down south and get mixed up with some radical bunch… I wouldn't be surprised if you'd gotten arrested. You always were a mouthy kid."

Charlene's mouth flew open. "Daddy!" she said, astonished at his insult.

He turned on Xander. "You talk her into that stuff?" he said, his anger palpable. Charlene's mother put her hand on George's arm as if to calm him, but he shook it off, jerking his arm free. She tucked her hand behind her back as if it had been burned and stared at the ground.

"Daddy, no. If anything *I* talked *him* into it. Don't blame Xander. I'm sorry, but I couldn't just sit by and do nothing. Not after we saw what was happening down here. Don't be mad at me or Xander. Nothing bad happened. We're here; we've graduated; we're fine."

"That boy said you were tear gassed. Don't sound like nothing to me. From what I read about Selma, you could have been killed."

"But we weren't..." she started to explain, but her father turned and walked away. "Daddy," she cried out. "Don't..." Charlene looked as if she were going to cry. Suddenly, her mother ran after her husband. George stopped as she called to him. The two stood apart from the group, heads together. Charlene could see her mother talking, her hands on his shoulders. Soon, the two returned.

"Daddy, I'm sorry you had to hear about all this from someone else. We'd have told you eventually." She looked at Xander's mother. "Mrs. Betts, I suggested that Xander not tell you, either. We just didn't want to worry any of you. We had some good experiences and learned a lot. I think it was a good thing we did. After all, if the young folks don't fight, nothing will ever change. And besides, we're here, we're safe, and we graduated. That's what's important, isn't it?" Out of the corner of her eye, she saw her mother smile, the first one she'd seen all day and she knew her mother secretly approved.

Both George and Livvie relaxed as they realized what she said was true. Their children, now adults, had done what they'd always dreamed of: they'd graduated from college and had their whole lives and careers ahead of them.

Mrs. Johnson, who had not said a word during this exchange, now spoke up. "I think it's time to celebrate, not fuss. Let's go have lunch. I'll treat." Surreptitiously, she winked at Xander as the group began to discuss where to eat. Xander knew it was her way of saying, "Atta boy!" In that moment, he thought of Gerald Baxter and of Leon. If only Baxter could have helped Leon like Mrs. Johnson had helped him. If only *he'd* done what he should have to help Leon. And, in that moment he resolved to continue fighting for the Leons of the world.

August 13, 1966
Xander

I'd been up since six trying to figure out how to tell Char what I'd decided to do. Now it was a bit past eight, and as always, the window fan of our one-room Moreland Avenue apartment was struggling against Atlanta's increasing heat and humidity. I watched her peacefully sleeping in the fetal position with one arm over her face to block out the light pouring in above the noisy fan. I'd struggled with this decision for a while without talking to her and now, as I watched her, I deeply regretted that. We'd always discussed our plans, our worries, together. This time, though, I'd made a decision without her. Her back was to me, so after I made her a cup of coffee and put it on the rickety bedside table left over from the previous tenant, I crawled in to spoon with her for a few minutes hoping she'd wake at my touch.

"Char," I whispered in her ear. "Wake up, sleepyhead. I made you coffee." Brushing back her hair and lifting her hand, I kissed her cheek. She didn't stir but a smile bloomed on her lips. "Char," I said again. She moved her arm and I kissed her again, this time on the ear.

"That tickles," she said, scrunching up her shoulder and turning to face me.

"Girl, were you playing possum?"

"Sorta." She smiled, yawned, then covered her mouth. "Sorry, morning breath."

I sat up. "Here's your coffee. I'll make breakfast if you're hungry.'

She swung her legs over the side of the bed and took the coffee from me. Looking at my jeans, she said, "You're awful chipper this morning. How long you been up?"

"Too long. I've got something I need to tell you. It's been bothering me way too long."

Now she was wide awake, her smile suddenly a look of panic. "What's wrong? Are you okay?" She reached to pull her nightgown strap back on her shoulder.

"Yeah, yeah. Nothing's wrong. I've just been trying to figure out how to get to law school."

"Whatta ya mean? With your new position and my teaching this fall, we're okay, aren't we? I thought we had this all figured out."

"Not exactly. I wanted to be enrolling now, but we just can't afford it."

Char put her free arm around me. "Aww, honey, I'm sorry. Are you sure?"

I nodded, "Yeah, I'm sure."

"What if we saved up for a few years? Then you

could go, right?"

"How are we gonna save? We're barely making it as it is. Even if we could, I've heard guys at the office say they tried to do that, but once they got caught up in their careers and started making a good salary, they never quit to go back to school. I don't want that to happen to me, to us."

"You got any other bright ideas, Mr. Magna Cum Laude?" She leaned back and looked at me with those piercing black eyes.

"Yeah, but I know you won't like it. That's my problem."

"Try me. You might be surprised. Can't discuss it if I don't know what it is."

I took a deep breath. "Well…" I paused, not sure how to start. "I've been asking around. I think… if I… you know when I graduated, I lost my draft deferment, right?"

"Hadn't really thought about it. Too busy with finals, I guess." She raked her fingers through her hair then took a sip of the hot black coffee.

"Well, I sure have. And it scares me. I don't want to have to go fight even if they're right and we won't be over there for long. I don't really believe in war but… if I go… did you know the G. I. Bill will pay for law school tuition?"

Her jaw dropped and she nearly spit out her coffee. "What?" she shrieked.

"Hear me out, Char. If I enlist… it could work. First, if I don't go to law school right away, I'll most likely be drafted. And, since we can't afford it, I'll surely be sent to the front." She sat mute but shook her head. I could see she was having a hard time coming to grips with this idea, so I rushed to finish. "Yeah, that's right, I could be and that would be the worst. I'll be cannon fodder for sure. But, if I enlist, since I'm a college graduate, I bet I'd get a desk job. No fighting. I'd serve my two years and then be eligible for the G. I. Bill. While I'm over there, I'd send you my Army pay. With that and your salary, you'd be fine. We might even be able to save some. Whatta you think?" I smiled, hoping she'd see the logic of my plan. Truthfully, I wasn't absolutely sure of it myself. I just hoped it would all work out because I didn't know what else to do.

The silence lasted longer than I thought it would. I stared at the floor. Finally, she sighed. "Xander, honey, you know I've always said I'd do whatever it took to support your dreams, but I gotta think about this. We just got into our own apartment, even if it is as small as a closet. We were gonna get married this year. I don't want my new hubby going off all the way across the world. And, you don't know if you'd get a desk job or not. You could be fighting just like all the rest."

"Yeah, but if I had to quit work to go to law school, we couldn't afford even *this* apartment. I seriously doubt I could do both school and work. And I don't think we could make it on your salary alone. I'd have to cut back to part time, again. Then, there's tuition. We couldn't begin to afford that, even at University of Georgia. Plus, there's always the possibility of the draft."

"I gotta go pee." She put down the coffee and slid off the bed. I sat there trying to think of any other argument I could offer. So often, during our relationship, she'd been the one that suggested what we did and I'd usually agree. Like protesting, going to Selma. Now, I'd decided something without her, and I could tell she wasn't happy.

She came out of the bathroom and said, "Look, you need to give me some time, so let's drop it and go out for brunch. We can talk about anything else but that. Okay? Maybe after dinner I'll be ready to talk again."

"Deal," I said, knowing that any further discussion right now would just make matters worse. "Where do you want to go?"

"How about that place where Dr. King and the others eat... Paschal's? I hear they've got great peach cobbler."

"Perfect, maybe he'll be there."

Despite Charlene's edict, the subject of Vietnam hung in the air at lunch along with the smell of fried chicken. We talked about the recent bombing campaign, Operation Rolling Thunder, they'd called it, and whether or not they thought it would end the war as the president hoped. I was sure it would; Charlene was fearful that it would not. "That's why I don't want you to go," she said. "I'm afraid things will only get worse."

She looked around the restaurant. "Who are you

looking for?" I asked.

"Dr. King." She chuckled. "Thought I'd ask his opinion about Vietnam."

"Come on, be serious," I said.

"Well, I was, sorta. I know he must be opposed just because he's anti-violence. But war is different, isn't it? If South Vietnam needs our help, don't we need to support them? I really would like to know how he feels about it."

"I don't know but I did read that his wife is against it. She's spoken out. But honestly? I just don't know."

In the end, I couldn't assure her that it wouldn't last long; after all, it was anyone's guess how America's involvement would play out. Finally, she sighed. "If that's the only way you think we can manage law school, I'll... that's not saying I like it... I don't. Not one damn bit, but if that's our only option, I'll go along with it."

I let out the breath I didn't know I was holding. "Oh, God, Char. I love you so much. I was so afraid you'd... I don't know... leave, maybe?"

"Alexander Lee Betts," she said, reaching across the table, "you should know better. I'd never leave you, no matter what. You're stuck with me, baby, for life."

With my heart about to burst with love and relief, I said, "I love you, baby, more than you'll ever know." I chuckled. "Want that cobbler now?"

"Damn right," she said.

OCTOBER 20, 1966 XANDER

After seven of the eight torturous weeks of basic training at Fort Benning, Georgia, I was about to graduate to eight more of advanced training after which I hoped to parlay my college degree into a position that didn't involve the fighting I was being trained for. Yes, I'd still need to know how to use my M16, my night vision goggles, and how to wriggle through the jungles of Vietnam like a snake, but dear Lord, I hoped and prayed I'd never have to do any of that.

I'd battled sand fleas, red ants, five-mile runs in full gear before and after most meals. I'd risen before dawn every damn day, gotten little sleep, suffered through interminable lectures, and endured the Army's idea of how to turn boys into men. I'd survived it all and still didn't regret enlisting, at least on most days, if it would get me the G.I. Bill for law school. *When I get home before shipping out, Charlene will be surprised at the ten pounds of pure muscle I've gained.* I was more fit than I'd ever been, even as a kid running from the cops in the projects. That, at least, was a positive.

Another was the good friend I'd made – another Negro named Philip Murphy. Phil was a skinny kid from Cordele, Georgia with skin much darker than mine. We both arrived the same steamy August day, although Phil had been drafted. From the moment he stepped off the bus, Phil seemed to draw the brunt of our bulldog drill sergeant's enmity. I thought it was because of his dark chocolate color since Sergeant Sudderth immediately began calling him derogatory names like "Hershey," "licorice whip," or "Black Beauty." This guy, whose breath could melt plastic, screamed at everyone, but his vilest taunts fell on Phil, and sometimes, by extension, on me. We were the only two Negroes in the company. I'd been drawn to Phil from the beginning, maybe because he looked a bit like Louie; maybe because of his persecution; or maybe I just knew we'd better stick together to survive.

Sergeant Sudderth wasn't the only one who tormented Phil. It shouldn't have surprised me, but I guess since I'd been at Morehouse for four years, I hadn't heard the hate on a daily basis. Of course, when Charlene and I had been out protesting, it was the language of the day. Most of these guys made cracks only periodically, but still, they rankled both of us. We tried to avoid the worst of it, but it was impossible. "Boy," was their favorite taunt. "Hey boy, you gonna get your bony ass over that thing sometime this week?" "You climb like a damn crippled monkey." "You boy, get your black ass outta my way."

One especially bigoted guy, bigger than both of

us by a mile, adopted the sergeant's pejoratives whenever Sudderth was out of earshot. Frankie Payne was
his name. "Hey boy, your dick's as skinny as a licorice
whip, black as one, too," he'd say as Phil exited the
showers. "Look at you, Hershey bar. You gonna melt
in this heat." The guy never let up. Phil ignored him
as best he could, but I could tell it got to him every
time. I'd see his jaw clenching, the veins in his head
straining, his Adam's apple moving to swallow the
comebacks he dared not utter.

But a week ago, Payne went a step too far. We
were in our barracks opening mail and packages
from home. Phil was unwrapping a fairly large one
when Frankie Payne spotted him. "Chitlins from your
mama?" he asked. "Or is it fried chicken? Or water-
melon. Something to fatten up your nigger ass?"

Phil yelled back, "Can it, asshole. I've had enough
of your shit."

With that, Frankie stormed over to Phil, jerked
him off his bunk and spilled the cookies his mother
had sent him all over the floor. Payne stomped the
mess on the floor, smashing the cookies into crumbs
as he dragged Phil into the aisle between the rows of
bunks. "What did you call me?" Payne snarled, his fist
twisted in Phil's shirt front and his face only inches
from Phil's.

"I called you what you are, an asshole. You've shit
on me since we got here. In my book that makes you
an asshole."

Phil looked defiant rather than scared. But I
knew he was no match for Payne if a fight broke out.

So, I grabbed his shoulder. "Fuck off, Payne. That's too much. Apologize, you sonofabitch."

Payne dropped Phil and swung around toward me, his fist connecting with my jaw. I staggered back but didn't go down. I charged at him and as we grappled with each other, I could hear some of the others yelling. "Fight, fight." "Get him, Frank." "Take him down, Payne." "You can take him, Frankie." Not a single person was cheering for me.

Suddenly, I saw Phil behind Payne trying to pull him off of me. But Payne was like a mad dog; there was no stopping him. Phil couldn't budge the two hundred and fifty-pound hulk from that angle, so he slipped around Payne's side and swung at him. It was a clumsy angle and Payne easily ducked the punch. With his head lowered, Payne slammed it into my solar plexus and knocked the wind out of me. I landed awkwardly on a nearby bunk.

He pulled me up and spit in my face. "This fight's between me and him. Back off, motherfucker."

"No," I yelled, wiping the spit off my face. "It's between your redneck ass and our black ones." I spit back at him. This was the third time I'd been spit at and I wasn't going to stand for it again. I threw a punch and it landed solidly on Frank's cheekbone, drawing blood.

As Frankie came at me again, Phil moved between us and grabbed Frank around the neck, his hands like a noose. I could see Frank's face redden from the force Phil was applying to his windpipe. The two stumbled across the room like ring-weary boxers until Phil slammed Frankie into the barrack's wall. Frank slid to the floor just as Sergeant Sudderth came through the door.

"What the fuck is going on?" he yelled. "Attention!" The room fell silent as everyone but Payne snapped to attention where they were standing. "Get your ass up, Payne. What the fuck are you doing down there?" he said as he marched across the room, extending him a hand.

"Murphy knocked me down. And Betts slugged me," he said as he stood and touched his swollen and bleeding cheek.

Sudderth looked around the room. "Anyone see this?" The entire company remained silent. He turned toward Phil. "Murphy, what happened here? You in the habit of beating the shit out of folks?"

"Sir, no sir. Payne called me a nigger. I couldn't take it anymore. He's been…"

Sudderth interrupted him. "Betts, what about you? You fancy yourself a big ass fighter?"

"Sir, no sir." I replied. "But, sir, Payne was attacking…"

Sudderth interrupted me as well. "Payne, what have you got to say for yourself?"

"Sir, those two guys… I was just ribbing them, but they took offense and attacked me."

"Get back to your bunk, Payne. Betts, thirty days latrine duty; Murphy, KP for the same. And both of you – no passes for a month," Sudderth barked.

"Sir, yes, sir," we said in unison. Sudderth yelled, "At ease," turned on his heel and stormed through the door.

As soon as he left, Payne started stage whispering, "Nigger, nigger, nigger." He knew we wouldn't dare accost him again. "Looks like your black asses'll be working like slaves… again."

I could see Phil lying on his bunk, his pillow over his head. Still seething, I tried to ignore Payne. *The military may be integrated, but there's no equal justice here, either. Fucked over once more even though, this time, I tried to do the right thing. I stood up for my friend but look where it got me – same place I'd have been if I'd stood up for Leon: in trouble. Sadly, Payne was right. I'll be cleaning latrines just like Mama used to do. Suddenly, I realized how she must have felt cleaning up other people's shit. She didn't deserve it and neither did I; but for me, it was worth it. I'd knew I'd done the right thing.*

MAY 3, 1967
NHA TRANG, VIETNAM
XANDER

This morning about six, I woke up with my right arm and shoulder in a cast and my arm resting on a wooden platform at right angles to my body. I couldn't move it at all. I had no idea what day it was or how the hell I'd landed in this hospital bed.

"Nurse! Orderly! Hello-o!" It felt like hours, but a few minutes later a Black nurse threw back the curtain with a scowl on her face. "What's all this fuss about, Private Betts? You need to hush up. Folks are sleeping in here," she said.

"What happened to me? Where am I? How'd I get here? What day is it? And when do I get out?"

"It's Wednesday. Can't answer your last question but you're in the base field hospital. From what I heard, one of your buddies brought in here about three in the morning on Monday. You were pretty busted up, but you weren't feeling any pain, they said. Little drinking going on, maybe?" She grinned.

"What did I do... fall off something? Trip over my own big feet?" I tried to laugh at my own joke, but everything ached, and I winced instead.

"I don't have any idea. You better ask your buddy." I wondered which buddy she was talking about – Phil or Jimmy? I *did* remember going out with them but nothing else.

She turned to go, then turned back. "Need anything before I go?"

"No, I guess not. Thanks." She started to leave again. "Wait," I said. "When will the doctor be back? I gotta get out of here. I've got work to do."

"Honey, I don't think you're going anywhere but home. But when he gets here, I'll be sure he comes your way." She flashed another smile and moved out of the curtained cubicle. *What did she mean, going home? To my barracks? Or home?* I fell asleep wondering.

Later that afternoon, when my buddy, Jimmy Gordon stopped by, he answered my question. He said my old buddy Phil Murphy had brought me to the hospital, then had gone back to Da Nang. He had called Jimmy around four in the morning to let him know where I was. Jimmy was another Black guy in our company and since I'd arrived in Nha Trang, we'd worked together processing orders for supplies. The base was home to the 14th Air Commando Wing and two medical helicopter units. Jimmy was a lanky guy, and he had the foulest mouth I'd ever heard, and in the Army that was saying something. Nevertheless, we had gotten to be pretty good friends. He was from the same town as Charlene: Columbus, Ohio. He'd been a civil rights protestor when he was at Ohio State, so we had that in common, too.

"Well, it's good to see your ass awake and somewhat upright," he said as he opened the curtain and looked in.

I turned at the sound of his voice. "Hey, Jimmy. Good to see you, man. Have a seat," I said as I patted the bed. "What the hell happened to me last night? I remember going out with you and Phil but…" I paused, tried to sit more upright, failed, and fell back on the pillows.

"Damn, Xander, don't you remember that dude on the motor scooter? Witnesses said he clipped you and that bicycle pretty damn good and just kept on going. Said he was Vietnamese, but they didn't know if he was RSV or VC."

I frowned. "Where the hell was I when he hit me? I remember Phil showing up at the office after he'd hitched a ride down on a medical chopper from Da Nang. And I remember all of us going to Soul Alley for some fried chicken and a little Marvin Gaye. I know I had a few drinks, and smoked some weed, but I wasn't that out of it. Still, after that it's all a blur. I don't even remember leaving."

"Good lord! You don't remember the fucking girls? They kept asking us to buy them Saigon Tea? Remember? They kept saying, 'You numba one' in those singsong voices."

I shook my head.

"Fuck! You must have really whacked that hard

head of yours. Okay; this one Mamasan kept trying to get you to go in the back with her. Plump gal with lots of bright red lipstick? When you wouldn't go, she said, 'You numba ten.'" Jimmy laughed knowing that meant she didn't like it that I wouldn't sleep with her.

"Hell, I got my girl Charlene back home pregnant and waiting on me. I sure wasn't gonna take home something I couldn't wash off, if you know what I mean. So, what happened then?"

"You left. Phil and I stayed a little while longer, but he left before I did. He said when he came out of Soul Alley you were lying in the street, unconscious. He said he flagged down a Jeep and brought you here."

"Damn, I owe old Phil a big one," I said. "Sounds like he saved my ass." I chuckled, "I guess now we're even. I saved his ass once in boot camp when this redneck asshole called him a nigger. I'd had it with his shit, so I took him on one evening. Of course, Phil and I got extra detail and he got nothing."

"Doesn't surprise me. Remember when you first got here, I told you that's why I stopped going to Saigon's regular bars? Too many southern crackers calling us names and itching to beat the shit out of you. Some old guy who'd been here a while told me about Soul Alley so I started going there instead." Jimmy grinned as if he had some very fond memories of Soul Alley.

"I'm glad you showed it to us. Great place to be, if you watch yourself and don't get tangled up with Mamasans." Xander laughed.

Jimmy turned as a doctor entered the room. "Good evening, Private Betts. How are you feeling?"

Before Xander could answer, Jimmy said, "I'm gonna take off. Let the doc here take over. Hope you get out soon." He gave me a short salute as he left the room.

I called after him, "Thanks for coming, Jimmy."

I turned back to the doctor as he again asked, "How are you feeling, son?"

"I hurt all over, but I think I'll live."

"Yes, you will, but you were lucky. Your head injury wasn't severe, but you could have a headache for a day or so. Your real problem is going to be that arm. Based on the way your shoulder was smashed, it's likely you won't be able to lift your arm much over shoulder height ever again. The break in the humerus was clean, but that shoulder… wow. Sorry son. Looks like your fighting days are over."

I could barely stifle a smile. "How soon will I be out of here, do you think?"

"I'm going to release you tomorrow if you think you can manage with your arm stuck out like that."

"Yes, sir. I can manage. Thank you, sir."

After the doctor left, I lay there dreaming of going home. I'd been in country only five months and had been counting the days until my tour ended. I'd gotten the desk job I'd hoped for, but I was worried about Charlene. She was battling terrible heartburn with her pregnancy and was having to stand on swollen feet teaching fourth graders. Every day, I'd wish to God I was home to at least rub her feet at night.

When her daddy found out she was pregnant and that we weren't married he'd stopped talking to Charlene. Her mother, however, snuck in calls and letters for moral support, but she was in Columbus. Char needed real help. I'd worried too, that I wouldn't be there when the baby came in August. Now, I would be.

I also tried to remember exactly what had happened. Even though Jimmy had told me, I wanted to recapture it for myself. I knew that on Sunday afternoon, Jimmy, Phil, and I had commandeered a couple of bicycles and had ridden into Saigon. The streets were packed with both our soldiers and the Vietnamese villagers. They made me nervous. During our indoctrination, we'd been warned that the Vietcong often roamed the streets intent on setting off small bombs in outdoor cafes or lobbing them at our Jeeps. And, of course, you couldn't tell the Vietcong from the South Vietnamese. In a way, it shamed me to be wary around them; it was too much like the way whites back home looked at all us Negroes – with suspicion.

On top of all that, the guys that were out on the front lines hated us rear guard guys. When they'd come back in, dirty, exhausted, and sometimes wounded, they'd make remarks about how our cushy jobs weren't really helping the war effort. If they only knew what it took to keep their shit coming to the front. Still, they called us Rear Echelon Motherfuckers. Of course, they didn't do it to our faces, but we heard it. If Frankie Payne were here, he'd have added *nigger.* Thank God, I'll never see his redneck ass again.

That was another reason we avoided the regular Saigon bars. Just one more chance to get our butts kicked. Like Jimmy said, that's why we went to Soul Alley. I lay there remembering Tran Minh Street – what we called Soul Alley – particularly the smells: heavy perfume, weed, the miasma of a hundred cooking odors, tobacco, and body odor. The noisy din: music, kids squalling, singing, shouts from food stalls, even barking dogs. I thought about how crowded that small area was with shops of all sorts. Whatever you wanted, you could buy in there – food, weed, booze, drugs, and sex. Plenty of sex. The place pulsed with the blues, jazz, and get-down rock and roll.

It was a heady place to go; the feeling of being safe was as intoxicating as the weed or the booze. I'd never felt that back home and maybe I never would. Still, the thought of going home to be with Charlene was far more intoxicating than Soul Alley. I knew I'd probably take some flak for being discharged because of a bicycle accident, but I didn't care. I couldn't wait to write and tell Charlene I was coming home.

JUNE 13, 2020

Xander Betts sits in his worn leather recliner watching the massive television that dominates their paneled den wall. Tears roll across his high cheekbones. He does not attempt to stop them even as they drip onto his shirt. CNN alternates between depressing news of the growing death count from the novel coronavirus pandemic, which reminds him of the burgeoning body count he saw when he was in Vietnam, and the coverage of yesterday's killing of Rayshard Brooks by Atlanta police. This latest killing has reignited CNN's repeated footage from last month's horrific video of George Floyd's murder, also at the hands of the police. He thinks of Leon. *Nothing has changed. Not one damn thing.*

He glances at the lineup of pictures on the credenza below the television set. There's one of him, his hair and beard as black as the judicial robe he's wearing. Today, he wonders why he didn't smile for that portrait, taken on the day he was sworn in. Beside the current and childhood photos of his three

boys and his wife, Charlene, all smiles and scrubbed
faces, there's one grainy black-and-white one of his
mother, Livvie Betts. He found it as he was closing
down the apartment after her death long ago. He
suspects it was taken at church because she's wearing a large-brimmed hat, something she only wore on
Sundays. There's one missing – their wedding photograph. Xander still regrets that they didn't take one,
but Charlene was embarrassed that a picture would
have immortalized the fact that she was seven months
pregnant when they eloped the week after Xander
came home from Nam.

Outside, the weather is glorious. Early June in
Atlanta brings summer weather without the humidity
that soon will cause clothes to stick to bodies and air
to feel as heavy as the leaden blankets dentists use.
But he takes no notice. With the mushrooming death
toll of Black boys and men and the frustratingly con-
flicting information presented at President Trump's
daily briefings about the pandemic, he has no heart
to do anything. The lawn mowing will wait, as will the
memoir he's been working on, mostly at Charlene's
insistence. She claims their children will want to know
how a poor Black boy overcame poverty, became an
attorney, a state legislator, and then a judge. She says
it's important and he agrees.

But today, of all days, he has no heart for writing.
*Nothing I've done has made a difference. Not the college protests.
Not becoming a defense attorney. Not trying to make the criminal justice system fairer for African Americans. Not the scores
of kids I've mentored. Why write about it? For that matter,*

Dr. King's marches didn't really change things. Some even say Barack Obama becoming president may have made things worse because now whites in power think we're going to take over. Instead, we're still the victims of police brutality. This killing is only one of hundreds. And maybe that's why they've increased. Still, I've seen this since I was a kid.

He counts on his fingers the names of others killed just this year. *George Floyd. Breonna Taylor. Ahmaud Aubrey. David McAtee. Sean Reed. Michael Ramos. Mannie Ellis.* Now he adds Rashard. He's been keeping track and it breaks his heart. To list them all, he'd have to go back to Emmett Till – a name he remembers well from his childhood. And to Leon, and what he didn't do to help him.

Charlene wanted to go to Sandy Springs today to march with the Black Lives Matter folks, but Xander said it wouldn't help. That saddened Charlene because he used to be an activist. But as he'd told her, we've been there before. Besides, there's the risk of COVID. She says he's being a wimp, that they would wear masks, but at seventy-five with a touch of high blood pressure, he knows the danger. And he worries that, as a judge, he shouldn't be there at all.

Unable to watch it any longer, he reaches for the remote and snaps off the set. He lowers the footrest and rises. "Charlene," he calls. "I'm going for a walk. Be back by lunch." From the back of the house he hears her. "Wear your mask, honey." She knows the danger, too.

Outside he glances up and down the block check-ing to see if he'll really need the mask, if folks are out and about. He sees no one; instead, he notices the houses on his street as if they'd just sprung up, all brick, well kept, with manicured lawns and gardens. He lives in an affluent area of Atlanta's suburb of Roswell. Some days that still surprises him, an African American who started life in the projects.

Where they live never did keep him from worrying about his kids, however. When they were young, he harbored the same worries every Black parent has regardless of where they live and despite his position. Years ago, he'd been stopped with Charlene and the boys in the car for an alleged traffic infraction where there was none. He was sure he'd been targeted for 'driving while Black.' So, he'd taught his three sons almost the same street rules his mama had taught him back in Blanchard's Bottom all those years ago. While things had changed and they no longer had to step off the sidewalk when white folks passed, no longer had to avoid looking a white woman in the face, he still had preached extreme deference to white folks. While it rubbed him – and most certainly Charlene – the wrong way, he'd done it. It ran counter to his years of protesting, marching, standing up; but he didn't want harm to come to them. As a father, he believed they should do as he said, not as he'd done. These days protestors sometimes got shot, not just sprayed with firehoses. And yet, as he thought about this, he realized the irony of it. Hadn't he spent his life trying to make up for listening to his mama when all along, he had known he shouldn't have? He shakes his head, dons his mask, just in case, and starts down the sidewalk.

JUNE 15, 2020

The day the email arrived, Xander had been thinking about his old law partner. When he saw Philip Murphy's name, he wondered if somehow he'd conjured his message into existence. If that were possible, it was because he'd been thinking about Philip ever since George Floyd was murdered, wondering if Phil's reaction had been as devastating as his own. The message was an invitation to visit with one another via Zoom. He'd been working from home since COVID hit and he really didn't like using the virtual platform, but he had no choice. The state supreme court had mandated the courts close for all in-person proceedings. He'd have been thrilled to actually *see* Philip, but with the pandemic, he knew traveling to Athens for an in-person visit was impossible. So, he wrote back asking when Phil wanted to talk.

Xander hadn't seen Phil in at least five years, although the two had made plans multiple times to meet somewhere between their two towns. Somehow, something always had come up. Phil had a class to teach. Xander had a thing with his kids. Charlene had made other plans. Phil's wife, Sheri, had gotten sick. Always something. Xander thought about when they met in boot camp and how they'd battled racism back then. He thought also about how close the two had been when they started their law practice together, when his hair was still coal black and Phil still sported those ridiculous mutton chops. Together they'd battled injustice and racial prejudice, and both still had the emotional battle scars to show for it. *God, it will be good to see him. It's been way too long.*

The next day he couldn't wait to see if Phil had scheduled a meeting. There it was… an email with several smiling emojis, and a link to a Zoom meeting that afternoon. He'd signed off with "let me know." Xander added the link to his calendar, wrote back, and said, "I look forward to seeing your ugly mug." He added a smiley face to be sure Phil knew he was ribbing him.

At 2:00 p.m. he fired up his computer again, logged on to Zoom, and waited. Five minutes later he was still staring at his own face. No surprise, he thought. *I swear, that man will be late to his own funeral.* He adjusted his glasses, realized his face was in shadow, and turned on another desk lamp to provide better lighting. Then, he began to worry that *he'd* misread the date or the time. He turned to check the email invitation he'd printed out to be sure he'd gotten the Zoom codes right. *No, I've got it right.* He glanced back to the Zoom screen and there was Phil.

"Where you been, mister?" Phil said as if he'd

been the one waiting.

"God, Phil, you'll never change, will you? I've been on here for ten minutes. Where the hell were you?"

"Getting a beer. Sorry. Sheri apparently hides them in the basement fridge. Took me a few minutes to get down those damn stairs. My knees just aren't what they used to be. So how you doing, old buddy? God, it's good to see your ugly mug, too." Phil took a pull on his Pabst.

"'Bout as well as anybody during this pandemic. I've about worn Charlene out with being here all the time. Before this, I'd go to the gym most mornings before court, and she'd do her thing. But now we're just here reading or watching television when I'm not on here listening to pleadings. I think she's pretty sick of me. She'd never say it, of course. How you holding up?"

"Same. Been teaching a law seminar at Georgia on Zoom but that's only a few days a week. Otherwise, watching TV's killing me, but I can't seem to quit. It's like seeing a train wreck, you know? You know you shouldn't look, but you just can't help it. I finally stopped watching our idiot president's daily briefings, though. Too hard on my blood pressure." Phil laughed.

"I hear you. I don't know which is worse. Him, the daily COVID death tolls, or the constant reports of Black men being killed by the police. Have you noticed how many there have been this year? God, I thought we'd gotten past all that long ago. It's like the lynchings of the 1920s all over again." Xander pulled a notebook toward him, opened it, and turned the open pages so Phil could see them. "I've been keeping a list. It's terrible. Charlene says I'm obsessing about it and maybe I am, but…"

Phil interrupted him. "I'm not keeping a list, but I sure know what you're talking about. It's an epidemic, isn't it? I think it's worse than the Civil Rights days. Hell, if I remember correctly, something like that… police misconduct… isn't that what made you go into law? Weren't you harassed by the cops as a kid? Didn't someone you knew get the chair when he wasn't guilty? Sorta the same thing, right?"

"Yeah, his name was Leon Pepper. His little brother was my best friend, and we had several run-ins with the cops when we were young. Nobody I ever knew was shot, but the cops sure didn't mind beating the living tar out of Black folks. And Leon, well, he was railroaded by an all-white jury. Remember me telling you that I could have stopped that but was too chicken to tell what I knew? That's really what changed my life. Sent me to law school."

"Man, you were one angry Negro back when we first met in boot camp. All those protests you told me about. I was always afraid you'd get thrown in the brig. That sure would have screwed up your plans to be a lawyer, wouldn't it? You been part of these Black Lives Matter protests?" said Phil.

"No. Charlene has been, but I'm done with protesting. Back in college, we went to jail once, but after that Charlene always managed to drag me out of the crowd before the cops showed up. Of course, we did get gassed at Selma." Xander chuckled at the memory. "Nowadays, it doesn't seem to do any good. Just gives the cops more reason to get violent even when the protest is peaceful."

"I know that's right. I never did protest, and I always felt guilty that I didn't. Maybe that's why I went into law. Trying to right that wrong. Funny, how our past creates our present, isn't it?" Phil's face had taken on that serious look he got in court when he was cross-examining a witness.

"That's a fact. Can't speak for everyone but my past sure shaped me," Xander said. "I've got a capital case coming up… a bench trial. Guy's name is Thompson. Sorta reminds me of Leon. This kid's also being ramrodded, I'm sure. But, if I turn him loose, the public will be up in arms. If I don't, it's Leon all over again. I want to do what's right… for once."

"I hear you. That's a tough one. But Xander, come on! You've done what's right dozens of times. You always wanted to take the cases of the underdog. You'll get it right this time, too. Remember that first pro bono case we had back in… maybe the second year after we hung out our shingle… that Black kid accused of assaulting a white cop? What was his name?" Phil asked.

"Man, you're going way back. Uh, let me think. I remember the case, but his name… was it Damien something? He'd been with a group of boys in Avondale Heights and the cops thought he'd stolen something from a bodega. What was it?" asked Xander.

"Don't remember… something small, like a candy bar, bottle of Coke, but I do remember he said he never raised a hand. That one cop swore he came at him when he tried to arrest him. Then the cop beat him up pretty good, as I recall. Would've been a case of he said, he said if it hadn't been for that woman watching it all out her window. She came forward and told what she'd seen. Corroborated that kid's story." Phil said. "If you hadn't believed that kid telling you somebody was watching, you never would have gotten him off."

"I learned the hard way to believe my clients. Like with Leon. If somebody had found out who was in that bar, things would have turned out a lot different for him. 'Course, in some cases that didn't turn out to be a good attitude." He laughed. "Lots of them would lie when the truth would have done better."

"Yeah, but you had an instinct. A nose for the truth. I always admired that in you." Phil smiled deeply.

"Thank you, Phil. We made a good team all those years. I'm damn glad we hooked up after Nam. Didn't always win, but we tried and did our best for our clients." Now Xander was smiling. "It's good to go back, remember the wins, don't you think? Helps me with this one, too. Thanks."

"Yeah… I wish we'd done more to keep a record of them. Make a hell of a book."

"I know that's right. Couldn't tell most of them, though. We'd be sued." Xander chuckled. "Just gotta keep them between us, I guess."

The old friends reminisced for a while longer until Xander heard Charlene calling him. "You still on that computer gossiping with Phil? You're like a couple of old biddies." She came up behind Xander's shoulder and leaned over. "Hey, Phil. Good to see you. Tell Sheri I said, 'hey.' Once this COVID thing's over, we need to get together. I hear they're working on vaccines so maybe it won't be long." She stood, kissed Xander on the cheek and said, "I'm running to Publix, honey. Don't forget... tomorrow's trash day. Be back soon." Turning to the screen, she said, "Bye, Phil." She waggled her fingers at both of them as she left the room.

Xander laughed. "Did you hear that? I think that's my cue to get off here and do my chores while she's doing hers. She's subtle but I always get the message. So, I better sign off. Let's do it again, though. Soon."

"Yeah, we ought to make it a regular thing. And don't spend too much time fretting over stuff you can't control, you know? Either join the protests or stop worrying about it. You did your part. Time to let the young folks deal with it." Phil shook his finger at Xander, reminding him of his mama years ago.

"I hear you, but it's just not that easy. Maybe I still have a guilty conscience, you know, left over from Leon. Hard to get rid of the notion that I could have made a difference, saved the guy. But I *will* try not watching CNN so much. And I will give this Thompson guy every benefit of the doubt. Promise."

"See you again, soon, buddy. Take care." Phil

said, as he closed the Zoom window.

Xander stared at the blank screen for a few minutes. *Did I really ever make up for Leon? All those cases. Did that make up for it? God knows I tried, but maybe it's time I tried some of Mama's praying. Ask Him for forgiveness.*

June 18, 2020

Xander's cell phone rang just as he climbed back in the bed after letting their dog, Sadie, outside to pee. He was just drifting back to sleep, Charlene at his side and Sadie near his feet. He fumbled for it on the bedside table. Without his glasses, he couldn't read the caller ID but he could see the time – 6:26 a.m. – on the digital clock next to his phone. "Hello?" he said, his voice full of sleep.

"Dad, it's me, Arthur. Sorry to call so early, but I'm in a bit of a jam."

Xander was awake immediately. He hurried out of bed and into the hall hoping to let Charlene sleep a while longer. Sadie bounded off the bed and followed him. "What is it, son? Are you okay? You didn't have a wreck, did you?"

"No, no. I'm just fine. I'm in jail, though," Arthur said.

Xander groaned. Arthur had always been their rebellious child, as middle children often were, according to all the books he and Charlene had read in an attempt to understand him. He'd been a slacker in public school, a party boy in college, and had already been married and divorced twice. Xander and Charlene were pretty sure he'd dabbled with drugs, too, but they'd never actually seen any evidence of that. In an effort to salve any guilt they felt for mistakes they might have made, they'd often told one another that judges' kids were just like preachers' kids. So, whatever Arthur had done now would come as no surprise to Xander.

"What? What have you gotten into? If you've been doing drugs, Arthur, I swear, you can find someone else to bail you out…" Xander shielded his mouth with his hand trying to keep Charlene from hearing the conversation, but his voice had risen several decibels.

"Shit, Dad. Do you always have to think the worst? I was protesting at the attorney general's house yesterday about Breonna Taylor's death and we got arrested for intimidating him. Dad, it's a felony. I'm in deep shit."

That took the wind out of Xander's sails, and he was at a loss for a response.

Arthur continued, his voice shaking. "Look, I know we haven't talked much lately and I'm sorry. I got this new girlfriend and the two of us decided to join a huge protest yesterday trying to get Cameron to press charges against the policemen who murdered her."

Finally, Xander recovered his voice. "Son, calm down. We'll get through this. Are you… is this your permitted… will they let you talk long enough to explain what happened?" Xander knew full well that his son was probably being allowed only one short phone call in order to get someone to bail him out.

"Yeah, I can talk."

"Good, so tell me what happened."

Arthur said he and Tanika had been so enraged by this blatant killing they'd joined a protest at a high school in Louisville, then marched with them to the home of Attorney General Daniel Cameron. Because he was also a young Black man, the organizers of the protest had thought he'd be sympathetic to their pleas.

"Dad, it was a peaceful protest. Just like those you participated in when you were young. We probably shouldn't have been in his yard, but we weren't doing anything but chanting and calling for him to take action."

"So, why were you charged with a felony? How many others were arrested? Were they all charged similarly?"

"Yeah, there were a bunch of us. Somebody said over eighty. Tanika's in jail, too. God, Dad, you gotta get me outta this mess."

"I'll do what I can, but a felony? Dear Lord. How'd they call trespassing a felony?"

"Beats me. It's bullshit. They said we were intimidating an official in a criminal matter. We didn't intimidate him, I swear. Yeah, they told us to leave, and we didn't, but, damn. No one, not a single one of us threatened him or anybody else. If anybody was being intimidating, it was the police."

"Not the first time, son. It's happened for years. Gonna continue, too, as far as I can see. Let me get off here. See if I can find someone I know in Louisville to take your case. I'll wire the bond. How much is it?" Xander said, dreading having to tell this to Charlene.

"I don't know. Maybe they'll let me call you again after I've been arraigned."

"They have to. Don't worry. I love you. Talk to you later." He started to hang up. "Oh wait, what about your girl? Does she have an attorney? Someone to bail her out?"

"Yeah, she's called her dad. He's coming down in an hour. She'll be fine. I just wish you and Mom were here." His voice wavered.

"Me too, son. I can come, if necessary. I don't think it will be, though; trust me. I'll find someone. Love you," Xander said, closing his eyes against the vision of his son in jail.

"Love you too, Dad. Thanks. I knew you'd understand. You been in my shoes, right?"

"Oh, yeah. Sure have. Bye."

Xander hit the red receiver icon on his iPhone to end the call and reached down to pat Sadie. "Our boy's in trouble, Sadie gal. Been there; done that." Too wired to go back to sleep, he padded downstairs and fired up the Keurig. He sat in the quiet sipping on a large mug of black coffee reflecting on the day he'd been arrested in 1963 at a protest in Birmingham. He'd been scared, too, maybe even more scared than Arthur had just sounded.

Xander rose to fix another cup of coffee and saw

Charlene standing in the kitchen doorway. "What in the world got you up so early? Sadie?" she asked.

"No," He sighed. "Arthur called. He's in jail and needs bail. Guess what he was doing?"

"Protesting," she said without hesitation. "That's my boy." She went toward the Keurig and fixed a mug for herself. "Let me guess. Breonna Taylor. Right?"

Just as Xander was about to tell her all about it, his cell phone rang again. "Arthur? It's too early for me to call anyone…"

Arthur interrupted his father. "No need, Dad. There's some group called The Bail Project that's gonna post it for all of us…"

"You still need a lawyer, son. Bail isn't the last of it," Xander interrupted.

"But there's talk of all the charges being dismissed, too. I'll be out of here today; then I'll let you know if I still need a lawyer. So, don't worry; I'll be fine. Dodged one this time, didn't I? Love you, Dad. Give Mom a hug for me," Arthur said.

"I will. Yeah, you did dodge one. A big one. You know, despite the fact that you might not have, I want you to know we're proud of you. Protesting takes guts. I just hate that we still have to do it. Love you, too, son. Bye."

Xander ended the call and turned to Charlene. "Well, looks like he's taking up the mantle for our rights. Never thought it would be Arthur, but I'm proud of him."

She rose and gave Xander a hug. "Me too. Me too."

August 5, 2020

By the time Xander arrived in Blanchard's Bottom, the summer showers had stopped, the clouds had receded, and the humidity was as oppressive as he remembered from childhood. Although he hadn't been back since his mother's funeral twenty-two years ago, he'd wanted to come for several months – since the June day when he'd gotten so upset about the growing racial tension in the country over the shootings of Black men, boys, and even women by the police. He'd made plans, cancelled them because of COVID or some other reason, and then made them again. Part of him didn't want to come back, didn't want to relive his past; but the urge to put that past behind him had finally compelled him to make the trip.

He had no trouble finding his way around town. Not much had changed; but, as is often the case, the town seemed much smaller than it had when he was a kid. On his last trip home, he'd been too caught up with his mom's funeral to notice that. Now, he was stunned to see there was no trace of the Booker T.

Washington projects where he had grown up. In its place were small clusters of apartments – each one with a small patch of green lawn and four parking places. As he drove by, he wondered if they were still government housing.

Tiny's Kitchen had been torn down, replaced with the golden arches of the ubiquitous McDonald's. *No pies sold there anymore. Unless you count those awful apple things that come in a cardboard sleeve.* Back home, Charlene often baked pies from the recipes Mama Livvie had shared with her daughter-in-law after she had retired, too crippled with arthritis to continue. She'd said if she couldn't keep on baking them, somebody should. Each time Charlene baked, the aroma wafting from their kitchen reminded Xander of his mother.

Pleased to see that Chicken Little's Restaurant was still open, Xander thought he might eat there after he finished what he'd come to do. Then, brought up short by reality, he remembered eating inside was dicey with COVID still afoot. *Maybe I'll get dinner to go and take some to Ladonna.* He wasn't staying with his sister, despite her pleas. Safer for you if I stay in a hotel, he'd told her. Truth was, he didn't want to have to talk to anyone after he'd been to the cemetery. He had private, unfinished business to tend to there. That's why he'd asked Charlene to stay home.

Satterwhite Cemetery also looked smaller than he recalled from his last trip there. It seemed tiny when he compared it to how it felt when he and Louie used to play hide and seek there, ducking behind tomb-stones and magnolia trees as dusk turned to dark. As he drove past its concrete signposts, past the section where the markers were still upright, pristine and shining, and into the Black section near the rear of the property, he noticed that some graves were sinking into the ground as though the weight of their markers was just too much to bear. *That's apt. Some sadness is just too hard to bear.* Many markers were chipped or vine covered. *What happened to the perpetual care we all paid for?*

He drove to his mother's plot first. As soon as he scuffed through the damp grass, tiny gnats rose around his head. *I don't miss those little suckers.* The simple flat stone of brown granite was clean, the carving clear – Janet Olivia Betts: 1927-1998. *Wonder who's keeping it clean? Probably Ladonna.* "I'm older than you were when you died, Mama. Bet you didn't think I'd ever be this old, did you?" he said to the silent space. "I was just lucky, I guess. Especially after Nam." He bent down, laid the small bunch of daisies he'd brought on the headstone and said a small prayer, still no surer of its efficacy than he had been as a child. As he walked back to his car, he pulled out the marked map he'd gotten from the cemetery office. Otherwise, he'd have had no idea how to find what he sought.

First, he found Mrs. Johnson's grave. He'd come to consider her his patron saint since she'd been responsible for him being able to go to college. They'd corresponded until she became so weak from cancer that she could no longer write. Her daughter had taken up the task and at the end, had written Xander when she died. He owed her everything. She'd believed in him, encouraged him, enabled him. He knelt and placed a second bouquet of daisies on her marker. It was only a token of what he'd always felt he should have given her. He had no idea what that could have been, but he sure felt like he owed her more.

Satterwhite Cemetery actually wasn't that large, but it took Xander a minute to wind around the circuitous road to the section where Leon was buried. Again, gnats swarmed his face as he trudged through the grass looking carefully at each marker. Finally, he spotted it. A simple grey stone, slightly raised at an angle – Leon Pepper, 1938-1962. MAY HE REST IN THE PEACE HE DID NOT HAVE IN LIFE. *Wow, who in the world put up that marker? I'll bet it was Mr. Baxter. He always believed Leon was innocent just like I did.* As Xander leaned over to put the final bunch of flowers on Leon's grave he noticed another marker next to it. Not as showy and with only the name and dates engraved on it – Louis Pepper: 1944-1974. It brought Xander to his knees. Tears stung his eyes. *Oh Louie, what happened? Look at you. You were so young. We used to be so close. I wish I hadn't lost track of you. I'm so sorry. God, I hope you went easily. Man, I wish I'd known.* With his tears threatening to spill, he divided the small bouquet and placed half on each brother's marker.

Still on his knees and ignoring the dampness seeping into his pants, Xander composed himself somewhat and began to talk. "Guys, I have spent my whole life wishing I'd done things differently. Regretting I didn't say something that would have helped. Louie, I wish I'd never slipped and told you. I don't blame you for not understanding, for thinking I'd lied to you. I'm sorry it ruined our friendship. I missed you so much after that. And Leon, God knows I wish I'd told what I knew." He sighed and the tears resumed. "I can't change what I did or didn't do, but I want you to know I tried to make up for it. So, you've got all the time in the world to listen. And I've got the rest of the afternoon to tell you. So, here goes. I know you can't hear me, but…" He cleared his throat.

"See, I knew you were innocent, Leon. But Mama had told me to keep my big mouth shut. I couldn't prove it so I never said anything, but I'm sure Bill Feeney killed Annie Sowards, not you. He came to work all scratched up the day after Miz Annie was killed. Besides, I knew there'd been something going on between them before. Mama said if I stood up for you against my white boss, no one would believe me and I would lose my job. I really wanted to tell. I've lived to regret that I didn't. Regretted it back then, too, but I tried to get on with life. I guess I did, but it – me being such a coward – always haunted me.

"I don't know why he killed her, but I thought they must have had a fight. Anyway, folks say he tried to confess later, but the police ignored him. That's when I should have spoken up. He eventually killed himself. So, that's sort of a confession, don't you think?"

He shifted off his knees, which had begun to ache. Now, sitting in the grass, still ignoring the damp, he pulled at a clover stem. As he put it to his nose, it brought back memories of childhood summers when he'd watched Ladonna make clover chains from those she found in the sparse grass plots in the project. A slight breeze carried the smell of wet pavement across the cemetery, reminding Xander of when he and Louie had turned on the fire hydrants at the projects so the kids could splash in the water. One memory led to another and soon Xander was back there, a young boy with his best friend.

"Louie, remember how we used to play here? Looks a whole lot smaller than it did back then. We sure had some fun, didn't we? Anyway, remember Miz Johnson, our Social Studies teacher? She caught me at home one day after Leon got convicted and I told her what I knew. She said, like Mama, that no one would have believed me even if I'd had the guts to tell. Then, she made me promise to do something to try to make things better and she got me a scholarship to start college so I could. I just put some flowers on her grave, too.

"Thanks to her, I graduated from Morehouse College. That's where I met my wife, Charlene. She's so smart and sexy! We went to protests about civil rights and heard Martin Luther King. We were even in Selma on Bloody Sunday. Every time I marched, I thought of you, Leon."

Xander's eyes misted over again but he wiped them with his forearm and continued. "For me, every protest was about making things better for kids like us, like you. Black kids who've been bullied, who've had the cards stacked against them since long before they were born." Then, a smile crossed his lips and the tears vanished. "Lord, I wish you guys coulda seen me back then. Big old Afro hair, dashikis. You wouldn't have recognized me.

"Didn't take long before I knew I'd marry that gal. Now, here we are, fifty years later we've celebrated our golden anniversary and she still wants to protest. You know, they got this movement now protesting cops killing Blacks. Called Black Lives Matter. There's one tomorrow but I told her I'd had it with protesting. Nowadays, it's even more dangerous than it was back in college. But she's still a firebrand. Says we've got to fight until we die.

"Got three kids, too. We named the youngest one after you, Louie. It took me a while to decide to name him that, though. I worried it would always make me feel guilty. We always call him Louis, though, so that helps. Now that he's grown, I realize it was a good choice. He's funny, like you were, and smart. Grew up to be a pediatrician. You should see him with little kids. I'm so proud of him.

"When I got to Morehouse, I realized Miz Johnson was right. If I didn't want to spend my life being miserable and feeling guilty for what I didn't do, I had to channel that regret into some sort of action. I think that's why I started going to the protests. And why I decided to get a law degree. Turns out both were good decisions. She was a constant supporter of whatever I wanted to do.

"Charlene worked while I was in law school. The G.I Bill paid my tuition, but she kept a roof over our heads with her teaching salary. Once I passed the bar, I opened a small practice in in Smyrna to defend African Americans. Charlene could have quit once I got a few clients, but it turned out she loved teaching. Didn't retire until just a few years ago. Raised all our kids and taught too. Amazing woman.

"While I was in boot camp at Fort Benning, I met this Black kid from Alabama. Philip Murphy, that was his name. We became buddies. After we both got out of Nam, he went to law school, too, and eventually became my law partner.

"Later on, I had another good African American friend. Sanford Bishop from Columbus. We served in the Georgia House of Representatives, and we thought the same way on most issues. I'd run and won on a platform of criminal justice reform. I didn't get as far as I'd like to have, but I did get a few laws on sentencing changed. Each argument I made, each law I fought over, were for you, Leon. I guess I hoped if I could make a difference for some kid down the road it would make up for what happened to you. What happened because of me. It was an uphill battle. Some folks treated me with respect but to others I was still a 'boy.' Sanford always stood up for me. As far as I know, he's still serving in the U.S. Congress trying to fight the good fight.

"I told Phil all about you. He knew I was still ashamed of myself. And he knew it was my way of trying to make up for... you know. Anyway, it was something I knew was needed. And he agreed with me. He'd seen bad stuff in Alabama, too. We agreed about the injustices perpetrated against Blacks. Typically, those boys we defended had been shuffled off to court-appointed attorneys who really didn't care, not like Mr. Baxter, huh? So, we tried to set our fees low enough that they could afford us. Neither of us ever got rich but it was satisfying work. And sometimes, I took cases where I didn't get paid. But every time I got a kid a good verdict, I thought of you, Leon. None were murder cases, but there were plenty of assaults and other felonies. Lots were totally bogus charges. And sadly, lots of those young men had been beaten up by the police. Black boys and men are still getting killed by them. Shot for bogus reasons or no reason at all. And they, the white cops, never get punished. Nothing's changed, has it?

"I'm actually glad you can't see what's happening these days. It's downright depressing. Racism is still alive and well. Maybe more so than when we were young. I haven't seen the Klan, yet, but white supremacy groups are everywhere. I sometimes feel so damn defeated. I'm too old. I guess all I can hope for is that my kids and their kids will make a difference, will make it better. Their generation is more accepting, less prejudiced. Maybe they can change the system. But it's gonna take a lot.

"Somewhere along the line, I got appointed to serve as an interim judge, so I left state politics. And then, by some miracle, I was elected the next couple times. The whole time I was on the bench I could see you, Leon, in those kids behind the defendant's table. Your tears when you heard that verdict. God, Leon. I'm so sorry." Xander's tears returned with the memory.

"I could see some of them would have a future if

they just got some help, just caught a break. So, I tried to give it to them when I rendered sentences. Sometimes, I couldn't because of the sentencing laws, but I tried." Xander reached into his pocket, pulled out a large white handkerchief and blew his nose.

"Now I've got a case where I can make a difference. It's so much like your case, it's eerie. I think the guy is being railroaded, but I get to decide, not a jury. It may cost me my job, but I need to do what's right. Maybe that will help me get rid of this guilt.

"There's nothing more I can say. But maybe wherever you are, you've become the forgiving type. You too, Louie. I only hope that something I did, someone I helped, or this one case will can make up for what I didn't do when I was that stupid, cowardly, kid."

He rose from the grass, pulled his wet pants' seat away from his body, and rubbed his stiff knees. "Gotta go. I'm getting hungry. Gonna stop by Chicken Little's." He leaned over, put his hand on Leon's marker and then Louie's once more. "Rest easy, guys. Maybe I'll see you on the other side." He turned, wiped his eyes, and walked toward his car; his step lighter than it had been when he arrived.

He started his car, then turned it off again. Staring out over the rows of graves, he watched the sky begin to turn pink. *I can't just sit back and do nothing, no matter how old I am. If I do, I'm still that cowardly sixteen-year-old. I've got to do whatever I can, no matter what the risk.* He picked up his cell phone and punched in Charlene's number. "Hey baby, I'll be home by noon tomorrow. Let's go to that Black Lives Matter protest you talked about. I'm ready to march again."

He smiled when she said, "I knew you still had some fight left in you, old man. See you tomorrow." He started the car again and drove toward Chicken Little's, the sun glowing orange in the western sky.

OCTOBER 22, 2020

Judge Alexander Betts settles into his high-backed chair behind the austere walnut bench. A tall, three-sided plastic barrier, necessary for protection from COVID, separates him from the nearly empty courtroom. Those few who are in the chamber − lawyers, the bailiff, the court reporter − sit or stand at some distance from each other, another COVID precaution. All are masked, as well. Judge Xander Betts looks out at the bizarre scene; it makes him think of the spaghetti western reruns he'd watched during the lockdown in which bands of masked bandits raided banks or burst into saloons. He stifles the chuckle that threatens to erupt.

Soon, Sylvester Thompson will be escorted into the room. Xander knows of all those who have appeared in his courtroom over the years, this one young man will remind him of Leon more than any other. Perhaps it's the facts of the case: the rape and killing of a woman; the evidence found in Sly's apartment that he swore he'd found on the street and that

Xander felt was circumstantial; shoddy police work, including botched DNA tests; and an easy target in the defendant. Or perhaps it's Thompson's demeanor. He remembers vividly the man's hangdog look when he first stood in the spot he would soon occupy to hear Xander's decision. His expression was just like Leon's as he awaited his jury's verdict sixty years ago. *Poor guy has been waiting for months to hear his fate. Leon had to do the same while Mr. Baxter appealed his case. I don't know how either one held up.*

While Xander is lost in memory, the door opens, the bailiff yells "All rise," and a spit-and-polish guard escorts Sly Thompson into the room. Both wear bright, white masks. "Court is now in session. Judge Alexander Betts presiding. You may be seated." The shuffle of chairs echoes in the domed courtroom. Xander glances at his papers one more time, picks them up, taps them on the desk to straighten them, and then replaces them on the desk, his hands folded across them.

He clears his throat and nods at the bailiff who calls out, "Sylvester Thompson, please rise."

Thompson does so; his face reflecting that defeated expression despite the mask covering his nose and mouth. It's in the eyes. Xander sees the expression, sees the same one in his memories of Leon. He recalls how Leon's knees buckled when the judge read the verdict. He has no desire to ever see that again; no desire to cause any man to feel that way in his courtroom. Yet, the law is the law. He can't rule from his heart alone; he has to use his head, as well.

Xander clears his throat again, speaks loudly assuming the mask is impeding his voice's normal volume. "Mr. Thompson, let me apologize for the unduly long time you've had to wait for this day. Couldn't be helped, as you know, but now here we are."

"I understand, sir," said Thompson.

"Very well. When you were here before the pandemic shut us down, you had been charged with first degree murder in the case of Maybelle Anderson. I believe you pled not guilty. Is that correct, sir?" Xander knows it is. He's trying to make the man feel a bit more comfortable.

"Yes, sir. It is," Thompson said, his voice barely audible behind the thick government-issue mask.

"And I assume that's still your plea?"

"Yes, sir. It is," Thompson repeats.

"Very well, Mr. Thompson. Having considered the testimony we heard, and the evidence presented by both the prosecution and your attorney, I have made my decision. In case number 246808 State of Georgia vs. Sylvester Thompson, I, Judge Alexander L. Betts, find the defendant, not guilty. You sir, are free to go."

"Hallelujah," Thompson yells, loud enough to be heard distinctly behind his mask. Then he turns to his attorney and envelopes him in a huge bear hug. Xander raps his gavel on the desk to regain order.

"Mr. Thompson, let me give you a word of warning. My verdict was based primarily on the rather shoddy case presented by the state. And I realize there is still another case pending against you but it's not in my courtroom, so it won't be up to me. However, if I ever do find you in my courtroom again, things may not go as well for you. Do you understand?"

"Yes, sir, I do. You won't ever see me in here again. I promise." Thompson's eyes sparkle with joy and relief. He turns to his attorney and hugs him again as the prosecutor slams his briefcase on the table, gathers his papers, and stomps out of the courtroom.

That evening, Xander sits at their kitchen's center island drinking a glass of wine as Charlene fixes dinner. Back when their children were home, they'd always eaten in the dining room, but now, the island suffices.

"Charlene, I wish you'd seen that man today. When I said not guilty, he actually hollered 'Hallelujah.' I almost yelled back, 'Praise the Lord' like we used to do in Mama's church. I think I was as happy as he was."

Charlene laughs. "I doubt that, baby. You weren't facing execution; he was! But I take your point. Bless his heart. I'll bet he didn't expect that."

"Maybe not. Of course, he's not out of the woods yet. There's still another murder charge against him. But, Lord, do I feel better. It's like I finally did something for Leon, you know? Thompson reminded me so much of him. Not his size or his looks, but his eyes. Just that defeated look Leon had."

"Are you okay with the consequences? I know that note scared you. Have you heard anything from the police about it?"

"No, but based on the handwriting on the address, they think it was some kid. Nevertheless, I decided to take what comes. We've been in tough situations before – jailed for protesting, registering folks to vote, Selma – we'll be okay. Don't worry." He smiles at her.

"I'll try," Charlene says. "I also know you're worried about the next election." She stirs the big pot of chili she's started for the weekend football games.

"Yeah, I am. President Truman once said he didn't decide issues based on the polls. I thought that was good advice. So, I finally decided I couldn't live with myself if I made my decision based on public opinion. I'm sure there'll be a backlash, but I'll just have to live with it. I think overall, my record speaks for itself. And Black voters usually turn out pretty good so maybe…"

Xander pauses for a moment, staring out the window into the darkness. "But I think I'm finally going to sleep better. Maybe Leon won't haunt my dreams as often. At least it's a start. I don't think I'll ever be completely rid of sixteen-year-old Xander, but it's a start."

Charlene put down her big spoon and turned toward Xander. "Well, whatever happens we'll manage."

"Yeah, and no matter what happens, I want to keep on protesting, too. I'm glad you forced me to do that back in college. When I went to the cemetery this summer, I told Louie and Leon I'd keep it up." He chuckles at the absurdity of making a promise to tombstones. "I know they couldn't hear me, but I meant it," Xander says, then takes another sip of his chardonnay.

"I know you did, baby. Like I said, whatever happens, I'm proud of you, really proud," she says as she leans over and kisses him on the forehead. "And I'll march with you any day."

ACKNOWLEDGEMENTS

Although *Guilt* is a work of fiction, the story grew from a tale related by my late cousin, Tom "T-Bone" Baker, and his good friend, Dave Harris.

Without the advice of a number of legal experts to whom I'm eternally grateful this book could not have been born. They include retired attorney John Hash, Cabell County West Virginia Judge Al Ferguson, Georgia Superior Court Judge Bobby Peters, former Georgia Superior Court Judge John Allen, and former Huntington Police Department Chief Hank Dial.

My undying gratitude goes to Dr. Dolores Johnson, a retired Director of Writing at Marshall University and a linguistics expert, who tirelessly schooled me on the nuances of African American vernacular. Each step of the way, the tale took shape through the much-appreciated workshop comments from my writing compadres, Eddy, Charles, and Gwenyth; the members of Patchwork Writers; and The Master's Review Editor, Deirdre Danklin.

Without those early readers who took the time to read the rough drafts and make much needed comments, the book would still be on my computer. Thank you, Austin Camacho, M. Lynne Squires, Eliot Parker, and Sheila Redling (who read it in one day!)

My gratitude for those at Blackwater Press runs deep. Elizabeth's editing saved me from several embarrassing mistakes and Eilidh Muldoon's cover design captured the spirit of the novel perfectly. Many thanks to Luca Guariento for his beautiful book design and his patience with my scores of questions. And to my friend Cat Pleska, who steered me in the direction of Elizabeth Ford and Blackwater Press: I owe you one.

ABOUT THE AUTHOR

Carter Taylor Seaton is the author of three novels: *Father's Troubles*; *amo, amas, amat... an unconventional love story*; and *The Other Morgans*, as well asnumerous magazine articles, and several essays and short stories. Her non-fiction works include *Hippie Homesteaders*, *The Rebel in the Red Jeep*, *Me and Mary Ann*, and *We Were Legends In Our Own Minds*.

She holds a Tamarack Foundation Fellowship Award for Lifetime Achievement in the Arts and the West Virginia Library Association honored her with the 2014 WVLA Literary Merit Award. In 2015, Marshall University's College of Liberal Arts honored her with an Alumni Award of Distinction. In 2016 she received the Governor's Award for Lifetime Achievement in the Arts.

She graduated from Marshall University in 1982 with a Regent's degree in English and Business, and worked as a marketing professional in West Virginia and Georgia for over thirty years. Now, also a practicing ceramic sculptor, she lives in Huntington, West Virginia with her husband Richard Cobb.

OTHER BOOKS FROM THE SAME AUTHOR

Father's Troubles, a novel
amo, amot, amas… an unconventional love story
Hippie Homesteaders
The Rebel in the Red Jeep
Me and MaryAnn
The Other Morgans
We Were Legends in Our Own Minds, a memoir of the rock era